Praise for t...
Curios Mysteries

"Written with verve and panache . . . Will delight mystery readers and elicit a purr from those who obey cats."
—Carolyn Hart, author of *Dead by Midnight*

"Quirky characters, an enjoyable mystery with plenty of twists, and cats, too! A fun read."
—Linda O. Johnston, author of the
Kendra Ballantyne, Pet-Sitter Mysteries

"[A] wild, refreshing, over-the-top-of-Nob-Hill thriller."
—*The Best Reviews*

"An adorable new mystery." —*Fresh Fiction*

"[A] merry escapade! It was an interesting trip where nothing was as it seemed . . . If you enjoy mysteries that are a little off the beaten path, ones that challenge you to think outside of the box, this one is for you."
—*The Romance Readers Connection*

Titles by Rebecca M. Hale

Cats and Curios Mysteries

HOW TO WASH A CAT
NINE LIVES LAST FOREVER
HOW TO MOON A CAT

Mysteries in the Islands

ADRIFT ON ST. JOHN

Adrift on St. John

Rebecca M. Hale

BERKLEY PRIME CRIME, NEW YORK

THE BERKLEY PUBLISHING GROUP
Published by the Penguin Group
Penguin Group (USA) Inc.
375 Hudson Street, New York, New York 10014, USA
Penguin Group (Canada), 90 Eglinton Avenue East, Suite 700, Toronto, Ontario M4P 2Y3, Canada
(a division of Pearson Penguin Canada Inc.)
Penguin Books Ltd., 80 Strand, London WC2R 0RL, England
Penguin Group Ireland, 25 St. Stephen's Green, Dublin 2, Ireland (a division of Penguin Books Ltd.)
Penguin Group (Australia), 250 Camberwell Road, Camberwell, Victoria 3124, Australia
(a division of Pearson Australia Group Pty. Ltd.)
Penguin Books India Pvt. Ltd., 11 Community Centre, Panchsheel Park, New Delhi—110 017, India
Penguin Group (NZ), 67 Apollo Drive, Rosedale, Auckland 0632, New Zealand
(a division of Pearson New Zealand Ltd.)
Penguin Books (South Africa) (Pty.) Ltd., 24 Sturdee Avenue, Rosebank, Johannesburg 2196,
South Africa

Penguin Books Ltd., Registered Offices: 80 Strand, London WC2R 0RL, England

ADRIFT ON ST. JOHN

A Berkley Prime Crime Book / published by arrangement with the author

PUBLISHING HISTORY
Berkley Prime Crime mass-market edition / March 2012

Copyright © 2012 by Rebecca Hale.
Cover design by George Long.

ISBN: 978-0-425-24665-8

BERKLEY® PRIME CRIME
Berkley Prime Crime Books are published by The Berkley Publishing Group,
a division of Penguin Group (USA) Inc.,
375 Hudson Street, New York, New York 10014.
BERKLEY® PRIME CRIME and the PRIME CRIME logo are trademarks of Penguin Group (USA) Inc.

PRINTED IN THE UNITED STATES OF AMERICA

10 9 8 7 6 5 4 3 2 1

For Jana, Felix, and Will—
who first brought me to St. John

*Her name was
Phuong . . . which means Phoenix,
but nothing nowadays is fabulous
and nothing rises from its ashes.*

—Graham Greene, *The Quiet
American* (1955)

Prologue

Deep within the murky, unlit darkness of the Caribbean waters skirting the northern tip of the Lesser Antilles, the stocky shadow of a catamaran powerboat rocked against a wooden pier off the tiny island of St. John.

The short length of the boat was built up over its center, providing an elevated captain's tower and, beneath, a small rounded cargo hold fitted with benches for passenger seating. A line of red letters in bold block print ran across the vessel's white-painted side. The text spelled out WATER TAXI.

The captain glanced impatiently at the empty dock and the path leading up to the sprawling resort laid out across the hillside above. He had a schedule to keep, and he was anxious to depart. But his last passenger was still en route, somewhere within the mass of palm trees and dense vegetation surrounding the cove. She had reportedly run back to fetch a forgotten item.

The captain skimmed the tip of his tongue over the plump surface of his upper lip as he surveyed the two passengers already on board. They were seated several feet apart on a bench that lined the boat's open back landing.

On the far right side of the bench sat a fleshy, pear-shaped man in a sweaty golf shirt and wrinkled chinos. He was a computer programmer, according to the resort manager who had scheduled the pickup. The resort's parent company had brought the man in to set up their Wi-Fi Internet system. With his work now complete, the programmer was on his way to the St. Thomas airport, where a series of red-eye flights would carry him to the next vacation destination in line for his specialized services. Following the prescribed protocol, the programmer had been waiting dutifully by the dock when the water taxi arrived.

The captain's eyes passed critically over the programmer's bulging form. This porky, pigeon-eyed man would look out of place, the captain thought, anywhere other than in front of a computer terminal. The shape of his body appeared to have evolved over many years of desk work, melding into a lumpy hump of colorless, amoeba-like flesh that could instantly surround and engulf a computer's console.

Even in the cool nighttime breeze, the programmer's pouchy skin glistened with a shiny layer of sweat. The captain watched as the man folded the puffy, swollen mitts of his hands and rested them on the uppermost roll of his stomach, sedate and seemingly unbothered by the delay. The round lenses of his wire-rim glasses stared, unseeing, into the blue blackness of the liquid night.

The programmer let out a tired yawn. He'd been bouncing around the Caribbean for several weeks now, and the endless stream of exotic island locations had begun to blur together. To his travel-glazed eyes, one hotel complex nestled beneath a cluster of planted palm trees looked pretty much the same as the next.

The programmer wiped the back of his hand across his damp forehead. He'd put on clean clothes not more than an hour ago, but already the cotton fabric of his collared shirt had begun to cling to his chest. He wasn't cut out for all this heat and humidity, he thought wearily.

A drop of perspiration slid across the bridge of the programmer's nose as he glanced down at his watch. They were running late, but not unusually so.

Everything in the Caribbean, it seemed, ran on a laid-back, unrushed, "island time" schedule. There was no use trying to fight the delay—he knew from long experience.

After the events of the last couple days, he was more than ready to get off this island, but the boat, he reasoned, would leave soon enough. He shifted his weight, trying to ease his back into a more comfortable position against the rounded curve of the bench, and closed his eyelids with an air of resigned acceptance.

The captain grunted testily and turned his gaze to the boat's second passenger. The elderly cleaning lady had been a last-minute addition to his roster. What was her name again? Beulah. That was it. Beulah. The captain angled his brawny arms out in front of his chest as he studied the feeble crimp of her body.

The old woman was but one of the hundreds of day laborers who supported the island's booming tourism and hospitality industry. The majority of this workforce lived on the neighboring island of St. Thomas, where low-income housing, however meager, was at least available, and the cost of goods and services, while still island-inflated, was somewhat more manageable.

Each day, a lumbering fleet of ferryboats shuttled the workers back and forth across the Pillsbury Sound, dropping them off in Cruz Bay on the west end of St. John in the morning, returning them to Red Hook on the east side of St. Thomas in the evening. Occasionally, circumstances arose that prevented one or more of the workers from making it to the last departing ferry, so their employer arranged for their passage back to St. Thomas on one of the private water taxis that filled in the late-night gaps in the ferry schedule.

Beulah had hobbled down to the pier just as the water taxi pulled up to the dock. She was the one who had reported the delay of the third passenger, the captain remembered with an irritated *thunk* of his thumb against the side of the boat. That girl had better hurry up. She was throwing off the entire night's schedule.

The old woman appeared distressed by her impending ride on the water taxi. Her bony face was drawn and pinched, her dark skin tinted with a grayish hue of concern. She crossed her arms over her chest and cupped her hands around the pointed tips of her frail shoulders.

"Ohhhh, no . . ." she muttered, her voice rhythmic in its lilting Caribbean dialect. *"What-ter taxi . . . what-ter taxi . . . ohhh, no . . ."*

The maid shook her head, as if trying to rid her mind of an unpleasant image. Her stiff, arthritic hands reached up and fretfully pulled on the frizzled gray wisps of her hair. Her muttering voice continued its singsong lament. *"Eye doon nut lyke thuh what-ter taxi . . ."*

Crazy old bag doesn't like my water taxi, the captain silently translated and rolled his eyes. The corners of his mouth curled into a slight grimace. She could bloody well swim across to Red Hook, then.

The captain slapped one of his muscular hands against the top of the nearest railing. His fingers wrapped around the curve of the piped trim; his smooth ebony skin stretched across the healthy bulge of his bicep.

What was keeping that woman? He couldn't afford to wait much longer.

A slender female figure sprinted across the resort's manicured grounds, her path marked by the soft glow of the intermittent lanterns that lined the concrete curb of the trail. The soles of her sandals slapped against the walkway's red brick surface as she passed through a cluster of villas and headed toward the wooden dock where, she hoped, the water taxi would still be waiting.

The woman clutched the handle of a small blue satchel in her left hand. The nylon bag swung wildly back and forth as she sped around a corner, startling a large iguana whose three-foot length skittered beneath the nearest hydrangea. From the safety of the bush, the giant lizard rose up on its crooked front legs and billowed out the frilly collar of loose skin that hung beneath its stubby neck.

The creature's affronted gesture was lost on the woman who had so rudely interrupted its nighttime stroll; she was already twenty yards farther down the path.

The air was moist with the forecast of a coming rain; its heavy, damp presence blanketed the resort. As the trail opened out onto a sloping green lawn, the storm's first sprinkling drops began to fall, pattering like the light drumroll of fingertips across the woman's shoulders, spattering over the cinnamon sun-kissed tops of her feet, dotting the flowering spin of her chiffon sundress.

A member of the grounds crew drove up beside her in one of the resort's ubiquitous motorized golf carts. He motioned for her to climb into the passenger seat beside him.

"Don't worry, Hannah," he assured her with a wink as the cart whizzed off down the path. "He will wait."

The captain huffed a sigh of relief when he saw the golf cart carrying his last passenger motoring down the dock.

"Come on, then," he bellowed as the cart screeched to a halt beside the boat.

Hannah clambered out of the cart's front passenger seat and lunged toward the edge of the water taxi. The captain grabbed her forearm as she stepped off the pier and firmly pulled her into the swaying boat. She quickly took a seat on the back bench in between the other two passengers.

Still clutching the nylon satchel, Hannah took in a deep breath and pushed back the sweaty mass of her curly dark hair. She ran her hands over the rumpled folds of her dress, trying to smooth out the wrinkles as she worked to calm her racing pulse.

The captain wasted no time in departing. Revving the engine, he steered the boat toward the mouth of the cove.

The black silk of the water lapped at the pointed prongs of the catamaran's bow, drawing the boat into the slippery crease of its thick, sensuous folds. Despite the glow of the numerous lights affixed to the masthead, sides, and stern, the misting darkness quickly swallowed the vessel whole.

As the boat's rudder met the rougher sea of the Pillsbury Sound, the hoarse voice of the elderly cleaning woman rose above the humming *pat-a-tat-tat* of the motor. Her dry, blistered lips smacked against the ending consonant of each syllable, making her thickly accented words difficult to distinguish.

After several repetitions, Hannah managed to make out the woman's mournful refrain. She closed her eyes as the small boat bounced across the current, but the old woman's haunting, singsong voice filled her ears with its chilling chant.

What-ter taxi . . . what-ter taxi . . . ohhh, no . . .
Eye doon nut lyke thuh what-ter taxi . . .
Beeg sheep go down slowe . . .
Small sheep go down fest . . .
Eye wurk und Eye wurk,
But steel Eye've gut to tek thuh what-ter taxi . . .
Ack, Eye doon nut lyke the what-ter taxi . . .

Water taxi . . . water taxi . . . oh, no . . .
I do not like the water taxi . . .
Big ship go down slow . . .
Small ship go down fast . . .
I work and I work,
But still I've got to take the water taxi . . .
Ack, I do not like the water taxi . . .

~ 1 ~

The Dumpster Table

The old woman had been right to worry. The water taxi reportedly sprang a leak halfway across the channel to St. Thomas and sank before the nearest Coast Guard vessel could reach it. The captain, the miraculously buoyant computer programmer, and the elderly cleaning woman had all survived by clinging on to the side of a hastily deployed inflatable raft. But the third passenger, Hannah Sheridan—a recent employee at my resort—had vanished into the sea.

It was late morning on the island, only a handful of hours after the water taxi's mysterious sinking, and I was already midway through my second cocktail. I sat on a white plastic lawn chair at a table outside a local dive bar called the Crunchy Carrot, waiting for news of the accident to filter through the porous island community of Cruz Bay.

My name is Penelope Hoffstra—at least that's what's printed on the nameplate that sits atop my desk at the resort. It's just plain Pen to everyone here on the island.

It's been four years now since I moved down to St. John, making me a veteran among the island's resident "Continentals"—a constantly rotating pool of pale-faced immigrants from the upper forty-eight.

There's no shortage of stateside applicants seeking jobs down here in the Virgins. The promise of an idyllic island lifestyle draws individuals from every social class and background. Once they arrive at their dream location, however, few make it longer than a year.

They all start out the same: so full of hope, so sure they've found paradise. After a couple of weeks, maybe a month or two, it begins to fall apart.

Some discover they actually miss all the mainland conveniences they'd come here to escape. Others run out of money—this isn't an easy place to earn a living, and a dollar doesn't go very far in the way of rent or groceries. Many find themselves feeling trapped on the island's meager landmass, confined by the surrounding acres of uninhabitable sea.

For a small number of us, though, somehow it just fits. As for me, I'll never feel at home anywhere else.

I flew down here on a whim, lured by the promise of an exotic, stress-free existence in the tropics. It was an impetuous act, spurred by an unusual relocation proposal from an admittedly questionable source. But before I could talk myself out of it, I'd hopped a flight and disappeared into this tiny U.S. territory ringing the eastern edge of the Caribbean.

The gamble had paid off. I'd never once regretted the decision. My only goal had been to make my time in the islands last for as long as possible.

I picked up my plastic cup from the table and stirred a straw through the liquored strawberry concoction inside. The fruity mixture retained just enough ice to resist the straw's swirling path and to sweat a coating of moisture on the cup's outer surface. I dabbed the end of the plastic tube into the fast melting slurry, watching as its frozen thickness dissipated in the rising morning heat.

You could still smell the aftermath of the heavy rains from the night before, a rinsing sheet of water that had freshened the streets and wiped clean the beaches, erasing my footsteps and obliterating all evidence of my last meeting with the missing Hannah Sheridan.

I leaned back in the lawn chair as a black rooster with colorful red and blue plumes strutted by on skinny yellow legs. Behind me, a scantily clad waitress in short shorts hefted a bag of refuse into a blue Dumpster located a few feet behind my table. Her cropped T-shirt was emblazoned with the bar's name and the image of a long skinny carrot.

My newfound exotic existence, as it turned out, frequently involved lengthy spells watching the foot, vehicle, and chicken traffic of Cruz Bay pass by my seat here at the Crunchy Carrot.

As the executive manager of one of St. John's larger resorts, I had a great deal of leeway, geographically speaking, on where I conducted business, and I typically spent several hours each day here at the Dumpster table. As a makeshift office, it had a lot to offer.

First off, the table's proximity to the trash bin meant that it was almost always left vacant by the island's scent-sensitive tourists, reserving plenty of seating space for the scent-diminished expat community. To be honest, the smell coming from the Dumpster wasn't anywhere near as offensive as that emanating from some of my sweaty compatriots. After much experimentation, I'd learned to strategically position myself upwind of both.

A little odor discomfort was a small price to pay for keeping up to date on the local gossip. The Dumpster table was *the* place to get the latest island news. Every informational tidbit of any significance passed through this central transit point.

In addition, I thought as I took another sip from the plastic cup, the Crunchy Carrot's policy of serving us expats on a loosely calculated bar tab made the food and drink at this slightly unaesthetic location the best deal in town.

Finally, the Dumpster table offered the certain prospect of camaraderie—you'd never sit solo for long. If nothing else, you could always count on the company of Richard, a free-roaming rooster who seemed particularly fond of the Carrot's greasy French fries.

It was from this spot that I reflected on the night's events and waited for the local reaction to Hannah's disappearance.

A wildfire of whispers had already begun to burn through the island's sparse population. Speculative rustlings rippled in the ocean breeze, spoken softly so as not to frighten the tourists, but voiced loud enough for anyone who was listening to hear.

I'd passed several clusters of cleaning staff, groundskeepers, and hospitality workers on my way through the resort that morning, each one a serious circle of quiet conversation. I'd tried not to meet the questioning faces that glanced up at me as I walked by, forcing out a solemn sigh to assure them of my inner sadness—all too aware of how quickly the worm of suspicion might turn in my direction.

I'd taken one of the island's many truck taxis into town from the resort, riding in the back bed of a cherry red heavy-duty pickup truck that had been outfitted with a canvas canopy and rows of plastic-cushioned benches. The driver had stopped several times along the route, parking in parallel with similarly decked-out trucks coming from the opposite direction. It had been pointless to protest the delay—on such a newsworthy day, these two- to five-minute stops were almost obligatory.

I had expected as much, and, in any event, I wasn't in any hurry. The Crunchy Carrot had never been known to run out of booze.

The waitress turned from the Dumpster and approached my table.

"How're you doing out here, Pen? Can I get you another one?" she asked, nodding at my half-empty cup as she dusted her hands off on her apron. "It's a strange day, isn't it?"

The waitress leaned in closer to me, her bare midriff

brushing against the side of the plastic table. "Hard to think she's gone like that. Drowned, they say. I don't suppose they'll ever find her body."

The waitress's eyes drifted to the ground. "You're not supposed to speak ill of the dead, but . . ."

I nodded with a knowing smile. No apology necessary, I thought bitterly. Not with me anyway.

Hannah Sheridan had worked as one of the many seasonal recruits my resort brought in at the end of October to help us gear up for the winter months of heavy tourist traffic. I typically ignored such temporary employees; their management fell into the large category of duties I delegated to my able assistant, Vivian. I might never have noticed Hannah's presence on St. John but for all the trouble she stirred up—and the disturbing familiarity of her name.

The waitress bent over my chair, her voice taking on a low, conspiring tone. "Do you know what they've been saying around town? The day laborers and the taxi drivers . . . about Hannah?"

I raised my eyebrows inquiringly, trying not to look too eager. I felt certain no one had seen me with Hannah the previous evening on the beach. No one else on the island knew the true coordinates of her current location. There was no reason for me to worry. I had to remain calm.

The waitress pulled a second plastic chair next to mine and perched tentatively on the edge of its seat.

"They're saying that Hannah was . . . taken," she whispered uneasily.

"From the boat?" I asked tensely. "From the water taxi?"

The waitress twitched her nose as if she were embarrassed to pass on the rest of the reported rumor.

"I always thought it was a bunch of superstitious nonsense," she said, fidgeting nervously with the frayed hem of her shorts. "But now . . . well, you can't help but wonder."

"What are you getting at?" I pressed, struggling to stifle the guilty blush rising on my cheeks. "What do they think happened to her?"

The waitress sighed and grinned impishly. "You'll think

I'm foolish, but here it is." She sucked in on her bottom lip, hesitating for a moment before her words rushed out.

"They're saying it was that spirit everyone's been talking about—the slave girl from the plantation days. They say she dragged Hannah down into the ocean while the others hung on to the side of the raft."

A pent-up volume of breath eased out of my lungs. There it was: confirmation of the rumor I had been waiting for, the seed that had been so carefully planted sprouting in the fertile ground of the morning's speculations.

I took another sip through the straw and shuddered—not out of fear or apprehension, but from the chill of the drink. The effect, nevertheless, appeared to satisfy the waitress, and, with a gracious smile, she stood up from the table and returned inside the bar. I leaned back in my chair, collapsing in relief.

It is no coincidence that a superstitious nature runs through the people of the Virgin Islands.

Life in the Caribbean has rarely been easy for its beleaguered inhabitants. They suffer continually beneath the unrelenting heat of the tropical sun. Each year, vengeful, seemingly self-willed hurricanes wreak wanton destruction across the area. Despite being surrounded by an endless horizon of ocean, these islands are particularly sensitive to drought and suffer from a chronic shortage of drinkable water.

Beyond the inherent ecological burdens of the region, the gloomy historical specter of three hundred years of colonial exploitation and brutal enslavement lurks just beneath the surface of nearly every aspect of society, an oft-cited excuse, justification, and alibi for exclusion, inequity, and entitlement.

For some portions of the population, it is easier to explain such a concentrated run of bad luck and geography with metaphysical, rather than scientific, rationalizations. Perhaps belief in such an elusive, overarching miasma is preferable to the harsh reality of human malice and greed.

Regardless, the persistent vein of these suspicions bleeds over into discussions of modern life's everyday mysteries. Anomalies, if not quickly explained, are frequently attributed to the work of ghostly hands.

Of late, many of the workers who ride the ferry back and forth to St. John have become convinced they sense a supernatural presence each morning when they step onto the dock at Cruz Bay—a presence leftover from the island's dark past—a spirit who has become known throughout the Virgin Islands as the Amina Slave Princess.

~ 2 ~

The Amina Slave Princess

I first heard the tale of the Amina Slave Princess a couple of years ago, not long after I moved to St. John. I had been out for the day on the neighboring island of St. Thomas, exploring the shopping district in its main town, Charlotte Amalie.

A tourist haven set up to maximize trade with day-trippers from docking cruise ships, Charlotte Amalie's downtown featured a thicket of narrow alleys lined with frigid, over-air-conditioned cubicles where beady-eyed merchants hawked duty-free merchandise and a wide array of gaudy jewelry.

Inside the cavelike showrooms, I walked past tray after tray of too-flashy-to-be-real diamonds glittering under the focused spotlights of florescent bulbs. My poorly feigned interest didn't fool the seasoned vendors. They immediately sensed that I wasn't a cash-dropping snowbird and only half-heartedly tried to entice me with their offerings.

Beyond the jewelry stores, the only other vendors of note displayed mass-produced T-shirts from China and kitschy tourist memorabilia constructed from recycled aluminum. To find stores stocked with merchandise tailored to the needs of the actual inhabitants of St. Thomas, one had to navigate away from the city center, along the edgier arteries that led toward the east end of the island.

I suppose I've spent too much time sitting around the Dumpster table listening to the tourist-mocking expats, but in the years since that first foray, I've never returned to the trinket shops of Charlotte Amalie. In any event, the most memorable aspect of that trip to St. Thomas occurred on the boat ride back to St. John.

I'd walked down to the waterfront to wait for the afternoon ferry to Cruz Bay. A nasty wind had picked up while I'd been trawling the alley shops, and the sky had begun to darken with the angry, streaking colors of a coming squall.

As I shivered on the pier in my sleeveless blouse and khaki shorts, a shuttle bus dropped off a handful of new arrivals from the airport. A typical collection of pale soon-to-be-sunburnt tourists joined me in the designated waiting spot for the ferry.

First came a harried husband and wife, dragging along two overtly bored, gum-popping teenagers. Familial relations had apparently been strained from the hours of airplane travel; not a word passed between them as the group stewed silently on the dock.

The family of four was followed by a spritely pair of white-haired retirees. The elderly couple hopped happily from the shuttle, clearly intent on enjoying their vacation. Nothing in the airline's arsenal of passenger torture had dampened their enthusiasm. They strolled patiently along the water, pausing every so often to admire the whirling colors of agitated atmosphere gathering above us.

The last of the shuttle's passengers stuck his head out the open exit door and loudly sniffed the ocean air. He was a wiry little man in tight, tattered blue jeans and a worn oxford shirt unbuttoned several notches down from its collar.

The man's thinning hair had recently been dyed a false

brown color, giving it a reddish chemical glow. He'd made the most of each surviving hair follicle, tying up the meager strands into a scraggly ponytail at the base of his neck.

The gray chest hair that poked out through the loose buttonholes on the man's shirt more accurately reflected his advanced age. Self-consciously, I ran a hand over the top of my own head, hoping my gray-masking attempts were somewhat less conspicuous.

The man hefted a guitar case out of the airport shuttle's back storage cavity and sidled up next to me on the dock.

"Howdy, love," he said smoothly, tilting his head with a broad, suggestive smile. "You headed to *Saint John* too?" He drew out the two-word moniker of the island's name, clearly anticipating the arrival at his final destination.

I tried to grin my way out of a reflexive grimace. "Mm-hmm," I replied, weakly nodding in affirmation.

"I'm from New York," the man said proudly, pointing to a faded "I heart NY" sticker on his guitar case. It was one of many appliqués plastered on to the side of the battered container.

"Mm-hmm," I replied again, trying to shift my gaze out toward the harbor, but the chatty hippie was intent on making my acquaintance.

"Brooklyn actually," he clarified affably. "To be specific."

I risked a quick glance at my new friend. The skin on his face was shrunk back against his skull, the tissue weathered and anemic from many years of hard living—and, I suspected, more than a smidgen of recreational drug use.

"I'm Conrad," he said, pausing as he waited for my reciprocal identification.

I sighed uncomfortably before complying. "Pen," I offered stiffly. "Nice to meet you."

"Pen, Pen, Pen . . ." Conrad mused speculatively. "That's short for . . ." He let the sentence hang in the air, waiting for me to complete it.

"Pen," I replied curtly. "Just Pen."

"Ah, well, just Pen it is, then." Conrad leaned back in a stretch, seemingly pleased at having extracted my name. The

wind plastered his shirt against his narrow barreled chest.
You could almost see his ribs protruding through the fabric.

"So, Pen," Conrad said, leaning against the guitar case as
he looked me up and down, "I've been coming to St. John
since, oh, let's see, 1971. I always stay out on the north shore
of the island—at the eco-campground near Maho Bay."

He pumped the narrow arches of his eyebrows at me.
"I've reserved one of their teepee tents."

Mercifully, the ferry's crew began to load us. I marched
purposefully into the lower deck of covered seating and slid
onto a bench seat about halfway down the boat's length,
grateful for the chance to get in out of the wind and hopeful
I might distance myself from Conrad's amorous overtures.

It was no use. I heard the clunking sound of a guitar
case sliding across the metal bench immediately behind me.

Conrad's squirrelly head popped up near my shoulders
as he leaned forward over the back of my seat.

"Now, Pen, let me see if I can guess your birthday."

My face furrowed skeptically.

"No, seriously," he insisted. "I have a knack for these
things. Here, first, let me absorb your aura."

I felt the pressure of his fingertips against my temples as
he began to rub them in a circular motion against the sides
of my head.

"Were you born . . . ah, say . . . between January and
March?"

I stared up at the ferry's ceiling. "No."

"Hmm," Conrad replied thoughtfully. From the confident tone of his voice, his faith in his powers of divination
appeared undiminished.

"How about . . . er . . . between September and December?"

"Nope."

"I know! I know!" he exclaimed as if suddenly receiving new information from his massaging fingertips. "It's
between April and May!"

I shook my head, my lips puckering with wry amusement at his luckless persistence. I turned around in my seat
to face him.

"July."

"Aaaah." He exhaled disappointedly, thumping the flat metal surface of his seat with the palm of his hand. "That was going to be my next guess."

Conrad slid slightly to the right and draped his arms over the back of my bench. "So, Pen," he began again, his brown eyes sparkling with interest, "what's your connection to the island?"

He twitched his mind-misreading fingers in the air near my face. "You're not in transit, not a tourist . . . I sense you're something a little more permanent."

I sighed tensely, not wishing to prolong the conversation. It would be at least another forty minutes before we docked in Cruz Bay. "I've just started a new job. I'm a manager at one of the resorts on the island."

"Mmm, interesting." Conrad made several exaggerated facial expressions while absorbing this information. "And where'd you come from before that?"

"Oh, up in the States," I said evasively.

Conrad assumed a critical stare, waiting for me to supplement my answer.

With another sigh, I relented. "California. I used to be a lawyer."

I bit down on my lip. The last phrase had slipped out before I could catch myself. I'd opened myself up to another line of questioning—one that I would rather not have to fudge the answers to.

"I'm a lawyer too," my companion stated immediately. "Self-taught," he added unabashedly. "Been in court dozens of times. I always represent myself, and I've always won."

He pointed proudly at his chest. "That district attorney man, he'll never convict me."

With a wan smile of relief, I leaned back in my seat.

"You should come visit me at Maho Bay," he invited eagerly. "I'll cook you dinner at my teepee tent."

Conrad quickly read the refusal on my face. He stroked his chin and tried another tack.

"You know, they've got a ghost up there at the camp-grounds. I've seen her lots of times."

I cleared my throat. This was quickly turning into a very *long* ferry ride. "You don't say."

"Oh, yes," he replied, pushing himself onto the edge of his seat so that he could crawl even farther over the back of mine. "If you walk into the woods and stay real quiet, become one with the surrounding nature—you know, let your Zen ooze out—oftentimes, she'll just sneak up behind you and tap you on the shoulder."

Conrad's bony fingers gently touched my shoulder blades.

"I bet I could introduce you to her, to the ghost that is, if you come for dinner at my teepee tent."

Wincing dismissively, I shrugged out from under his grasp.

Conrad continued, undeterred. "This ghost, she's from the 1700s, back when the islands were full of sugar plantations."

His eyeballs bulged, stretching his skin against the tight contours of his face.

"She was part of a group of slaves that were brought over from West Africa. Her people were called the Amina. They were one of the most powerful tribes in the Gold Coast area, fierce warriors that all the others lived in fear of.

"But I guess the Amina had a run of bad luck and lost a couple of battles. A rival chief sold them to the Danish slave traders."

Raindrops began to spit against the windows of the ferry as the sky grew darker, dimming the light inside the cabin. Conrad's pale face glowed in the shadows. He licked his upper lip, warming to his narrative.

"Before her capture, the woman who became this ghost, she'd been part of her tribe's nobility. She was the king's daughter, the tribe's princess. A delicate flower of a woman—just like you."

Conrad paused for a lecherous wink in my direction. I rolled my eyes and looked pointedly at my watch. He cleared his throat and returned to the tale.

"The Princess managed to survive the ocean passage across the Atlantic to Charlotte Amalie; that's where she and several other members of her tribe were auctioned off. Most of them were bought for plantations over on St. John. You can still see the ruins of the sugar mill where the Princess used to work, just off the North Shore Road on your way up to Maho."

Conrad smacked his lips together. "It was a hard life, being a sugar slave—rough, I tell you." He wiped his brow for emphasis.

"But from the moment of their capture and enslavement, the members of this warrior tribe began plotting their revenge. A couple of months after they arrived on St. John, they organized a massive revolt and took over the island. It was a bloody siege that caught everyone by surprise. Some of the plantation owners and their families escaped to St. Thomas, but most of them were"—Conrad twisted his face into a lurid expression and made a slicing motion across his bobbing Adam's apple—"slaughtered."

The rain was coming down now in nearly horizontal sheets, slamming against the windows of the ferry. I gripped the side of the bench as the boat heaved sideways in the rolling waves.

"These rebel slaves, they held on to the island for six or seven months before reinforcements of French troops arrived to help the Danes. Once the slaves saw the size of the incoming fleet, they knew they were outnumbered. And they knew what would happen to them if they were captured. So, as the troops advanced on their camp"—he drew in his breath, his thin face wrinkling under the force of an exaggerated cringe—"they committed suicide.

"Some of them used the muskets they'd stolen from the plantations. Some slit their throats with their knives. But one of the rebel slaves, the Princess, she chose a different method. She hiked up to the northern rim of Mary's Point, just beyond the curve of Maho Bay. There on a cliff, overlooking Tortola, she stepped to the edge, closed her eyes, and jumped off"—he made a whirring flap with his lips, followed by an imitation of a loud splash before completing the sentence—"into the ocean."

Conrad leaned even closer toward me, the pale skin on his skeletal face shining in the storm's eerie half-light. His voice dropped to a whisper.

"Something about her death—the way the water swallowed her up—it didn't quite do the job. Her spirit was too strong. It survived even after her body perished. The waves tossed her out onto the beach there at Maho, and she's been haunting the island ever since. Everyone at the campground has seen her at least once or twice."

He *thunked* his chest solemnly. "Every year, the Princess, she comes to visit me."

He paused, switching his expression to an impish grin. "In my teepee tent at the far end of the campground."

Wearily, I shook my head. I'd heard more than enough about Conrad's teepee tent.

"No, no, honest, I swear," he protested. "Late at night near the beach, you can hear her voice. It's kind of a mournful, wailing chant."

He made a strained caterwauling sound before nodding informatively at me. "They call her the Amina Slave Princess. The Ghost of the Slave Princess. Ask anybody. She hangs out most nights at Maho Bay."

Conrad collapsed onto his bench and stretched his arms wide across its back metal railing. He was convinced of the ghost story, even if I wasn't buying it.

"I tell you what, St. John, it's an amazing place," he said reverently. "I look forward every year to coming down here. This island, it will pull you apart, then put you back together again—if you let it."

In the years since my first encounter with Conrad the charismatic hippie, I have heard many versions of the Amina Slave Princess story. The legend has been repeated over and over again, particularly among those of Afro-Caribbean descent.

Of late, some have come to believe that the Princess

walks among us—that she has taken on human form to protect the sanctity of the shoreline where her lifeless body washed up, all those many years ago.

I leaned back in the white plastic lawn chair and took another slurp from the strawberry drink. If the rumor that Hannah had been done in by the Amina Slave Princess was circulating among the waitresses at the Crunchy Carrot, it was well on its way through the island's gossip chain.

Of course, I knew Hannah hadn't been sucked into the water by a wrathful sea spirit. I knew exactly what had happened to her—because I was the one responsible for her disappearance.

~ *3* ~

A Dark History

Setting aside Conrad's constant references to his teepee tent, his ferryboat recounting of St. John's slave rebellion did manage to capture the overall gist of the event. He glossed over a few aspects of the historical record, however, that are worth mentioning.

Christopher Columbus stumbled across the Virgin Islands in 1493, during his second trip to the Americas, a region he inaccurately identified as the West Indies. (Columbus's vehement geographical assertions to the contrary, the islands he discovered were nowhere near India, Asia, or any other Far East spice-trade landmass. Nevertheless, the people of this region are still commonly referred to as West Indians.)

For the most part, Columbus and his Spanish cousins passed up the Virgins in lieu of the Greater Antilles islands to the east, which, they believed, were more likely to hold the fabled gold mines they so desperately sought. Beyond the Virgins' lack of obvious mineral riches, the European explorers were eager to avoid the area's militant Carib inhabitants—their warriors considered the Europeans' tender human flesh to be a tasty delicacy.

So the Spaniards gave the Virgins a wide berth and focused the brunt of their marauding efforts on the island of Hispaniola (now divided into the countries of Haiti and the Dominican Republic). Unfortunately, even brief contact with the Europeans was enough to do in the Virgins' native tribes. Many died from the strange new illnesses the explorers brought to the area. The rest were subsumed in the first wave of colonial slave trading. With the exception of a scattering of British settlements to the east, by the time the Danish set their sights on St. Thomas in the mid-1600s, the Virgin Islands were largely wild and uninhabited.

Despite the island's unoccupied status, the Danes had a tough time getting their new colony started. Their fledgling settlement was raided and obliterated several times over by the pirates that plied the Caribbean waters. It wasn't until 1672 that a permanent township finally took root in the area now known as Charlotte Amalie.

As reports of these trials and tribulations filtered back to Denmark, fewer and fewer Danes volunteered for the trip across the Atlantic. The government was forced to recruit nationals from neighboring Nordic states, and, as a result, there were soon as many Dutch as Danish in the Danish Virgin Islands.

Once the foothold on St. Thomas was finally established, the colony grew quickly. Before long, most of the island's arable land fell under the control of a few wealthy plantation owners.

In 1718, searching for unclaimed fields to cultivate, a small group of farmers crossed the Pillsbury Sound to the neighboring island of St. John. They circled around to Hurricane Hole, the protected cove on the island's opposite side, and set up permanent camps in what is now known as Coral Bay.

The meager contingent of Danish troops who accompanied the settlers built a rudimentary fort on a hill overlooking the settlement and the surrounding soon-to-be sugarcane fields.

Sugar production was the all-consuming obsession of the Caribbean during the colonial era, and this labor-intensive industry rapidly burned through the few native workers who had survived the Europeans' initial invasion. Before long, it became clear to the colonial powers that the only way to maintain and harvest the islands' valuable sugar crops would be through the use of imported labor, most readily found in the form of slave trade from Africa. The Danes soon turned to this approach for their primary source of manpower.

For the chattel on board the Danish slave-trading ships, it was a terrifying trip from the Gold Coast of West Africa to the auction yards on St. Thomas. During the months of ocean passage, the slaves were chained together and frequently packed into the fetid cusp of the ship's hull. The extreme heat and unsanitary conditions in the below-deck quarters often led to the outbreak of illness and death among the hapless captives.

Those slaves that survived Danish transport across the Atlantic were put up for auction at Charlotte Amalie. The bidding price for each slave varied depending on the individual's age, gender, and physical condition—but the most important criterion for determining a slave's value was his African tribe affiliation.

By the early 1700s, the majority of slaves entering the Danish trading system were casualties of tribal warfare. Danish forts along the African coast traded with various tribal chieftains for slaves that were captured as part of ongoing intertribal conflicts in the region. As the Colonial demand for sugar slaves increased, the situation in West Africa grew more and more turbulent, destabilizing the established power structure and destroying many long-standing alliances.

Caribbean plantation owners lived in constant fear of slave rebellions and uprisings; if at all possible, they steered clear of slaves they suspected of having a militant background. Individuals from tribes thought to be more easily pacified brought a premium price at auction and were generally sold to the more prosperous plantations on St. Thomas, leaving those from tribes with warmongering reputations to the struggling farmers on the backwater island of St. John.

Despite the hopes of those first migrating planters, St. John turned out to have minimal agricultural potential. The island had a much smaller landmass than St. Thomas, and the available acreage suitable for farming was limited by its hilly topography. Many of the sugar plantations on St. John were eventually deeded to absentee landowners, who in turn relegated their responsibilities to largely unsupervised overseers.

As a result, the least desirable land in the Virgin Islands ended up with the least desirable slaves, that is, those most likely to resist their enslavement. It was no coincidence, then, that one of the most significant slave rebellions in the history of the Virgin Islands happened here on St. John.

In the fall of 1733, after a miserable crop season besieged first by drought, then hurricanes, a group of recently arrived warrior slaves planned and executed an uprising that took over the island for almost seven months. Some if not all of these rebels belonged to an African tribe the Dutch called "Amina."

The rebel slaves sought to establish a new Amina empire that would encompass all of St. John and eventually extend east across the Virgins to the sparsely inhabited island of British Tortola. As envisioned by the rebels, this Amina territory would be ruled by their designated king and his noblemen. Theirs was not, by any means, a pan-emancipation effort. They expected, as was typical among the warring tribes in their previous West Africa homeland, to profit from the slave labor of other African ethnic groups as well as any of the homesteaders who survived the rebels' initial attack. Given the prospect of Amina enslavement, many of St. John's non-Amina slaves sided with their white owners during the revolt.

The Amina assault began November 23, 1733, at the Danish fort overlooking Coral Bay when a group of slaves purportedly delivering firewood overpowered the seven unsuspecting Danish soldiers manning the fort. The Amina rebels killed all but one of the soldiers (the lone survivor escaped by hiding under a bed); then they fired the fort's cannon as a signal to their fellow conspirators throughout the island.

The cannon shot was followed by the blowing of conch shells, a call to arms for a bloody slaughter that commenced on plantations across St. John. The Amina wrought their vengeance against white slave-owning families as well as overseers of any color who failed to flee their path. Their reign of terror extended across the island's north coast from Brown Bay, where an entire family was gruesomely slain, to the front gates of the plantation now occupied by the Caneel Bay resort.

Within a few weeks' time, Danish troops from St. Thomas managed to recapture the fort at Coral Bay, but the Amina rebels maintained their grip on the rest of the island. They dispersed into the heavily forested jungle interior, many taking refuge in the dense woods of Mary's Point, a bulging knob of hilly land that curves out from the modern-day eco-resort at Maho Bay to form the island's northernmost point. Every so often, the rebels emerged from hiding to ambush patrolling soldiers or to raid and ransack another plantation.

Over the next several months, the Amina fought off assaults by both Danish and British troops. It wasn't until an elite squadron of French colonial soldiers began a systemic sweep of St. John that the rebels finally gave up their Amina empire aspirations and faced the inevitable grim reality of their immediate future. In the slave-driven society of the colonial-era Caribbean, punishments for even the slightest act of slave disobedience were well publicized and severe. Recriminations for escape were, by design, so egregiously horrifying that only the bravest, most desperate souls dared make the attempt.

If caught, runaway slaves were subjected to a public display of hideous, sadistic torture, usually involving hot irons and crudely executed dismemberment, generally culminating in a slow and painful death. The heinousness of the penalty that would be exacted for seven months of open rebellion, not to mention the murder of several white plantation families, was simply unimaginable; for the Amina rebels, suicide before capture was the only alternative.

The majority of the Amina chose to take their own lives; the few who couldn't bring themselves to make that sacrifice soon regretted their decision.

The tale of the Amina Slave Princess, the one Conrad so vividly recounted, offers a somewhat romanticized twist on this story's sad ending. According to the legend, instead of slitting her throat, the Princess opted to take a suicidal leap into the drowning depths of the Caribbean Sea.

The actual site of this jumping-off point has, of late, become the subject of some discussion on the island. Although Conrad and others place the Princess's fateful plunge at the tip of Mary's Point, many agree the more logical location is from the cliffs of Ram Head, a narrow peninsula of land that protrudes from the arid southeast corner of the island.

From the two-hundred-foot height of this barren, windblown peak, one can see the low shadow of St. Croix to the south and the flat-faced boulders of Virgin Gorda to the east. Directly below, the roiling churn of the ocean surrounds a bone-crushing array of volcanic rock.

As one stands on this dramatic spot, the image of a

lonely, desperate woman leaping from the cactus-strewn precipice fixes the imagination. It is the ultimate act of rebellion, self-sacrifice in the name of self-preservation.

Despite the Virgins' modern-day reputation as an idyllic vacation destination, the evanescent remnants of those tormented souls still float through the islands' ether. The area's dark history is reflected in the faces of many of the Territory's current inhabitants, who have inherited their ancestors' numerical advantage along with much of their seething resentment. Fixation with the Virgin Islands' tragic history dominates and divides the modern political landscape, a deep fissure straining beneath the surface, threatening to rupture the fragile foundations of the Territory's still-nascent democracy.

Every year, as the November 23 anniversary of St. John's 1733 revolt approaches, commemorations of the event fill the calendar, culminating in a public march to the site where the attacks began, at the original Danish fort overlooking Coral Bay. Of late, the dramatic story of the Amina Slave Princess has infiltrated these festivities. She has become a community icon, worshipped with the reverence of a patron saint.

Hannah Sheridan arrived on the island just as this annual frenzy was beginning to build, and our new employee quickly became caught up in the local whirlwind of obsession with the Princess and her tragic death. Somewhere in the midst of this melee and confusion, she set off down the murky path that would culminate in her disappearance.

In a way, it was the public's fixation with this historic figure that pulled Hannah from the water taxi into the waters of the Pillsbury Sound.

It certainly wasn't the ghostly hand of the Slave Princess.

After the events of the last twenty-four hours, of this, I was certain: while the Amina revolt of 1733 was real enough, the Amina Slave Princess herself was nothing more than a vivid figment of someone's imagination.

~ 4 ~

A Disturbing
Introduction

As I sat there at the Dumpster table on the morning after Hannah's disappearance, swirling the straw through my melting daiquiri, my thoughts drifted back to the day our pesky employee first arrived on St. John.

It was the end of October—a Monday—not that the start of any given workweek signified more than a different digit on the calendar. Here in the lazy vacationland aura of the resort, each new day looked pretty much the same as the one that came before it. The only change of any significance would occur with the next drenching rainstorm, and its respite, however temporary, from the oppressive heat.

I woke that muggy morning in my resort-appointed quarters—an older one-bedroom condo unit that was scheduled for renovations in about six months' time—swatting at the high-pitched drone of a gnat hovering near my forehead.

We were nearing the sweltering end to the watch and wait of hurricane season. A couple of storms had come close to grazing the Virgins, but it looked as if we would make it through this year's danger months unscathed.

The smothering humidity was torture enough. The stagnant air and heavy listless heat had dampened the energy of all but the island's insect inhabitants. Even the tiny yellow-chested bananaquits that typically twittered along the tree-tops in nonstop frenetic harmony had lost some of their pep.

With effort, I pulled myself out of bed. After shrugging on a white T-shirt and the cleanest pair of khaki-colored capri pants I could find in my dresser, I staggered across the resort to my office.

There's a lot to be said for a job of actionless supervision. I'd grown comfortably careless in my leisurely lifestyle, delegating most of the resort's day-to-day operation to my assistant, Vivian.

Having clocked another late-night session at the Crunchy Carrot's Dumpster table, I decided a low-key start was on order—one that would allow plenty of recuperation time from the hangover pounding against the inside of my forehead.

A quiet morning on the couch inside my office should do the trick, I thought as I stumbled down the dimly lit hallway on the second floor of the administrative building.

It was with rueful surprise, then, that I found a young woman in a brightly colored sundress waiting outside my office. I stifled a yawn into the half-drunk paper cup of coffee I'd picked up on my way past the breakfast bar and braced my still sleeping brain for the mental rigors of conversation.

The woman pushed a curly tangle of dark hair from her face to expose a timid smile. Nervously, she gripped the pouch of a blue nylon satchel slung over her right shoulder. Then she stepped forward and grabbed hold of my coffee-free hand.

"Good morning, Mrs. Hoffstra."

Her voice hesitated with a bashful tic as I took another swallow from my paper cup.

"I'm Hannah, Hannah Sheridan. I'm supposed to start work for you today."

I nearly choked as the liquid clogged my throat. Hannah Sheridan? Surely, I hadn't heard her correctly.

"It's Pen, just Pen," I replied hoarsely. My vocal cords rasped as I gasped out the short response. "And I'm definitely not anybody's missus."

I drained the last drop from my wilting paper cup and warily surveyed the resort's new employee. She was a tall slender girl in her early twenties with creamy cocoa-colored skin that showcased high cheekbones and emerald green eyes. It was a beautiful, exotic look, the result, I suspected, of a mixed-race heritage.

"I'm sorry. What did you say your name was?" The words stumbled over my sleep-numbed tongue.

"Hannah . . . Sheridan," she repeated, slowly measuring out each word.

Her face bore an honest expression, as if she hadn't noticed the disturbing effect of her introduction.

I coughed loudly at the confirmation. The throbbing in my head intensified, this time from an entirely nonalcoholic source.

"Hi-umm, yep, good morning," I replied, tugging my hand free from her grip as my mind struggled to process the information. "Nice to meet you—Hannah."

I unlocked the door and held it open for her.

"Please, come into my office," I said, still puzzling as she sped past me through the entrance.

A slight breeze eddied in her wake. In the long hot history of the Caribbean, no one had ever walked with the fast-paced vigor of this Hannah Sheridan.

I followed my unexpected visitor through the door, my feet shuffling across the floor at a much slower, more island-appropriate pace. Tossing my crumpled cup into a trash can, I motioned for her to take a seat on the couch at the far side of the room.

"You'll have to bear with me for a moment," I mumbled as I riffled through the papers scattered across my desktop, a maneuver meant only to buy myself a moment to regroup.

It was a coincidence, I told myself. The name had to be a coincidence.

Hannah spun a tight pivot in front of the couch; then, smoothing the folds of her dress, she dropped neatly onto the middle cushion. Despite her shy, diffident manner, she was as bright-eyed and bushy-tailed as they come.

I returned her ardent gaze with a skeptical one. My mouth flattened into an unpleasant grimace, only partly due to the bitter residue I'd sucked down with the last gulp of coffee.

Any second now, I thought, she'll drop the act—and give me the real reason she's sought me out.

I drew in my breath as Hannah leaned forward in her seat.

"You were a lawyer before you came to St. John, weren't you?"

My gut clinched queasily. Aside from the one slipup to Conrad on the ferryboat four years earlier, I hadn't divulged that information to anyone else on the island.

Who was this woman, I wondered silently, and what did she want from me?

"My uncle told me," she added simply, as if this explained her unique fountain of information.

"Your—uncle?" I asked weakly.

"Yes." Her forehead crinkled in confusion. "I thought you knew him?"

She paused and then opened her mouth as if she was about to continue, but I cut her off.

"Yes, well . . ." I said, patting my hands once more across the disarray of papers, trying to suppress my growing panic. I didn't need to hear any more about her omniscient relative. I could think of only one man who knew about my lawyer past—only one man who would have sent a Hannah Sheridan to the resort to see me.

"I'm sure we have your orientation materials here somewhere. Let me see if Vivian can track them down."

Hannah shifted her weight toward the back of the couch, crossing her legs as she studied me curiously. "Do you miss it?" she asked, her green eyes flickering with interest.

"Miss what?" I replied quickly, my pulse accelerating.

"Practicing law," she supplied with an innocent blink of her eyes.

With a weak smile, I picked up the receiver from the telephone on the right side of my desk and pushed a quick-dial button that rang through to Vivian. I needed to get Hannah Sheridan—or whoever the heck she really was—out of my office as quickly as possible.

"Yes?" a steady female voice answered on the other end of the line.

Vivian was a short-statured woman of solid build, stern demeanor, and skin the deep espresso brown of roasted coffee beans. She'd grown up in the Bahamas, an island chain that, she never tired of telling me, greatly surpassed the Virgins in natural beauty and splendor.

"So, uh, Vivian, I have one of the new employees here in my office. A Hannah Sheridan . . . ?" I let the end of the sentence trail off into a hopeful half question as I glanced uneasily across the room at my couch.

After a long moment of silence, she issued a stiff, "Yes?"

It was a typical Vivian response, one that conveyed the full brunt of her frostiness. She wasn't about to volunteer a single syllable more than absolutely necessary. She never did; the woman lived to make me suffer.

Vivian was my right-hand man—or woman, as the case may be. In truth, she practically ran the place all on her own. Any issue requiring substantive study or analysis, I immediately delegated to Vivian. She gruffed and complained constantly, and never missed an opportunity to point out my obvious incompetence, but I suspected she secretly enjoyed the responsibility. The rest of the staff went to her first with their requests, knowing I would immediately rubber-stamp anything that had received her preapproval.

"Well, uh, are you busy right now?" I asked somewhat testily into the receiver, twirling the phone cord with my fingers.

I glanced nervously at the woman seated across the room from me. The sooner I dropped this Hannah egg in Vivian's basket, the better.

"Yes," Vivian said slowly and suspiciously, clearly sensing I was about to push some unwanted task in her direction.

"Can you come up to my office anyway?" An urgency crept into my voice. "Please," I added, even though it pained me to do so.

There was another pause during which time I imagined Vivian's pained expression on the other end of the line. This was followed by a nearly silent grunt, indicating she had lifted her hands, palms upward, in supplication to some unknown deity in the hopes that it might deliver her from the earthly torture of my perpetually unreasonable demands.

Finally, her voice came back through the line, short but rigidly polite. "I'll be right there."

With a relieved sigh, I set down the receiver. "So, Hannah . . ." The name struck a constricting chord as it came out. "Have you found your room yet?" I asked with forced breeziness. "I'm sure Vivian can take you there next."

"Oh, I'm not staying at the resort," Hannah replied swiftly, uncrossing her legs as she inched once more toward the edge of the couch.

She was like a hummingbird, her wings beating a thousand times a minute . . . draining every last ounce of energy from my bleary-eyed being.

"I reserved an eco-tent over at Maho Bay. I dropped my bags off there on my way in this morning." She stood from her seat and stepped anxiously toward my desk. "I hope that's okay."

"Sure, certainly," I replied lightly, pondering as I leaned back in my chair. I'd never known any of our workers to turn down a free room at the resort for a tent in the woods. But, then again, this was no regular employee. "No problem at all."

A sharp knock rapped against the open door frame to my office.

"Ah, Vivian!" I called out briskly, waving the reluctant woman into my office. "Please, let me introduce you to . . ." The name hung in my throat. "Hannah Sheridan."

Vivian stalked heavily through the door, her square face warily surveying the newcomer.

Hannah bounced toward her, bumping into a stack of papers on the side of my desk as she crossed the room. "Hi, Vivian," she said, awkwardly thrusting her hand toward Vivian's stoic figure.

"Welcome," Vivian replied, her flat, even tone unmatched to the sentiment expressed.

"*Vivian* will be showing you around today," I announced boldly, ignoring my assistant's instantly rebuking stare.

Hannah slapped her hands together girlishly. "Great! When can we start?"

She seemed not to notice the revolted expression on Vivian's face as I hurried the two of them out of my office. No rain could wilt her effusive flower.

As Hannah skipped down the hallway, her voice floated back to us. "I want to learn as much as I can about the island. I've got so many questions for you . . ."

Vivian scowled at me with silent but livid recrimination. Then, she spun around and stormed off after Hannah.

I pressed the door shut and firmly twisted the lock, breathing out a temporary sigh of relief.

In the four years since my arrival on the island, not a single question had been raised about my assumed identity. My metamorphosis from down-and-out estate lawyer to disheveled and frequently inebriated resort manager had gone off without a hitch—until now.

How much did this young woman know about my past? The "uncle" she'd mentioned—why had he sent her here, and what did he want?

Even more important, I thought as I thumped the back of my head against the door, why was she using my name?

~ 5 ~

The Amina Record

In the dusky basement of a New York City library, a wiry little man with thinning gray hair dyed an unnatural shade of reddish brown crept through a dusky maze of bookshelves. Humming softly, he skimmed his fingers over the spines, searching through the overloaded stacks for the Dewey decimal code number scrawled across the scrap of paper he held in his hand. It was a listing for an obscure title he'd found at the computer terminal on the main floor, several levels above.

At last, Conrad Corsair located the item on a top shelf, several rows removed from its designated location. Standing on his tiptoes, he wiggled the book free from its wedged position, releasing a poof of dust and cobwebs. Yipping out a series of light nasal sneezes, he carried the heavy volume to a small table near the center of the basement and flicked on a reading lamp. The yellowed pages creaked as he flipped the book open to the desired selection.

Clearing his throat, Conrad glanced around the room to confirm that he was alone. Then, with a slight pump of his eyebrows, he pulled a crumpled packet from the back pocket of his tight-fitting blue jeans and set it on the table. The paper bag rustled as he fished around inside for one of his special self-rolled cigarettes. Once he'd made his selection, he brought the lumpy cylinder to his lips, waved the flame of a lighter beneath the opposite end, and took in a deep doobie-infused breath.

Exhaling with a relaxed sigh, Conrad unfolded a pair of dime-store reading glasses, slid the frames onto his thin face, and bent his head over the open book.

As he began to read, the basement's cramped ceiling faded into the pale arid blue of a cloudless sky. The dingy, graffiti-marked reading table became a dry parched savannah, framed by the purple-mounded humps of distant mountains. A hot, dry African sun burned down on the wide listless plain, wilting the field of grassy reeds, browning the scattering of scrubby, low-slung trees. What few creatures quivered beneath this searing atmosphere flattened themselves against the curve of the earth, seeking even the slightest shadow as a reprieve from the parching heat.

A young woman's galloping footsteps suddenly broke through the baking stillness. The calloused soles of her feet slapped against the dusty red dirt as she sprinted headlong across the savannah, hurtling down a narrow goat trail.

The sizzling sun cooked the smooth surface of the woman's cocoa brown shoulders, searing the tender scalp beneath her curly mop of dark hair—but the Amina Princess dared not stop to search for shade. Nothing could slow her frantic, fleeing pace.

The woman's eyes squeezed shut as she raced across the field. Her pounding legs needed little visual guidance for the path whose every twist and turn was etched into her memory. She rubbed her hands over her pinched eyelids, trying to blot out the sky's blazing light, but no amount of blackness would ever erase the scene she had just witnessed. Life as she knew it had come to an abrupt and horrible end.

*   *   *

A few hours earlier, the Princess had risen from a restful night's sleep. Leaping up from her mat, she'd set off on an early hunt, stalking a guinea fowl through the thickets at the savannah's edge, not far from her tribe's encampment. It was her favorite time of day, the crisp morning half-light before everyone else awoke—a moment of solitude that she shared with her wild surroundings.

She moved with the soundless ease of a lion, her body a weightless spirit slipping noiselessly through the swaying grasses. Her senses came alive as she tracked the bird's skittish cluck. It didn't take long for her keen eyes to find its frozen shape, immobilized in the shadows beneath the thorny cover of a mulberry bush, nearly camouflaged by the brown speckled coloring of its feathers.

Carefully, she aimed the sharp tip of her body-length spear at the guinea's gangly neck, honing in on the throbbing vein whose rapid tempo provided the only evidence of the bird's racing pulse.

In that single moment, the seconds stretched out across the rigid rule of time, and both the Princess and the guinea knew that it was done for.

A slicing draft whistled through the silence, the sound representing the volume of air displaced by the spear as the weapon drove through the prickly spines and pegged the guinea to the ground.

The Princess watched as the bird thrashed against the dirt, fruitlessly heaving its weight against the spear's piercing grasp. She felt no remorse, no pity for the dying creature. It was the natural order of things in the African plains, a matter of survival. She was a hunter, like all of her ancestors who had come before.

When at last the bird had expired, the Princess pulled the spear's tip from its anchor in the soil. She twirled the pole in her hands, gingerly threading the dead bird out from the twisted branches. Lifting her prize, she judged the bird's size and weight. Even her haughty brothers, she thought proudly, would be impressed by her contribution to the morning's breakfast.

Clutching the guinea's limp neck, the Princess skipped off down the path to her tribe's circle of huts, sniffing the air for a smoky hint of the day's first fire. The cooking servants should have gathered the kindling by now. A savory gruel would be bubbling in the camp's large iron pots.

But as she neared the edge of the encampment, her forehead creased with concern. The plume of smoke rising from the trees up ahead had a dark ominous color, its billowing char indicative of a far greater volume of combustion than that produced by a single fire pit.

Her anxiety heightened as she reached the edge of the village. There was no sign of the typical morning bustle, no evidence of the regular foot traffic between the huts—and everywhere a dense choking smoke.

She had only been gone a short while. What had happened during her brief absence?

Tentatively, the Princess rounded the corner to her father's hut. A fog of smoke and red dust hung over the entrance. The air was thick with the scent of a recent struggle, stinging her eyes, blurring her vision. The morning's busy chatter had been replaced by an eerie silence and the rancid smell of death—one far more potent than that of the guinea.

The bird fell from the Princess's grasp as she leaned into the hut's dark hazy entrance. Her stunned gaze sank to the stiff body sprawled across the scuffed-up ground and the ragged, blood-soaked heap of her father's clothing—piled up next to his severed head.

The Princess's oldest brother knelt on the floor next to the corpse, his face blanched with shock as he examined the cut below their father's once proud chin. Her mouth opened to set loose the horrified scream coursing through her body, but a hand quickly reached out to muffle it. A second brother wrapped his arm around the Princess's trembling shoulders while together they stared in disbelief at the gruesome display on the floor.

The pounding *thud* of human feet sounded in the distance, cutting through the awed hush of the hut. The older brother snapped his head up from his father's mangled figure. Lurching forward, he shoved the Princess out of the tent.

"Run!" he yelled hoarsely.

She stumbled, her feet tripping clumsily on the red dirt. She shook her head, numb with confusion as her brother grabbed her shoulders and spun her body toward the savannah.

"Go!" he ordered firmly. "Don't let them take you alive!"

The Princess panted heavily as she reached the end of the goat trail on the far end of the open plain. Her body was drenched with sweat, and her throat rasped for liquid, but she immediately began the rugged hike up into the mountains. Picking her way through the thickening forest, she slowly gained altitude. She had to put as much distance as possible between herself and the sabotaged encampment.

All the while, her head pounded with questions. How could this have happened? What had become of the rest of her family? Who had attacked her tribe? Which of her father's allies had turned against them?

She reached a stand of trees overlooking a steep cliff and slipped into the shadows beneath their canopy, melding her body into a nest of branches. It was a hiding place she had used many times before—usually after playing a joke on one of her brothers for which she feared retribution. Never before had she stood in this spot with such urgency, desperately willing the smooth contours of her skin to harden into the shape of the surrounding wooden limbs.

Trying to steady her frightened nerves, the Princess reached a hand up to her collarbone and cupped it around an amulet that hung from her neck on a thin leather strap. Her fingers, still sticky with the blood of the guinea fowl, ran along the raised ridges of the iron-forged medallion.

The circular piece of metal had been crafted into the

shape of the sun. It was the symbol of her tribe—her father's emblem, known throughout the region.

Her ragged breathing began to slow as she took a calming strength from the amulet. Her thoughts focused on her immediate needs, how she would survive alone in the bush for the next twenty-four hours.

But as the Princess began to sift mechanically through her available resources, she felt the presence of another being lurking in the woods behind her. The hopeful breath within her chest instantly evaporated.

In that long elastic moment, she stood, paralyzed, fervently praying one of her family members had escaped to meet her—all the while knowing, like the guinea, that it was not a friendly companion who had tracked her to this spot.

Her eyes drifted to the edge of the cliff as she heard her brother's voice, calling out his last cautionary warning.

"Don't let them take you alive."

The ledge was just a few footsteps away. A short sprint would take her to it—and the endless drop into the abyss. The Princess swallowed hard, trying to summon the will to throw herself forward.

Her feet dug defiantly into the rocky soil; the muscles of her legs ached with stubborn resistance.

At long last, she overcame her body's instinctive objection and lunged from her hiding place, committed to the fateful jump . . . but it was too late.

A swift blow to the back of her head knocked her unconscious, and her body crumpled to the ground.

Conrad slammed the book shut and pushed back from the table. He wiped the sleeve of his shirt across his face; then he reached his hands up to massage a stiffness that had crept into his shoulders. As he popped a loud crick in his neck, he noticed his cigarette had burnt all the way down to its end.

"Whoa, whoa, whoa . . . what happened here?" he muttered as he twisted the stub in his fingers.

He'd been so engrossed in the story, he had missed out

on the most pungent puffs. He puckered his lips and sucked in a last stale puff from the charred paper. Lifting his head, he tried to inhale a large volume of the air above the table, a futile attempt to recapture the lost smoke. Still snorting loudly, he climbed onto the seat of his chair and tilted his head toward the basement's low ceiling.

He suddenly stopped, midsniff—someone had entered the room. A shadowed figure lurked among the stacks, just out of view.

"Hello?" Conrad called out warily, hopping off the chair as the remains of the cigarette dropped from his fingers to the floor.

Crushing the stub beneath the toe of his boot, he brushed the bag of cigarettes off the side of the table and kicked it into the bottom shelf of the nearest bookcase.

"Who goes there?" he asked suspiciously.

The shadow issued no response.

"District Attorney Man," Conrad grumbled under his breath, "you've got yourself one heck of a persistent streak . . ."

A slender, barefoot woman stepped into the half-lit corridor on the far side of the basement. She wore a close-fitting beaded vest on her torso and a knee-length sarong around her waist. A dizzy mop of dark curly hair bounced youthfully around her shoulders. Despite the frosty New York winter outside the library, her cocoa-colored skin glowed with an equatorial warmth. Her neck was encircled by a narrow strip of leather; it had been threaded through an amulet whose shiny metal glinted in the dim glow of the nearest lightbulb.

"Wha—well, hello there." Conrad quickly smoothed over his surprise. He ran his hand over the balding crown of his head as the Amina Princess peered bashfully around the corner of a shelving unit.

He cleared his throat. "I . . . I was just reading about you."

Cautiously, the Princess approached the table. She gave Conrad a timid smile; then she wrapped her fingers around the edge of the book and slowly reopened it.

"You want me to . . . ?"

Nodding silently, she pointed to the text.

"Yes, of course," Conrad said, shrugging his shoulders as he returned to his seat.

Pushing the reading glasses farther up the bridge of his nose, he resumed the story.

~ 6 ~

The Miami Encounter

I stood on the small balcony outside my office, hidden from passersby on the brick path below by a dense bank of trees that had grown up against the railing. Through the mass of limbs and leaves, I watched as Hannah accompanied Vivian up the hill toward the resort's main reception area.

Even from a distance, the young woman exuded an inquisitive vigor. Her curly hair bounced in time with her energetic step as she carried on a lively one-sided conversation with Vivian, who sulked silently beside her.

My eyes followed the mismatched pair until they disappeared from view; then I returned inside my office, my earlier headache now amplified by a raging apprehension.

Scooping up the "Penelope Hoffstra" nameplate from the surface of the desk, I began to pace back and forth across the room, smacking the flat side of the triangular-shaped wedge against the palm of my hand.

"Hannah Sheridan," I muttered grumpily as I tried to make sense of the morning's events. "Not very likely."

It had been four years since I'd last heard anyone utter that name—four years since I'd left behind my life in the

States—four years since a mysterious airport encounter had changed everything.

An eternity had passed since that fateful scene.

When I looked back, I hardly recognized the harried woman in the tired business suit, nylon stockings, and high-heel shoes, wearily rolling her suitcase through the Miami airport. It was as if I were seeing someone else.

I was on the return leg of an unsuccessful business trip, the latest in a never-ending series of increasingly fruitless endeavors.

The airport was midway through a lengthy renovation project, and the wing where I was stranded had yet to receive the benefit of the coming improvements. After a long walk through a construction detour, I'd finally reached a crowded row of uncomfortable plastic bucket seats next to my gate.

I picked an open chair and slumped into its hard curvature, awaiting news on my indefinitely delayed flight home to LAX. A thin volume of air circulated through the failing ventilation system, overlaying a stale, moldy scent to the departure area's overall sense of disarray and disruption.

Groaning, I kicked off my left pump, cracked the stiff bones in my big toe, and sized up the blister I'd worked up during the hike. Accepting the inevitable fate of a long sit, I unbuttoned my suit jacket and loosened the top buttons of my blouse.

The outfit had begun to show wear after one too many circuits through the dry cleaner's, but there wasn't any room in my diminishing budget for a replacement. I would have to make do until I figured out a way to reverse the current downward trend in income.

I'd spent the day with an elderly client in Boca, a cranky septuagenarian who was trying to determine which of her heirs would inherit her estate. She was still mulling over her options, but after numerous rants about her unworthy offspring, I was willing to bet her favorite tabby would end up with her most valuable asset, a nicely appointed ocean-front beach house.

The old lady looked to have a good year or so left in her, giving me, I hoped, time to solidify my relationship with the soon-to-be affluent feline.

I glanced around the dingy waiting area and thought gloomily of my pending coach seat to Los Angeles—six hours trapped in the confines of a middle seat with nothing but a can of soda to look forward to. Kneading my forehead, I propped my feet up on my suitcase, took a long sip from the now cold cup of coffee I'd purchased halfway through my marathon trek through the terminal, and opened my laptop computer.

After nearly a decade of struggling to build my solo legal practice, I was finally coming to the conclusion that the lawyer life wasn't all it was cracked up to be.

As I began tapping away at the keyboard, searching for alternative flights, a heavyset man waddled down the narrow aisle in front of my row of seats. Glancing up from the computer, I pulled my knees to one side to allow him space to pass through. He turned, pivoted like a stuffed penguin, and squeezed himself into the seat beside me.

I swiveled further sideways, trying to avoid the extra folds of padded skin that spilled out over the armrest as he settled into his chair. My eyes scanned the waiting area, searching for another empty seat, but, predictably, they were all now taken.

The swollen fingers of the man's right hand tugged against the collar of his golf shirt. A thin layer of sweat dotted his brow, and a light fog clouded the round lenses of his wire-rim glasses.

The gate attendant's voice boomed through the intercom, providing a noninformative update to my flight's status as the man over-occupying the next seat bent down to the floor to sift through his briefcase. A moment later, he emerged with a large manila envelope.

"Hannah Sheridan?" the man asked, politely clearing his throat.

A sudden intake of moist, moldy air flooded my lungs. I snapped shut the lid of my laptop and turned to give him a suspicious look.

My first instinct pegged him as a process server. I rolled my eyes internally. Another malpractice lawsuit, I thought grimly—that was all I needed.

After a moment's pause, I dismissed this option as unlikely. If he were one of *those* guys, he would have already slapped the papers in my lap.

Perhaps he was from the state bar's ethics committee, I considered ruefully. They were due to issue their ruling on the latest complaint against my law license any day now . . .

But, upon consideration, this too, I rejected. The bar wouldn't have sent someone all the way to Miami just to deliver that news in person, and it was too soon for the Florida boards to have caught onto my activities in their state.

Hmm, I mused, tapping my fingernails against the metal surface of my computer. Maybe he was some sort of petty-crime bounty hunter, cashing in on the stack of unpaid parking and speeding tickets registered to my name.

The possibilities were numerous, I concluded with a sigh, and none of them promised a pleasant outcome. This ballooning walrus of a man had caught mc at a point of minimal resistance. Whatever bad news he had to dump on me, there was no point in trying to avoid it. If this poor fellow had tracked me all the way through the airport's maze of dusty construction detours, I supposed he deserved to deliver his coup de grâce.

Nevertheless, I glanced down at my feet. Both shoes were kicked off. I was ready to run if necessary, and I stood a greater chance of escape without the high heels. Clutching my laptop with one hand and the handle of my roll-around with the other, my face flattened into an acquiescent grimace, and I nodded my confirmation.

Yes, he'd found Hannah Sheridan—at least some depleted version of her.

"Please, I have something for you," he said in a measured, even tone. "A proposal I think you might want to consider."

I stared at him as if he'd lost his mind.

"Please," he repeated. "Take a look. I think you'll be surprised."

Skeptically, I took the envelope. Pursing my lips, I pulled open the end flap and slid out the contents.

The papers inside outlined an unusual offer—one unlike any I had ever seen or imagined.

It had to be a joke, I reasoned, and glanced around the terminal, expecting to find someone smirking in a corner.

There were no obvious suspects; the area was a typical sea of introspection. Cell phones, tabloid magazines, and any number of handheld devices dominated the landscape. I was surrounded by strangers, each occupied by one means or another of self-amusement.

I returned my gaze to the puffy-faced man seated beside me. How had he located me, I wondered, and what was the catch? More important, what did he stand to gain?

He noted my perplexed expression and cleared his throat.

"I had someone else in mind for the job, but she fell through at the last minute."

A puzzled stare was all I could muster. He tried again.

"I need someone on the ground there . . . someone with your skills."

"Skills?" I asked dubiously, finally finding my voice.

"Yes," he replied calmly. "Your legal training, your"—he paused and raised a suggestive eyebrow—"adaptive abilities."

I squirmed uncomfortably in the hard plastic chair. Clearly, this guy knew far too much about me and my slightly illicit operations.

As it became harder and harder to pay my bills, I had slipped into somewhat less than honest and aboveboard relations with my clients. A couple of my creative variations on the truth had come back to haunt me—to be honest, the California malpractice suit was the least of my legal troubles.

The man gave me a reassuring smile and nodded at the

papers I'd removed from the envelope. "Take a close look. Let me know what you think."

As the rain continued its numbing patter against the windows behind my seat, I returned my attention to the short sheaf of papers and began studying the details. The pay was minimal, but housing and meals were included; the scenery, it went without saying, came for free. When it came right down to it, what else did I really need?

I found myself giving the proposal serious consideration. The more I thought about it, the more the idea gained in appeal. Assuming false credentials wasn't exactly new territory for me. Stepping into another person's dream job on an idyllic tropical island where cell phone reception was spotty and pantyhose were a rare, even extinct invention— what was the worst that could happen?

"Penelope Hoffstra," I murmured out loud, trying the name on for size. It was almost like slipping into a new pair of clothes. The moniker felt a little stiff at first, but it softened to my shape the more I repeated it in my head.

I avoided asking myself what might have occurred to the real Penelope Hoffstra that would have left her so conveniently unavailable for this assignment.

Desperate times call for blind leaps of faith. If it didn't work out, I told myself, I would simply head for home after a much needed week of sunny rest and relaxation; I could regroup and remake myself from there.

And so, strange as it may seem, at the end of my conversation with the mysteriously marshmallow-ing man, I took the package from him, walked up to the ticket counter, and changed my destination to STT, the airport code for St. Thomas, U.S. Virgin Islands.

That had led to the best four years of my life, I summed up as I glanced across my office to the balcony doors and the tropical surroundings beyond. I wasn't giving up this gig without a fight.

Once more, I replayed the morning's conversation in my

head. Try as I might, I couldn't dismiss the interaction as one of luckless coincidence.

"Hannah Sheridan," I repeated warily.

The young woman's presence here at the resort was meant to send me a message, to provoke a reaction. Someone—most likely, my large friend from Miami—had sent her here.

I slid behind my desk, pulled open the bottom drawer, and retrieved my not-so-secret bottle of Cruzan rum. After a deep steadying gulp, I marched resolutely to the door of my office.

The next step was to figure out why.

~ 7 ~

Government House

A short distance offshore from St. John, a white catamaran motored across the Pillsbury Sound, heading toward St. Thomas. The current splashed against the red-painted lettering on the side of the boat and the words that read WATER TAXI.

Twenty minutes later, the vessel angled around the island's craggy bottom lip into Charlotte Amalie's protected harbor. Slowing to an idle, the boat pulled into an open slot along the waterfront near the mint green block of the Legislature Building.

The brawny captain swung himself down from the upper deck and tossed a heavy rope around the nearest concrete piling. Following the rope onto shore, he pulled the boat up against the side of the wharf. With expertise gained from years of repetition, he quickly cinched a knot in the line and slipped a lock around the mooring.

His boat secured, the captain set off across the shoreline's main thoroughfare. Selecting a narrow road heading inland, he tromped up the incline through the downtown area, his worn flip-flop sandals popping against the rough asphalt. Past Fort Christian's bright red edifice, he veered right to cut through the edge of Charlotte Amalie's primary public green-space, the Emancipation Garden.

At the opposite side of the park, the captain's path turned sharply steeper. A sheen of sweat broke out across his dark chiseled face as he labored another block up the hill to his destination.

Built in the 1860s, the three-story Government House held the main offices for the Territory's governor and much of his cabinet. The ornately decorated interior showcased several paintings by Pissarro, a native of the island. A white iron railing formed a delicate trim around the building's front porch and balcony, which looked out across the hillside to the cruise ships docking in the harbor below.

The captain wiped a dingy handkerchief against his brow as he skipped up a short flight of red-carpeted steps into a wood-paneled foyer. He was recognized at once by the receptionist, who ushered him toward a mahogany stair-case leading to the building's second floor. At the top of the stairs, she led him down a hallway into the governor's well-appointed office.

Wordlessly, the captain took a seat at a small oval table, next to the governor's other guest, who had arrived a few minutes earlier. The receptionist discreetly departed, shutting the office door behind her.

The governor waited until he heard the receptionist's footsteps treading down the staircase before he opened the meeting.

"Thank you both for coming this afternoon," his deep, gravelly voice intoned.

Then, he turned toward the first guest and asked with thoughtful curiosity, "Please, tell me more about this Amina Princess."

~ 8 ~

The Empty Folder

I cracked open the door to my office and, after confirming that the hallway outside was clear of the perplexing Hannah Sheridan, headed for the exit at the end of the corridor. A concrete stairwell attached to the outside of the building led down to the first floor and the resort's main administrative suite.

Generally, I avoided Vivian's frigid lair of purposeful efficiency, lest she use the opportunity to coerce me into doing some manner of substantive work. But, given that she would be tied up with Hannah's orientation on the opposite side of the resort for at least another hour, I proceeded without hesitation into her office suite—for once, without first conjuring up a ready excuse as to why I was immediately needed elsewhere.

I wrapped my fingers around the door handle and steeled myself for entry. Vivian controlled the thermostat on the opposite side of the glass. For a person who'd been born in the tropics, the woman had an unnaturally strong preference for cold environments.

Wincing in anticipation, I pulled open the door and released the interior's icy blast. My breath began to crystallize within my chest, and an icicle, I felt certain, was forming off the tip of my nose. Shivering, I hustled inside.

The administrative suite was the central hub of the resort's business activities. It occupied a large room that had been partitioned with five-foot-high prefab walls into a half dozen office cubicles. Within each cell sat one or more of Vivian's busy worker bees, tapping away at their computer keyboards, speaking softly into their telephone headsets, or otherwise performing the essential functions that kept the resort running smoothly.

The office buzz fell silent as I slipped behind the cloth wall that demarcated Vivian's corner space. A few heads poked up over the top of the dividers, watching suspiciously as I slid into the seat behind her desk.

"I . . . uh . . . just need to check on something," I offered with an awkward shrug.

There was no use trying to disguise my actions. These were all Vivian's people—local hires who reported to her directly. She would be informed of my visit as soon as I was out of earshot. Likely, several of them were texting her my whereabouts that very instant.

The chair groaned as I swiveled around to survey the surface of the desk. Per Vivian's exacting standards, everything on her workstation was laid out in a neat and tidy arrangement: a pair of pens lay precisely placed in parallel with the stapler, while a stack of paperwork sat center stage, waiting to be processed.

I paused to admire a photo of her six-year-old son, Hamilton, displayed at a forty-five-degree angle on the desk's far left side. There wasn't a speck of dust on the frame; it looked as if it had been polished that very morning.

The first numbing pricks of frostbite brought me back to the purpose of my visit, and I turned my attention to the drawer where Vivian kept the resort's confidential personnel files. After plucking a bobby pin from a small plastic kiosk sitting on a nearby bookcase, I unfolded it and fed it into the keyhole.

"Not my first time performing this maneuver," I muttered to myself as still more obvious stares emerged over the top of the cubicles.

Gently, I twisted the slender metal rod, searching the interior of the lock for its tumbler. After a quick toggle of the bobby pin, there was a slight releasing *click* of moving metal, and the drawer rolled open.

One of the onlookers picked up a telephone receiver and began to dial as I blew a warming breath on my fingers and started thumbing through the files.

The interior of the desk was as precisely ordered as the top. It took only a few seconds to find the paper tab labeled with the hand-printed name "Sheridan, Hannah." I pulled the folder out of the drawer and eagerly flipped it open.

My loud sigh of disappointment reached all of the room's listening ears.

The folder was completely empty.

On the opposite side of Vivian's frost-covered window, the resort's maintenance activities were proceeding through their regular daily schedule. Across the lawn from the administrative building, a group of dark-skinned men crouched beneath a row of bushes, trimming and weeding the shrubbery.

The resort's ground crew had been at it since daybreak; this was their fifth targeted location of the morning. They had started the shift with vigor and enthusiasm, but as the sun rose and the muggy heat intensified, their movements had grown more and more languid. There was only so much fight the human body could put up against such an oppressive environment.

At last, the group's leader stood and waived his hand in a circle over his head, signaling the end of the pruning session. Manto began loading the gardening tools onto the short bed of a modified golf cart while his men reached for their water bottles. There was still more to do—there was always more to do—but it would soon be too hot to continue.

Manto and his ground crew waged a never-ending battle against the encroaching jungle that surrounded the resort. The front lines pitted the men's rusty metal shears against a dense foliage of invading tendrils whose reaching grasp could progress several inches over the course of a single day. The vegetation resumed its guerrilla assault the moment the men packed up their gear.

One day, Manto thought wearily, the jungle would be victorious.

He wiped the cleanest section of his shirt across his eyes and mouth. A grimy layer of the island's black volcanic earth covered his skin and clothing. His feet steamed inside his floppy oversized boots; his arms ached from the constant hacking motion of the hoe.

Manto reached for the throbbing muscles at the small of his back as he glanced across the field at the fogged glass on the first floor of the administrative building. Despite his aches and pains, the sight of the resort's head manager seated in the chair behind Vivian's desk caused him to momentarily forget his exhaustion.

"Hmm," he mused curiously as he reached a grubby finger up to the flat round of his nose and tapped its smushed center.

Vivian had stomped past the ground crew half an hour earlier. She'd been in an unusually foul mood, even by her standards. Presumably, it was the young woman bouncing along beside Vivian that had soured her demeanor—the girl in the spinning sundress had been asking a lot of questions about the resort.

In response to Manto's raised eyebrows, Vivian had jerked her head at the girl and spit out a curt one-word explanation.

"Peen-ello-pee."

Manto's brown face creased into a broad smile. He ran his tongue across the top row of his ragged yellow teeth.

The cheery plump of his cheeks pillowed out over the flat skin above his mouth.

He shook his head as Pen jimmied the lock on the filing cabinet-sized drawer beneath Vivian's desk.

"Pin, Pin, Pin," he rumbled into a loud guffaw. *"Viv iz nut goin' to bey happ-ee about dis."*

The two women were constantly spatting at each other, and Manto loved to egg them on. Their daily fights provided endless fodder for the resort's numerous gossiping tongues. He took a mental note to ask Vivian about Pen's unauthorized pillaging of her desk—that would be sure to provoke an entertaining reaction.

Then, he directed his attention to the nearest palm tree and the cluster of plump coconuts tucked beneath the crown of fronds at its top.

He motioned to one of his workers. The man immediately stripped off his shirt and shoes, tucked a machete into the hem of his pants, and began scaling up the tree's ribbed trunk.

Manto watched anxiously as his worker clung precariously to the tree, thirty feet or so above the ground. He wasn't sure which was more dangerous: the threat of coconuts falling on unsuspecting guests or the risk a machete-whacking worker might accidentally cut off a limb.

"Aye!" he called up with concern. *"Wach' ya-self up there."*

The man waved the machete in casual acknowledgement.

"Hmm." Manto's calloused hands gripped nervously at the slight paunch that had begun to thicken his aging waistline. The wrinkled lines etched across his forehead deepened with worry.

Thwack. Thwack. Thwack.

A coconut sprang loose from the cluster and dropped slowly through the air, hitting the grass below with a loud *thump.*

Yawning, Manto glanced down at his watch. As soon as this grove was de-nutted, he would be off for a quick shower and a change of clothing. His afternoons and evenings he spent driving one of the island's many truck taxis. His wages supported an extended family that included numerous grandchildren. Even working double shifts, he found it difficult to make ends meet.

Another coconut bounced across the lawn as Manto turned to stare up at the sky. It was clear and blue at the moment, but he detected a slight change in the atmosphere's stagnant swelter.

He'd lived in the Virgins all his life; these islands were in his blood. After seventy years, he knew every culvert, cove, and crumbling stone ruin. The feeling in his bones was a far more accurate predictor than all the fancy radar equipment used by the weatherman on St. Thomas. A heavy brooding storm was gathering in the Atlantic, somewhere off the west coast of Africa, soaking up energy and moisture that it would later dump on the Lesser Antilles.

"Storm's komin'," a scratchy voice whispered in his ear. *"A week hout, mey-bey two."*

With a start, Manto turned to face the frail, bony woman who had sneaked up behind him.

She wore a loose-hanging cotton jumper, the official uniform for the resort's large cadre of housecleaners. Her skinny legs poked out from beneath the garment, feeding into rubber-soled sandals that were as oversized as her dress.

Manto had known Beulah Shah his entire life, ever since they were both small children squirming in the pews at the local Moravian church. Even when Beulah was a little girl, she'd had an unnerving knack for suddenly appearing out of nowhere, noiselessly and without notice.

She leaned toward him, her wizened face unsettlingly close to his. A stale breath oozed out of her nearly toothless mouth.

"Yes, ma'am," Manto replied, gulping as he nodded in agreement with her weather assessment. *"I kin' feel it too."*

Beulah stared, trancelike, into his brown eyes; then her gaze swept across his sweaty shirt, narrowing in on his throat.

Manto felt his chest constricting, the air stagnating within his lungs. It was as if she were looking right through his skin, visually clamping off his breathing capacity. After a long moment, he managed to clear his throat and took a wide step backward onto the lawn.

Beulah gave him an odd, spooky smile; then she tottered off down the walk toward the administrative building.

Manto's eyes followed her frail figure as she crept up to the window beside Vivian's cubicle. Pen had already vacated the administrative suite, but it appeared something on Vivian's desk had caught Beulah's interest.

Manto watched as the old woman pushed up on her tiptoes and pressed her forehead against the glass. He shivered with involuntary apprehension as he wondered what Beulah was up to—before jumping briskly to the side to dodge an incoming coconut.

~ *9* ~

Fred

I returned to my office a few hours later with a boxed sandwich from the food kiosk by the pool, still none the wiser about how the recently arrived Hannah Sheridan had found her way into the resort's employment. I'd left the empty file laid open on Vivian's desk, a pointed question I felt certain she would understand as soon as she returned to the administrative suite. For the moment, there was nothing left to do but resume my daily routine.

I grabbed the contents of my inbox from the side of my desk and set up camp on the shaded balcony outside my office. After plopping down into a plastic recliner (one I'd "borrowed" several years ago from the pool area), I poured myself a generous shot of rum and offered a toast to Fred, an iguana who spent most of his afternoons in the treetops just beyond my balcony's railing.

"Alley-oop and down the hatch," I called into the greenery.

It sometimes took ten minutes or more of searching through the dense foliage before Fred's long lizard shape jumped out at me from the leafy maze of tree limbs. Once spotted, however, his leathery green body was impossible to ignore.

A ruffling of spines rose like a crown from the top curve

of Fred's neck and extended along the sharp ridge of his
back. The rounded plump of his belly was decorated on
either side with swirling circles of lighter and darker shades
of green, a color combination that continued into alternat-
ing stripes on his tail. A sprinkling of shiny purplish nod-
ules rose up through the skin beneath his stiff shoulders,
adorning his chest like medals of honor. When a direct ray
of light reflected off his coat, the surface shimmered like
an armored chain-mail suit.

He turned his head to look me as I issued the toast. The
frozen contours of his angular face transmitted a dignified,
regal expression. He was really quite beautiful—for a giant
scaly lizard.

Beyond his rugged good looks, Fred, I'd found, was an
excellent listener. I sought his counsel on a regular basis. He
took his time forming his opinions, but his judgments, once
given, were unassailably sound in their logic and reasoning.

"What are we up against here, Fred?" I mused, still pondering Hannah's inauspicious arrival.

Fred blinked cryptically at me. Then, he tore off a nearby
leaf and began the slow process of breaking it down with
the sharp points of his tiny teeth.

Sighing heavily, I refilled my shot glass and began to flip
through the day's pile of paperwork. Fred's advice generally became much clearer after a couple doses of Cruzan.

The sheets on the top of the stack had been dropped off
earlier by one of Vivian's minions. A red sticky note cut into
the shape of a pointed arrow had been affixed to each paper,
indicating where my signature was needed. It was all business as usual: routine approvals for overtime, applications
for leaves of absence, and a couple of bills for the water taxi
that picked up day workers who'd missed the regular ferry
back to Red Hook.

I glanced only briefly at the contents of each page as I
scrawled a hurried rendition of "Penelope Hoffstra" next to
the sticky-note arrows—the sloppier the signature, the better. I'd never quite got the hang of the original Penelope's
capital "P."

"Fred," I said as I finally turned to the last arrow-marked sheet, "why don't we get you some signature authority?" I spun a wide-tipped autographing pen in my fingers before flourishing it across the paper. "You'd put more care into this than I do."

Once more, Fred blinked his beady lizard eyes, this time in placid agreement.

With a shrug, I turned my attention to a heavy manila envelope that had been lying beneath the sheaf of red-flagged papers. Both sides of the package were stamped in red ink with the word CONFIDENTIAL.

Another tedious missive from the head office, I thought, estimating the heft of the contents as I slid my fingers beneath the envelope's end flap.

My resort was one of the largest vacation properties on St. John, but it was a minor player in the parent company's worldwide holdings, several star rankings below its most prestigious resorts. We were but a minor blip on their radar, which in part explained why my surreptitious substitution into this relatively obscure management position had gone undetected all this time.

Vivian handled the bulk of our correspondence with the headquarters up in the States, keeping me safely out of the loop. In the four years since I'd taken up Miss Hoffstra's station, she'd received the regular ream of standard-issue memos and a few information packets generically addressed to the resort manager. Only a small handful of personalized acquisition proposals had been specifically designated for her input.

This package had the overall feel of the last category. Tilting the envelope toward its now open end, I slid out a portfolio of glossy promotional materials.

The bulk of the content looked as if it had been put together by an outside consultant—I recognized the handiwork from a real estate stint I'd done early on in my legal career. Apparently, the resort's parent company was considering another land development proposal.

"Lots of pretty pictures of people on a beach," I yawned to

Fred—but I cut it short as my eyes scanned the contents of the cover letter. This proposal was for a new resort on St. John.

"Oh no," I groaned, my earlier anxiety resurging as I glanced across the balcony railing at the munching iguana.

Fred issued his all-knowing I'm-way-ahead-of-you stare.

I rubbed my forehead wearily. There'd been rumors that something like this might be coming. Our tiny island was about to receive a visit from a boatful of fancy-pants executives, and I, no doubt, would be on the hook as hostess to shepherd them around.

"What property are they looking at?" I mumbled as I flipped open the embossed folder and fished out the summary sheet. I suspected I already knew the answer.

"Maho Bay," I confirmed as I read the description of the targeted land.

I drifted slowly off into my thoughts, which Fred always seemed perfectly capable of reading without any verbal translations.

The plight of the Maho Bay land parcel had been the talk of the island for the last several months—that it had been put up for sale was no secret. The multi-acre plot included a beautiful stretch of beachfront property along the island's undeveloped north shore. It was surrounded on all sides by a national park that encompassed almost two-thirds of the island's landmass.

For the last thirty years, Maho Bay had been leased to an eco-resort, one renowned throughout the Caribbean for its environmental stewardship and innovative design. It had a unique setup, visually different from any of the island's other accommodations.

To minimize the camp's footprint on the heavily forested property, all of its buildings, including a hundred-plus individual screened tents, were constructed on platforms raised ten to twenty feet above the ground. The tents were connected by a network of elevated walkways to protect the natural flora that thrived beneath.

The resort was popular with vacationing families as well as the tree-hugger hippie set. Its staff acted as camp counselors, providing a constant lineup of activities: arts and crafts, nature walks, and water sports. The resort also found favor with the budget conscious; the rustic lodgings were some of the most affordable on the island.

All of this, it seemed, would soon be gone. The eco-resort's current lease was set to expire at the end of the year, and the proprietors had been unable to negotiate an extension. A few months from now, the campground would be closed for good.

The Maho Bay property had hit the real estate listings last spring—igniting an uproar of public protest. The eco-resort and its quirky proprietors were beloved by most of St. John's permanent residents. Few welcomed the prospect of a high-end resort complex taking over this pristine stretch of the island.

Shaking my head, I returned my attention to the brochure, wondering how our home office planned to compete for what was sure to be a pricey bid. Maho Bay would be far more expensive than any other transaction they'd attempted during my tenure. I didn't think they had that kind of cash to throw around.

Property values on St. John were among the highest in the Caribbean, due in large part to its national park. This massive federal holding made the island's remaining private land relatively scarce; proximity to the park's undeveloped beaches further enhanced real estate assessments.

The park's origins went back to the 1950s when financier and wealthy heir Laurance Rockefeller began purchasing land on a then largely unknown St. John.

Using a private broker to mask his identity, Rockefeller bought up huge tracts from unsuspecting owners—a move that was still controversial among many of the sellers' descendents, who felt they had been cheated out of their properties' true values.

Once Rockefeller had acquired as much property as possible along the island's north shore, he consolidated his land holdings and donated the bundled plot to the National Park Service, reserving a renewable lease back to the lavish resort he'd built on the parcel's west end, the site of the former Caneel Bay plantation.

The owners of the Maho Bay property were one of the few landholders who had been able to resist the negotiating power of Rockefeller's bankers. Sixty years later, the trustees representing these property rights were now ready to cash in. It was hard to imagine any other development prospect in the Caribbean that could match Maho's unique features.

I reached for the shot glass as I turned to the last page of the prospectus. I wasn't looking forward to the extra eyes such a high-profile land sale would draw to me and my rum-soaked fiefdom. I wasn't sure how well my Penelope Hoffstra routine would hold up to the parent company's corporate diligence committee.

Another swallow of rum helped tamp down my concerns. Vivian would make the necessary arrangements for our soon-to-be-arriving friends in suits. I would just have to hope no one knew enough about the original Penelope Hoffstra to recognize the difference. It would probably be prudent, I reflected somberly, to keep a low profile in the coming weeks.

I dropped the prospectus onto the pile of papers from my inbox, and my focus returned to the troublesome issue of the resort's new employee.

"Maybe Vivian hadn't had a chance to put her file together," I offered to Fred. "Simple as that. Maybe it's all just a coincidence."

Fred continued to chew on his leaf. He was still considering the pros and cons of the Maho Bay land deal; he didn't like to be rushed from one topic to the next.

I took another steadying gulp from my glass. The rum was beginning to numb my Hannah concerns. "Plenty of people have the same name."

If only she had been a strung-out party girl, like most of kids who came to work for us, the strange happenstance of her name would have been much easier to dismiss.

The bulk of our temporary employees were college students, free spirits looking for a semester's break from the books. They spent far more time enjoying the island atmosphere than actually working in it.

I shook my head. There was no way to deny it. Simply put, Hannah didn't fit the mold.

Fred began to carefully back down off his limb, rustling the branches as his stiff, awkward movements caused the tree to sway wildly back and forth.

I glanced at my watch. It was time for his daily afternoon swim at the beach that fronted the resort. Several guests would be lined up along the sand, waiting with their cameras, eager to capture the event on film. Fred, the body-surfing iguana, was something of a legend on the island. He seemed to enjoy his fame; his adoring fans were rarely disappointed with his performance.

As Fred hit the shaded ground below the balcony, I drained the shot glass and set it with a loud *clink* on a small metal table beside my chair. My gaze fell once more onto the prospectus.

"Fred," I mused aloud as he waddled off down a concrete path leading toward the water, "she's staying at Maho Bay. Hannah's staying at the eco-resort."

The narrow tip of Fred's long dragonlike tail swished back and forth, a wordless critique of how long it had taken me to finally make the connection.

~ *10* ~

Maho Bay

Alden Edwards sat at a short wooden desk in a rustic cabin nestled in the woods on the hillside above Maho Bay.

The floor of the cabin, like that of the other semipermanent structures spread out across the eco-resort, was mounted on stilts made out of thick rounded posts, elevating it fifteen feet or so above the forest floor.

Alden often felt as if he lived in a tree house. It was a boyhood fantasy he had been acting out for almost thirty years.

An abundance of wildlife frequented the open area beneath the cabin. Throughout the day, the jungle of leaves and underbrush rustled with activity. Hermit crabs moseyed past with their slow shell-dragging crawl, tree frogs hopped happily about, and geckos skittered in sporadic stop-and-go sprints.

Several members of the last category ventured up the support posts and sneaked in through openings in the cabin floor's wooden slats. Once inside, the tiny creatures skimmed fearlessly across the walls, comically pumping their front legs in mock push-ups whenever he glanced up from his desk to watch them.

Then, of course, there was the occasional mongoose

meandering blindly through the leaves, clumsily oblivious to the noisy ruckus it created.

More than once, Alden had leaned out over the edge of his front porch to check an overenthusiastic rummaging on the ground below, just to make sure the campgrounds hadn't been invaded by a large bear that had somehow managed to migrate to the tropics.

Brought in by the Danish in the 1700s, the island's now-entrenched mongoose species had been meant to help dampen the mice population inundating the sugarcane fields. Unfortunately, the brown rodentlike beasts hunted primarily during the daytime hours when the mice were tucked in their dens, fast asleep. Three hundred years later, both species continued to thrive in peaceful coexistence.

Overlaying all the crustacean, lizard, and mongoose activity that surrounded the cabin, there was the steady din of insects, ceaselessly chittering and chattering through the trees. These multitudes operated in their own separate kingdom, remaining mostly out of sight as they constructed elaborate nests that hung down from tree limbs and dug intricate underground bunkers that tunneled through the volcanic earth.

Of all the creature sounds Alden had come to know and love, it was that of the insects he found most endearing. Their soothing, buzzing hum calmed his nerves each night and sang him off to sleep.

This fanciful lifestyle was not without its spoilers. While the vast majority of the bug population had no interest in the eco-resort's human residents, the jungled forest was home to a certain species of biting gnats that posed a constant nuisance. The screens that covered the cabin's windows were no impediment to these nasty pests.

Alden kept a can of bug repellent within arm's reach, and the burnt-out stubs of a half dozen citronella candles filled the counters near his desk. A tattered flyswatter hung from a nail in the door frame, a weapon of last resort.

Alden hated to be the cause of any living being's destruction, but he had long since assuaged his conscience when it came to the island's infamous no-see-ums.

He scratched absentmindedly at the top of his knobby left knee, brushing a piece of fuzz tickling his skin. Beneath the wooden desk, two of the outlawed insects hung in the air, scheming as they swooped to avoid his large calloused hand.

Alden didn't know it yet, but a rash of small red welts had begun to rise on his hairy shin. The line of microscopic bite marks spread from the soft flesh beneath his ankle all the way up to his knee.

As his hand returned to the desktop, the tiny gnats circled his leg, proudly surveying their work. They weren't called "no-see-ums" for nothing.

Alden was a tall, lean lumbering man whose wild, unkempt beard conveyed the wooly look of someone who camped for a living. The top of his head, in contrast, he kept closely shaved.

After many years of experimentation, he'd determined that this was the optimal grooming combination for the island's hot, humid conditions. He couldn't care less that his friends told him he looked like a coconut on a stick.

Together, Alden and his wife, Sherry, had opened the Maho Bay eco-resort back in the early 1970s. They'd started with fewer than twenty elevated tree house tents, but the concept had proved so successful that the resort now boasted over a hundred units. The eco-minded campground was known throughout the Caribbean for its environmentally sensitive footprint as well as its close proximity to St. John's seven-thousand-acre national park.

The resort's infrastructure was laid out along a labyrinth of stairs, ladders, and elevated walkways that the guests navigated to reach their treetop lodging quarters. Each tent unit sat atop stilts similar to the ones beneath Alden's cabin. The walls of the tents were covered with interlocking screens and thick waterproof canvas—barriers that were, despite all bug-proofing attempts, still easily breached by the tiny gnatlike no-see-ums.

Meanwhile, the nefarious pair beneath the desk had finished up with Alden's left leg and had begun planning their attack on his right one.

The campground's network of stairs and elevated walkways led down the hillside toward Maho Bay's scenic beach. The round, protruding bulge of Mary's Point curved out from the northwest side of the area, sheltering it from the larger waves that sometimes hit St. John's north shore. The calm water was safe and easy for kids of all ages to swim in and explore, a perfect fit for the family-friendly camp.

Alden, Sherry, and their crew of similarly minded outdoor enthusiasts provided a daily offering of water sports and arts and crafts activities, frequently supplemented by nighttime gatherings and star-gazing programs. Meals were served throughout the day, cafeteria style, in a circular restaurant with a partially tented open-air roof.

Alden leaned back in his chair, squinting his left eye. He thought he felt the slight twinge of an itch somewhere on his body. His hand reached down and brushed against his right leg, but his thoughts drifted elsewhere.

Hovering about a foot off the floor, the naughty pair of no-see-ums continued their feast.

The eco-resort boasted some of the island's least-expensive lodging. The nightly rates weren't cheap, by any means, but they were far less than that of the rest of the available vacation housing. Given the camp's greater financial accessibility, it hosted a much broader range of visitor types than seen at the island's pricier establishments.

Alden and his crew were an easygoing, laid-back bunch, and he generally managed to get along with all of his guests, no matter how strange or bizarre the personality. Any problems arising in that department he left to his wife,

Sherry. In their thirty years of running the eco-resort, no one had ever dared to cross her.

Alden preferred to sit back and observe. After decades of practice, he had developed a keen eye for outliers—that's the term he used to describe his more eclectic guests. These were folks who seemed to float along, oddly detached from the regular threads of society.

Outliers, as carefully defined by Alden's well-honed analysis, lived by a different set of rules than the rest of the campground's patrons—their "unique" lifestyle choices frequently warranted extra staff attention. They marched to their own drummer, so to speak, in a way that was both frustratingly unpredictable for his role as site manager and maddeningly intriguing for his far more dominant biologist persona.

Conrad Corsair—outlier exhibit number one, Alden thought as he scrolled through a list of guests who were scheduled to arrive in the coming days.

Conrad was the sole reason Alden had devised the outlier term in the first place. The crazy hippie from New York had been flying down once a year ever since the eco-resort first opened.

Alden sighed ruefully. He could already hear the little man's twangy voice. For some reason, the moment he stepped off the plane, Conrad began layering his sharp New York accent with a strained, drawling affectation.

"How-dee, Eddy. How's it hangin'?"

Alden ran his fingers over the shaved crown of his bald head. He had never been able to convince Conrad—or, for that matter, anyone else on the island after Conrad started the trend—that Edwards was his last and not his first name.

This was but one of Conrad's many endearing quirks. Another was that he insisted on referring to the accommodations at the eco-resort as teepee tents. Alden had given up trying to understand why—there wasn't anything about the units that even remotely resembled the structure of a teepee.

Conrad apparently thought the teepee reference made his Maho Bay digs sound more alluring to the ladies.

Alden groaned and rolled his eyes. To his knowledge, none of Conrad's persistent pickup lines had ever panned out. And if they had, Alden thought with a cringe, he'd rather not know about it.

He and Sherry had dealt with countless complaints from the campground's female guests over the years. The New Yorker's over-the-top charm could sometimes be a bit too much to take.

Shaking his head dismissively, Alden slid his eyes across his desk to the day's stack of mail and the legal-sized envelope that lay on top. He felt his blood pressure begin to rise as he stared at the familiar gold-embossed printing on the return address label. It was the monthly notice from his landlord's lawyers, repeating, for the umpteenth time, the date of the eco-resort's coming eviction.

Alden scowled at the repugnant envelope. How would he break the news to Conrad? That man lived for his annual two-week trips to the island. He was going to be crushed when he found out.

The fourteen-acre site beneath the eco-resort had been put up for sale several months earlier, in anticipation of the end of the campground's multiyear lease. The legal envelopes providing formal notice of the termination had been arriving like clockwork every month for the last year to ensure there would be no possibility of legal redress.

Alden tossed the latest communiqué into a file folder packed with similarly embossed envelopes. He didn't even bother to read the letters anymore. It was just too painful.

The development interests had been circling the property for some time, eagerly anticipating this moment of opportunity. There were few plots of undeveloped land like this left in the Caribbean; there were certainly no others of similar potential in the U.S. Virgin Islands. It was the perfect site, according to those in the business, for an expansive, new, high-end resort.

Alden winced, imagining the transformation. A suffocating mass of concrete and pavement would quickly swallow this forested hillside, carving a permanent scar across the island's north shore. He closed his eyes, trying to erase the painful vision. It hurt him down to his soul.

The global economic downturn of recent years had deterred several interested buyers; the upheaval in the financial markets had made it difficult to raise funds for the multimillion-dollar asking price. But Alden knew that impediment was only temporary. Time was running out.

It would sicken Alden to see this place, his life's work, morphed into a monstrosity of condos, villas, and swimming pools, but his hands were tied. In the back of his mind, he had already accepted defeat. This would be their last year in operation.

At the end of the winter tourist season, they would tear down the tents, the elevated walkways, and the stairs leading down to the beach, then, he promised himself, never look back.

Alden shrugged his shoulders dejectedly. As he reached once more beneath the desk, his fingers found the first raised bump on the top of his left knee.

Cursing, he scooted his chair back to survey the damage. *This* was something he would not miss. He pulled open a desk drawer stocked with anti-itch medications and applied a thick coating of alcohol-based gel across the reddening surface of his skin. After propping his gel-soaked leg on a nearby stool, he returned his attention to his paperwork.

Below the desk, the no-see-ums continued their ravenous assault on his skin, their devious work unabated.

Unaware of the ongoing no-see-um activity, Alden scanned through a list of new arrivals and their activity requests, mentally ticking each one off.

First, there was the elderly lady from Connecticut who had signed up for tomorrow's craft class. Done. Sherry had prepared a stained-glass project for her.

Next was a young married couple from Atlanta. They'd asked to take a day cruise to Virgin Gorda on Friday. He checked his notes. Sherry had signed them up with a charter that serviced the larger resorts.

Alden set his left leg back on the ground as he came to the third entry: Hannah Sheridan. She was working for the next couple of months over at the big resort on the island's southwest side. He rubbed his fingers into the scruff of his beard, contemplating.

It was too early to know for sure, but he suspected Hannah might fall into the "outlier" category. You couldn't always pick them out right at first, but she certainly showed some of the signs.

Hannah had been quiet, almost shy when she approached the check-in desk that morning. But not long after they started talking, she began peppering him with questions: about the island, about the eco-resort, and then, most memorably, about the pending termination of the lease.

What a way to start the day, Alden sighed wearily. The whole sordid lease situation was like a persistent cloud that he couldn't escape. Its lurking black shroud followed him wherever he went. He scrunched up his lips and gazed out into the forest, his mood darkening with an overwhelming sense of defeat.

It was as Alden stared out the window screen, the no-see-ums munching hungrily on his lower extremities, that he sensed a slight uptick in the previously deadened breeze. The tree outside his window rustled with movement. A forest of wooden limbs creaked in unison with a low mournful moan. It was as if a restive spirit had suddenly been awakened.

Maybe, Alden thought wistfully, maybe there is hope after all. He was a spiritual man, in the naturalist sense of the word, and this forest was his chapel. He'd been praying for months, in his own meager, diminutive way, for some sort of miracle to save it from ruin.

But then, just as quickly as it had started, the stirring in the trees fell silent. The wind evaporated as if it had existed only in his imagination. Alden slapped hard against his right leg, nearly crushing the mischievous pair of no-see-ums, and swore out loud as he saw the second track of welt marks.

Probably just a mongoose, he thought bitterly.

Alden let loose another long sigh, this one laced heavily with remorse. He was really going to miss those stupid mongooses.

~ 11 ~

The Surfing Iguana

Fred had already drawn a sizeable crowd by the time I reached the beach near his favorite surfing spot. Several of the resort's excited guests were clumped together beneath a row of palm trees, clicking their cameras as his scaly body cut through the waves. Every so often, his bony head rose above the water's foaming surface to reveal a crooked lizard grin.

As I stood on the beach admiring Fred's surfing prowess, I heard the distinctive stomp of Vivian's footsteps charging up behind me. After four years of working together, I was well acquainted with her heavy, accusing gait. Fixing my face with a calm expression, I turned to greet my hot-tempered assistant.

Sure enough, I spied Vivian chugging toward me at full speed. Her entire being steamed with a heated mixture of consternation and exertion. She must have spotted me leaving the administration offices and immediately set off to catch me.

Vivian looked as if she'd run all the way down the hill from the reception area, which was positioned just off the main road near the entrance to the resort. A network of curving pathways connected the reception area to the guest accommodations sprinkled across the resort's ocean-facing slope. Several wide lawns tastefully edged by colorful mounds of blooming vegetation filled in the rest of the space.

The reception's open-air pagoda-style structure swallowed the rounded top of the hill, capturing whatever breeze blew in off of the ocean. The shade beneath the exposed wooden beams of the soaring vaulted roof made it one of the most comfortable spots on the resort, a cool oasis from the humidity-soaked environs. It was the only location other than the goose-pimpling administrative suite that I would have expected to find Vivian on such a sweltering afternoon.

Instead, my overheated assistant stood panting on the beach, her dark skin slick with perspiration, her sweat-drenched shirt clinging to her sturdy torso like a wrinkled sausage casing.

There was something about Vivian's obvious physical discomfort and disheveled appearance that gave me a pleasant sense of confidence and superiority. I'd scored a temporary win in our never-ending game of one-upmanship—but every ounce of that smug satisfaction withered as my gaze traveled to our new employee.

In contrast to Vivian's state of near heatstroke, Hannah still looked fresh as the daisy who had greeted me earlier that morning. She moved effortlessly in the island's swampy heat, her creamy cocoa-colored skin flushed with only the slightest tinge of pink.

What was with this strange woman? I thought as my palms began to moisten. No file, no background, and, apparently, no sweat glands.

"Oh, hello. There you two are," I greeted the pair with a forced brightness. "I've been searching for you all day. You look like you've been busy. How's it going?"

Vivian scowled sternly, not the least bit amused by my remarks. She marched forward and steered me into a row of hydrangea bushes ringing a sidewalk near the beach.

Before I could protest, she latched hold of my sleeve and tugged down on my shoulder so that she could speak into my ear. Her harshly whispered words curved with the inflection of her usually muted Caribbean dialect.

"She ask'd me if I waz a nate-teev."

"She asked you what?" I replied in bewilderment.

I was unaccustomed to hearing Vivian speak with such a thick accent. She'd long since anglicized her speech patterns after tiring of me constantly asking her to repeat the words I couldn't understand.

"A nate-teev. She ask'd me if I waz a nate-teev of thuh Ver-gene Eye-lands."

Vivian glared with a fierce determination as she waited for me to interpret her hushed phrase. Several sharp branches from the hydrangea bushes poked painfully into my back, but I could see Vivian wasn't budging until she confirmed I'd understood her message.

"She asked if you were a—native?" I repeated warily, trying to keep my voice inaudible to Hannah, who had wandered over to the iguana-watching group a few feet away.

"A nate-teev, a nate-teev . . . she ask'd if I waz a nate-teev!" Vivian hissed into my ear again, giving me a look of great affront. *"Mark mye words. Shee's tr-rouble, that wone!"*

And with that, Vivian stormed off down the pathway, her stocky figure quickly disappearing as the trail circled into a clutch of villas.

I remained for a moment in the prickly embrace of the hydrangea bushes, contemplating Vivian's words as I watched her depart.

Like most of my fellow expats, I didn't pay much attention to local politics, but I was vaguely aware of the identity-based tensions that dominated the opinion pages of the local papers.

Loosely defined, "Native Virgin Islander" referred to someone who could trace his or her ancestry back to a resident of the Danish territory at the time of its 1917 transfer to the United States. It was a way of differentiating those with a specific tie to the Territory's colonial-era past from the numbers of West Indians who had immigrated to the islands in recent years to work for the booming tourism industry.

The distinction cut a strong undercurrent through almost every aspect of political debate; candidates for public office were clearly identified as Native—or not.

Native Virgin Islanders currently represented about forty percent of the population, and they had historically controlled the legislature and governorship. Nearly one-quarter of the Territory's residents were employed in sought-after government jobs, and almost all of those positions were held by Native Virgin Islanders.

Falling outside the "Native" crowd were the expats, who couldn't care less, and those of other West Indian or Afro-Caribbean descent, like Vivian, who cared a great deal about any perceived slight to herself, her son, or her beloved Bahamas.

While Native versus non-Native friction commenced soon after the transfer, the current tensions started to build in the 1960s.

After the Cuban revolution and the rise of Fidel Castro, Americans started looking for alternative Caribbean vacation destinations to replace Havana. The subsequent flood of tourists into the U.S. Virgin Islands triggered a substantial uptick in new construction, mostly in the form of hotels and lavish resorts, as well as an influx of much needed cash. With the resulting labor shortage in the service and construction industries, the USVI began issuing work visas, and the population exploded.

Much of the expanded workforce came from neighboring Caribbean islands. With the exception of those immigrants from the U.S. Territory of Puerto Rico, many of the newcomers were aliens and unlikely to gain U.S. citizenship or voting rights. Non-Native political influence soon began to grow, however, through the voting power of the immigrants' offspring. At last count, more than half the residents of the

Territory were descended from a parent who had arrived on the islands after the U.S. purchase.

Over the past thirty years, the increasingly testy public discourse over the title of "Native Virgin Islander" had derailed the last two initiatives to draft a USVI constitution, and it was well on its way toward defeating another.

Delegates to the Territory's Fifth Constitutional Convention were now meeting on St. Thomas to try to agree on the document's language. Certain delegates were insisting on insertion of a clause that would explicitly define who among the citizenry qualified as a Native Virgin Islander. The implied and, in some cases, explicitly asserted rationale for the phrase's inclusion was to form the basis for special rights that would attach to persons falling under the classification.

The subject of Native Rights was an increasingly touchy topic among the island's long-term residents. The passionate debate on this issue showed no signs of abating.

From the prodding couch of the hydrangea bushes, I continued to puzzle over Vivian's communication. Why would Hannah raise such a divisive question on her first day at the resort? Was it simply a matter of misplaced curiosity, or was she intentionally trying to rile people up?

Before I had time to decide which, Hannah left the group of iguana enthusiasts and began walking toward me. Given the expectant look on her face, I wouldn't be able to dodge the handoff any longer.

Advantage Vivian, I thought as the sun focused its merciless beam on the top of my head. The heat here on the beach was rising by the minute. Pretty soon, I would match my assistant in terms of sweat production.

I attempted a gracious smile at Hannah as I finally extracted myself from the hydrangeas' poking grasp.

"Why don't we head into town?" I suggested with a glance at my watch. Since I'd been unable to glean any information from Hannah's file, I reckoned it was time to see what I could learn from the young woman directly. Plus it was never too early for a stop at the Crunchy Carrot. "I'll introduce you to some of my friends."

Hannah's face immediately registered interest. "Vivian said you had a way with the locals," she said in an admiring tone.

"I bet she did," I muttered under my breath. Vivian was not a fan of my frequent Dumpster-table sessions.

"Right this way," I added in response to Hannah's confused expression as I ushered her toward the nearest path that would lead up to the reception area, where we could catch one of the truck taxis heading into Cruz Bay.

I suppose it was the rum shots dulling my senses, but it never occurred to me that Hannah might have had in mind a totally different group than the people I was taking her to meet.

~ *12* ~

A Ticklish Situation

Manto's red hemi drove up the resort's horseshoe-shaped front drive and pulled into one of the designated truck-taxi spots by the front entrance. In his loose-fitting collared shirt, dark pleated slacks, and huarache sandals, he was almost unrecognizable from the man who had led the grounds crew through their paces earlier that morning.

Still groaning from the soreness in his lower back, he eased out the driver's-side door and limped around the flamingo-painted hood to help Vivian's son from the cab's high front seat. Per their long-standing arrangement, Manto coordinated his taxi pickup schedule so that he swung by the elementary school in Cruz Bay right as Hamilton was getting out of class.

Vivian never spoke of Hamilton's father. As far as anyone at the resort knew, she had left him behind in the Bahamas. Manto had stepped in as a surrogate grandfather figure—a role for which he had plenty of practice.

All of the children on the island recognized Manto's red truck. He kept a well-stocked tin of candies in the glove compartment and could always be counted on for a free ride in the case of inclement weather. Manto's cab was the best place to hide if you'd received a poor report card or were having trouble with a schoolyard bully. His understanding ears had heard countless childhood confessions over the years; his kind hands had dried thousands of tears.

Happily, Manto's counseling skills weren't needed that afternoon. Hamilton was nothing but smiles as he hopped down onto the pavement, holding his sticky fingers out from his body to avoid wiping them on the white shirt and blue shorts of his school uniform. The large piece of candy he'd eaten on the way to the resort had proved a little more than he could handle without making a mess.

Manto steered the little boy by the elbow into the reception building, behind the front check-in desk, and down a short hallway to a break room used by the resort staff.

"All rig't, Ham. Les clean you-up 'fore your momma get's hold of ya," Manto said with a chuckle as he trotted ahead to a counter by a sink.

After ripping off a paper towel, Manto wadded up a corner and waved it under a trickle of water from the faucet. Turning, he bent down with it to clean up the boy.

Hamilton, well accustomed to this routine, held his palms upward, tiny fingers spread apart.

Several West Indian women in resort-issued shirtdresses shuffled in as Manto began wiping the sugary coating from Hamilton's skin. Some of the women were tasked with cleaning guest rooms; others supported the resort's various dining facilities. One by one, they slid their time cards into a wall-mounted clock to punch out for the day.

A hardened, crowlike woman with short grizzly hair and a hooked nose shoved her card into the machine and shuddered.

"Akk, Eye'm glad to bey gettin' off on tyme tu-day."

A younger maid standing nearby broke into a grin, as if she'd just heard the punch line of an oft-repeated joke.

"Come on, Glenna, you know you like to work late," she said with a wink. "Then you get a *special* ride home."

Glenna shook her head violently back and forth. *"Ohhhh, no. Noooo, no. Nut me, Eye doon't. Eye doon nut lyke thuh what-ter taxi."*

All the women giggled, offering encouragement. "Tell us, Glenna. Tell us. Why don't you like the water taxi?"

Glenna's eyes widened with an exaggerated terror; the sharp corners of her face hardened into a dramatic expression.

"Eye doon nut lyke thuh what-ter taxi," she repeated vehemently. *"Ack, what-ter taxi, what-ter taxi . . . oh, no."*

Manto shook his head with a rueful grin as the women doubled over with laughter. Hamilton, despite having seen the performance several times before, stood spellbound, his gaze fixed on Glenna's charismatic face.

Glenna hunched over and began to circle the room, all the while wagging a crooked finger at the other women.

"Eye doon nut lyke thuh what-ter taxi . . . Beeg sheep go down slowe . . . Small sheep go down fest . . . Eye wurk und Eye wurk, but steel Eye've gut to tek thuh what-ter taxi . . ."

By the time she reached the end of the chant, her hoarse voice had been drowned out by the women's loud cackles.

"Bah," Glenna said, straightening her shoulders as she approached her locker. *"Eye doon't know why you-all mek may do that a-very day."*

Still letting out a stray guffaw or two, the group dispersed to their individual metal lockers to collect their belongings.

Someone switched on a portable radio, and its broadcast added to the room's overall background noise. A man's deep voice intoned through the speakers, but he could barely be heard due to the ruckus near the lockers.

"We welcome you to the proceedings of the Fifth Constitutional Convention. Today's session is being held at the Starlight Hotel here on St. Thomas . . ."

A young waitress walked up to Hamilton, holding her hands behind her back.

"Tell the truth, Ham," she ordered with mock sternness, a twinkle in her eye. "Were you a good boy at school today?"

Hamilton's round face contorted into a serious expression. He looked up at her and nodded affirmatively.

"Well, then," she said with a wide grin as she swung her arms out in front of her waist, revealing a small plastic-wrapped plate. "You deserve some cookies."

Manto threw his hands up as the little boy broke into a toothy grin. Hamilton quickly removed the plastic wrap and crammed a cookie into his mouth. The women all turned to coo at him, leaving the radio to take over the room's primary audio.

Through the speaker, the murmuring rumble of a distant crowd fell to a hush as the leader of the event tapped a microphone and began his opening remarks.

"As most of you know, this is our fifth attempt to draft a constitution for the U.S. Virgin Islands. If approved by Congress and ratified by the voters, this document will supersede the current governing document, the Organic Act, which was put into place in 1954."

The break room's cheerful atmosphere dimmed as a cloud moved across the occupants' faces—all except for Hamilton, who was still munching blissfully away on his cookies.

The waitress who had prepared the cookie plate tugged the worn belt of her shirtdress. Her smile disappeared as she returned to her locker.

On the far side of the room, near the shelf holding the radio, Beulah Shah sat on a bench watching the group's reaction to the broadcast. She crossed her right leg over the left and began kicking it up and down, causing the toe of her loose rubber sandal to *thunk* against her foot.

"Speaker, speaker," a female voice cut through the room's growing silence. "I would like to make a motion."

Manto cleared his throat uncomfortably and leaned over to brush crumbs from Hamilton's mouth as the voice continued.

"I move to amend the draft to introduce the following language defining a Native Virgin Islander . . ."

One of the housemaids sighed out a volume of pent-up breath. "It's a very ticklish business, this."

Glenna slapped her hand against one of the lockers. *"Eye doon't lyke it. Nut wone bit."* She pointed accusingly at the radio. *"Eye doon't trust thuh people who are on it."* Then, she made a curdling sound with her mouth. *"They should jus' leave things thuh way they are."*

She was seconded by a sharp-eyed cook with dark pitted skin. "Special privileges," the woman said venomously. "They are trying to set themselves up with special privileges. They are going to take over the island. They are going to lord it over the rest of us."

A gavel pounded in the radio static as the leader of the meeting asked for order, but the heated discussion in the break room had now overwhelmed the convention proceedings.

A third woman, this one with round hips and a heavy chest, stepped forward, shaking her head in fervent disagreement.

"My grandfather was here at the time of the transfer. He didn't have any say in the matter. That twenty-five million, the U.S. didn't pay any of it to him. It's time. We have to stand up and protect what is rightfully ours."

The cook spun around to face the dissenter. "And what about the rest of us? What happens to us? Are we second-class citizens?"

The door to the break room suddenly burst open and Vivian stormed through. The women all stopped, some of them midsentence, and gaped as she strode forcefully across to the radio and flicked off the switch. Then she grabbed Hamilton by the wrist and herded him brusquely out the door.

Manto quickly followed, fretfully stroking his balding skull. The rest of the workers silently filtered out, leaving only Beulah, who had watched the entire episode from her bench at the far side of the room.

The old woman reached over and thoughtfully stroked the side of the now silent radio, her frail fingers twiddling aimlessly with the dial.

"A tick-leesh situation," she said softly. *"In-deed."*

~ *13* ~

The Dearly Departed

Hannah and I arrived at the reception area to find Manto's truck taxi parked out front of the resort. It was already half full with women from the restaurant and cleaning crews who had finished their shifts and were headed into Cruz Bay to get on the four o'clock ferry.

The women were abnormally quiet for that time of day. The afternoon ride into town was typically filled with their energetic chatter, playful joshing, and colorful recountings of the latest salacious gossip, of which, it seemed, there was never any shortage.

The strained silence in the truck taxi deepened as Hannah and I climbed into a row of empty seats near the front of the bed. Something had clearly disrupted the group unity.

Boyfriend troubles, perhaps? A petty jealousy that had blown up into a quarrel?

I recognized most of the women's faces, but I didn't know their names. Vivian handled all of the hiring at this level. I glanced curiously over the back of my bench at the nearest stony-faced housemaid, but she merely swung her head sideways, so that her eyes stared blindly at a flower bed next to the curb.

Thankfully, Manto scurried out of the reception area and slid into the truck's front cab. The roar of the engine, with its loud disruptive rumble, broke the tension, and a moment later we were bumping down the resort's front drive.

I turned toward the still smiling Hannah, searching for some topic upon which to build a common ground through conversation. After studying her flowery sundress, youthful physique, and doe-eyed expression, I sighed and asked, "So, how do you like the weather down here?"

The tip end of Hannah's perky nose began to twitch as we hopped off the truck taxi and crossed the street for the Dumpster table.

There was an extra pungent stench coming from the south side of the Crunchy Carrot that afternoon. The fumes from the trash bin were in fierce competition with the rank aroma of the two sweaty men collapsed in the white plastic lawn chairs. Even my Dumpster-hardened senses picked up on the unusually strong odor floating in the air.

I cast a sideways glance at my new employee as we approached, wondering how well her perky enthusiasm would hold up against this crowd.

Clearing my throat, I waved a brief hello. "Hey guys, meet one of the resort's new employees." With effort, I managed to force the name out casually. "Hannah Sheridan."

I grabbed two empty chairs and positioned them on the opposite side of the table, motioning for Hannah to take the one to my right. I'd given her the seat of honor, farthest upwind from the stench, but her face took on a pale greenish shade as she stared at me with an expression of marked surprise and confusion. Her mouth guppied open and shut without making a sound, as if she were unable to find a suitable comment to express her thoughts.

The two men looked up, their reddened faces showing a faint, wearied interest as I slid comfortably into my chair and Hannah perched gingerly on hers.

"Jeff, César," I said, making the introductions, "this is . . . Hannah."

Hannah smiled nervously across the table. Her green eyes passed slowly over the growing collection of half-empty beer bottles and paper boats that littered the surface, coming to rest on the rooster who was perched discreetly near the table's edge.

Richard's sharp yellow claws gripped the table's curved plastic rim as he stretched his scrawny black neck toward a few discarded French fries that had fallen out of their plastic basket container.

César, a short balding Puerto Rican, was finishing off a blackened fish sandwich. My stomach rumbled at the sight of it—the Carrot's fish sandwich was renowned throughout the island, by far and away the best item on their menu.

César stuffed the last bite into his mouth and chomped uncomfortably for a moment, his chubby cheeks bulging from the pressure of the contents he had just crammed inside. After a stiff swallow, he tilted his head back and drained the last half of a bottle of Jamaican beer down his throat. Smacking his lips, he wiped the back of his hand across his grease-smeared face. Then, he reached across the table and offered Hannah a shake.

"Welcome to the Dumpster table," César said heartily in his pinched, slightly nasal voice. He nodded at the wrappings and debris that Richard was now nosing his way through and winked. "Finest dining in town."

César was the head sous chef at Pesce, an Italian restaurant on a bluff overlooking Cruz Bay. Pesce was one of the nicest restaurants on the island, but César took most of his meals at the Crunchy Carrot. Despite the culinary wonders of the Carrot's fish sandwich, I suspected his frequent appearances at the Dumpster table had a lot more to do with escaping the pressures of Pesce's stress-filled kitchen than the quality of the bar's food.

César had spent the bulk of his eight-hour day shift on prep work for the evening meal. A splatter of fish guts and tomato juice decorated his gray sweat-stained T-shirt. His already thick fingers were bloated and blistered from the lengthy chopping and peeling session.

As a Puerto Rican, César wasn't exactly an expat—at least, not in the way we all thought of the term—but he had been given honorary membership to the Dumpster table gang due to his hyper energy and offbeat sense of humor. He was a nonstop source of entertainment. With a stomach full of food digesting in his plump belly, I expected that, at any moment, he would launch into his latest shtick.

My gaze shifted to his dining companion—the human one, not the rooster.

Jeff was an entirely different type of character. A young man of few words, he wore the quiet subdued air of his native New England like a mask that concealed all expression of emotion. In response to Hannah's introduction, he had simply shrugged his shoulders and grunted a greeting. That was his rendition of a warm welcome.

A full head of frizzy brown hair towered over Jeff's freckled face. The tangled matting suggested his head had gone several months without the application of shampoo. I often teased him to steer clear of the bananaquits for fear they would build a nest in it.

My speech-thrifty friend worked for the company that ran the dive shop at my resort. He had been out on their sailboat all day, tying up ropes for the captain and slinging rum and cola drinks for the passengers. Per company policy, he'd turned his red dive-shop-issued T-shirt inside out, so that the logo wasn't visible to the Crunchy Carrot's other patrons.

You wouldn't know it from his scruffy, rumpled exterior, but Jeff dreamed of moving up the company ladder, maybe even manning his own boat someday. He was taking nautical classes in St. Thomas on his days off and would soon finish the necessary qualifications for a promotion to first mate—a job that focused more on tying ropes and less on pouring drinks.

Jeff and César lived in a small basement apartment tucked into the side of a hill a few miles east of Cruz Bay—they were just two of many in an ever-rotating list of roommates.

Long-term accommodations on St. John were expensive and hard to come by. At last count, there were at least seven people crammed into the apartment's dark moldy living space; the number fluctuated between high and low tourist seasons.

St. John wasn't the kind of place where one spent a lot of time indoors, but in such cramped living quarters, the occasional petty conflict was inevitable. Roommate grievances were often aired out at the Dumpster table. As Hannah leaned forward and gingerly shook César's greasy hand, I thought I sensed the friction of a pending dispute in the air. César, I mused, was about to let loose.

"We've had a death in the family," César announced somberly as Hannah settled nervously back into her plastic seat. "A member of our family has passed away."

Jeff took a long sip from his beer. The slightest hint of a question creased his placid expression.

Hannah carefully studied César's short round Hispanic face and Jeff's long Anglo one. She rolled in her bottom lip, apparently sizing up the slim possibility of the two sharing a direct blood relative.

"I'm so sorry for your loss," she said sympathetically, opting for a neutral tact in her response. Despite her initial reaction to the trashy smell of the Dumpster table and the disheveled appearance of its occupants, she couldn't tamp down her innate curiosity. "Was it someone who lives on the island?"

César nodded emphatically up and down, as overemotive as Jeff was reserved. "Yes, yes, yes, she lived in our apartment, in our home. We were very close." He sighed with exaggerated sadness. "She was like family to me."

Hannah leaned over the table, her tender face filled with compassion. "One of your roommates?" Perplexed, she glanced back and forth between César's exaggerated show of grief and Jeff's blank stare. "That must have been . . . tragic."

A quizzical wrinkle furrowed Jeff's forehead as he rotated his chair toward the chunky Puerto Rican.

César tilted his face skyward. His eyelids fluttered shut in remorse. "Yes, it is a sad day for Kaká."

I slouched back in my chair, watching the scene play out, as Richard gulped down the last stray French fry. He cocked his head toward César and clicked his beak hungrily.

Jeff stared skeptically at his roommate. His blue sea-worn eyes narrowed suspiciously before he murmured a barely discernable, "Who?"

César pouted in frustration, then huffed indignantly, "Kaká, Kaká! Surely you remember Kaká?"

Hannah pushed even farther forward in her seat, her face muddled with confusion. I picked up the plastic cup of water our waitress had just placed in front of me and hid my face behind it, trying to straighten the grin tugging at the corners of my mouth.

César strummed his thick fingers on the table's sticky surface, reflecting.

"Each day, when I got home from work, I would walk through the door, and there she'd be, peeking around the kitchen counter at me, welcoming me home."

He shook his head, his plump lips tutting with remorse.

Jeff sighed, his expression one of silent resignation.

Hannah ventured a tentative guess. "Was . . . Kaká . . . a pet?"

César thumped his hands against his chest. "Aaaaye, yes, yes, yes, Kaká, you could say that. A pet. Yes, she was a pet."

He stroked the air with the point of his finger, his voice pipping coarsely up and down. "But, but, but—she had her own spirit. She was free!" He wagged his blistered finger back and forth in the air. "She never lived in a cage."

The left side of Jeff's face twitched with the shadow of a grimace as César continued to build momentum. The Puerto Rican knew when he'd hooked a live one; he would take his time reeling Hannah in.

"She couldn't see very well, so she would sniff the air to tell if it was me. Her tiny pink nose would quiver, just like this." César made a wet snorkeling sound into his beer bottle. "And I would call out to reassure her, 'Kaká, I'm home!' "

He let out another sad sigh. "But she will never be waiting to greet me again."

César *thunked* the bottle back down on the table, causing Richard to squawk and fly off. He leaned across the debris-strewn surface toward Hannah, the fleshy contours of his face squishing up around his mouth.

"Kaká, she was always glad to see me. Her whiskers would wiggle back and forth . . . and the tip end of her tail, it would sort of rise up in the air. That was her way of saying hello. I tell you, Kaká, she was so friendly."

Hannah's eyes widened. She thought she had figured out the species of the deceased pet. I moved the plastic cup even closer to my face as she began, "Was Kaká a ca—"

Jeff sighed tiredly, cutting her off. His voice, flat and unemotional, rolled out, "It was a rat."

César fell back in his chair as if he'd been slapped. "But, but, but—she was a *good* rat, man. You know what I mean? A *good* rat."

Jeff rolled his eyes as César bounded forward again in his seat.

"You remember, man. There was the thing she would do with her tongue, flashing it in and out."

César performed his best Kaká imitation, ending the effort in a loud *slurp* as Hannah's face returned to its previous green pallor.

"And her fur too," he said, rubbing his hands together in the air above the table. "It was so smooth and silky. A rich brown color. She was very clean for a rat."

Hannah had now plastered herself against the back of her

chair, but she managed to issue a second condolence, this one far more shocked than sympathetic.

"I'm so sorry for your loss."

Jeff slowly blinked his eyes in derision and muttered, "Dude, it was a rat."

This was turning into an extremely verbose afternoon for Jeff. In all his visits to the Dumpster table, he'd never been known to issue so many complete sentences.

But César ignored him, focusing all his attention on Hannah. He wasn't quite ready to let his fish off the lure.

"I guess *some* of our roommates didn't appreciate Kaká's contributions to the apartment. They just couldn't see how she was such a *good* rat."

He swiveled in his chair and glared furiously at Jeff. "They put out some poison," he said accusingly. "That's what killed her."

Jeff bent his head, threading his fingers into the tangled mass of curls as César pointed reproachfully at him.

"I bet she had babies, man. Cute little rat babies, and now they're wondering what happened to their momma. Like she said, it's *tragic*, man. They're going to hunt you down and get their revenge."

Jeff glanced up and sent me a pleading look across the table.

I coughed lightly and tilted my cup toward César. "What did you do with the body? Is there going to be a funeral?"

César nodded up and down, welcoming my contribution as Jeff sent me a withering glare.

"I found her under the refrigerator. There was just the tip end of her tail sticking out on the floor."

He reached his chubby hand into the air over the table and wrapped his fingers around an imaginary tail. "I grabbed hold of it and tried to pull her out from under there, but the skin just—*whomp*—slipped off."

Standing up from his chair, he gestured as if his hand were still wrapped around the loose skin.

Hannah looked as if she might throw up at any minute.

Jeff sighed, finding one last comment. "That's gross."

César plunked back down onto his seat. He reached into the pile of refuse at the center of the table, pulled out a cold limp French fry that Richard had somehow missed, and popped it in his mouth.

"Aaaaye, Kaká, she was a *good* rat, man," he said sadly. "I tell you, a *good* rat."

That was the first and the last time Hannah joined us at the Dumpster table.

~ 14 ~

On the Danish
Slave Ship

Just as Manto's truck taxi pulled out of the resort's driveway
onto the main road to Cruz Bay, Beulah Shah scrambled into
the last bench at the rear of the bed. She hunkered down
behind the backrest of the next-to-last row of seats, her eyes
level with the bench's upper edge. Her gaze focused in on
the two women at the front of the canvas-covered seating
area: the resort manager and her new curly haired employee.

All the way into town, Beulah maintained her hunched
vigil, even as the truck bounced over the numerous bumps
and ruts in the pavement. When at last the taxi stopped outside the Crunchy Carrot, she waited until Pen paid the driver
and ushered Hannah toward the Dumpster table before making her own exit.

Taking care not to be seen, Beulah circled around the
block to the narrow alley that ran behind the Crunchy Carrot, her bony feet clunking in her loose rubber sandals as
she crept along the rough dirt path.

Ignoring the rancid odor, she crouched in the dirt behind
the Dumpster's metal wall and pressed an ear against its
rusted iron sheeting. She gazed, unseeing, at the dusty

ground as she listened to the conversation unfolding at the table on the opposite side.

Tonight, Beulah was only marginally interested in the woman who called herself Penelope Hoffstra—she had recognized her as an imposter the moment she first set foot on the island nearly four years earlier. She had kept a close eye on the lazy resort manager and knew her routine. The phony Pen was, predictably, settling in for another long night of drinking with the other expats.

Beulah spat at the dirt dismissively. On this particular evening, she was primarily concerned with the younger woman, the new arrival with the empty personnel file who was staying out at Maho Bay.

Beulah rocked back and forth behind the Dumpster, listening to Hannah Sheridan's debut with the expats. As the banter at the table followed its typical banal course, Beulah's thoughts drifted back to a tale she had once heard as a small child—about an Amina Slave Princess with dark curly hair and skin a creamy cocoa shade of brown.

It didn't take long for Beulah to decide that she had heard enough. Dusting off the worn threads of her navy blue jumper, she emerged from the alley behind the Crunchy Carrot and hobbled the short distance to the ferry dock, where she joined the regular afternoon crowd waiting for the four o'clock boat to St. Thomas.

The truck taxis had filled their designated line of parking spots on the road running perpendicular to the dock, waiting to pick up fares from the incoming load of tourists. The bright-painted metal and fluttering canopies provided a colorful contrast to the orange stucco building that contained the ferry company's ticket booth and operating offices.

A gated barrier stretched across the concrete dock, holding back the ticketed passengers until the ferry pulled into its slip. Several clumps of workers, most still in their service-industry uniforms, waited under the open-air pavilion attached to the building. Many more spilled out into the shaded park across the street where a half dozen green wooden benches flanked a statue memorializing the 1733 Slave Revolt.

The iron bust commemorated the moment the Amina stormed the Danish fort on the opposite side of the island and sent shots from its cannon to signal the start of the rebellion. As cannon fire reverberated across St. John, the bellowing blast of conch shells passed the message on to every plantation, mill, and field.

The memorial depicted the head and torso of a shirtless man, positioned defiantly on a plinth looking out across the Pillsbury Sound toward St. Thomas. One hand wrapped around the smooth curve of a conch shell, holding its horn piece to the statue's firm lips, which were puckered in a defiant blow.

The figure's bare chest rippled with muscles, the powerful physique accenting the item clutched in its opposite hand. Raised above the statue's head, ready to hack, waved the menacing blade of a machete.

Beneath the sculpture, one word was written in bold capital letters: FREEDOM.

Beulah shuffled through the day laborers congregated around the memorial, slowly pulling one of the wooden benches behind her. Conversations quelled to a murmur as she climbed onto the bench to address the crowd. Her hoarse, dry voice began to tell the story she had recalled behind the Crunchy Carrot's rancid Dumpster, the tale of the Amina Princess.

"Eeet waz thuh sum-mer uv 1733 . . ."

From the bird's-eye view of the seagull gliding on the trade winds several hundred feet above the Atlantic Ocean, the Dan-

ish slave ship was nothing more than a brown speck of wood
tethered to a tiny mast of billowing sails. The gull circled,
spiraling down through the clouds until the ship's deck—and
its miserable human cargo—came into sharper view.

Several hundred dark-skinned figures tromped slowly
up and down the length of the boat, each tortured being
anchored to the next by a heavy rusted chain. An army of
bare, blistered feet pounded against the weathered floorboards as the human centipede snaked along its well-worn
path. The harsh whip of the sun beat down on the sweating
slaves, roasting their backs with its unrelenting heat.

The ship rolled on a passing swell, pitching sideways in
a sickening heave. The column broke as the chain-hobbled
captives scrambled to regain their footing. Then, under the
sharp orders of the taskmaster, the dreary march resumed,
an endless procession down a trail without purpose, without destination.

With each plodding step that *thumped* against the deck,
a seething hatred burned deeper into the hearts of the
oppressed.

Hours later, the Amina Princess huddled amongst her tribesmen in the ship's dark fetid hold. The slaves had finally been
given a reprieve from the day's exercise regimen, but the
stench below instantly made them long for the fresher air
on the upper level.

As each day passed, one long effort of extreme endur-
ance after the next, the restive warriors that made up much
of the ship's human cargo grew more and more agitated. The
on-deck sessions, instead of letting off steam, only intensified the pressure-cooker atmosphere inside the hold's sweltering enclosure.

The Princess kept her eyes tightly shut, trying to block
out the sensory overload of her surroundings—a terrorizing
mixture of stale sweat, decaying human tissue, and growing rage.

She reached her hand up to the bare skin of her neck,

fumbling at the empty divot at the top of her chest where her medallion had once rested. The iron emblem was long gone—she'd noticed its absence the moment she awoke in the holding cell of the Danish fort—but its image was emblazoned in her memory, its phantom weight a constant presence at the base of her neck.

As she concentrated on the medallion's circular shape, its strength coursed through her body, giving her the courage and the will to survive the nightmare of the ocean journey to St. Thomas. After a long moment of fortifying concentration, she slowly opened her eyes.

In the dusky half-light, she spied the body of a dead rat. Its stiff, lifeless form sprawled across the damp floor just a few feet away, where a narrow crack of moonlight illuminated its long hairless tail.

~ 15 ~

Something in the Air

Those early days of November passed slowly, seemingly the same and yet strangely different. The humidity continued to rise, an ever-increasing pressure without the release of rain. It felt as if the island were a pot on a stove, its liquid contents coming closer and closer to a boil, a suffocating prelude to the whomping storm headed our way.

I had little direct contact with Hannah in the days following her Dumpster table debut. There had been no more impromptu visits to my office, no more unsettling questions about my past. When our paths did cross, she was still painfully polite and sickeningly eager to please, but I sensed her opinion of me had diminished significantly after our afternoon session at the Carrot.

Her presence at the resort—and the coincidence of her name—remained disturbingly unexplained.

As for Hannah's interactions with Vivian, I was similarly in the dark. Whatever exchanges passed between them were not reported to my ears. I was a week and a half into a Vivian-imposed silent treatment, my penance for breach-ing the barrier of her office and breaking open her personnel files.

I had enough experience with the testy Bahaman to know that she would be the one to decide when I had completed my punishment. It was best for me to stay out of her way until then.

I was left to my observations.

Hannah and her rotating wardrobe of flowery sundresses appeared to be settling in nicely to her designated post at the reception desk. After quickly mastering the resort's computer and electronic key systems, she now spent the bulk of her time diligently checking in guests, answering the phones, and fielding the numerous requests directed to her station.

Every so often, I noticed, she wandered away from the other interns—slipping into the break room when the housemaids were getting off from their shifts or down to the lawns when Manto and the grounds crew were working.

Slowly but surely, she appeared to be breaking into their closely guarded society. From the balcony outside my office, I heard her voice calling out names that were unfamiliar to me, and their, at first tentative, replies. Through the leaves of Fred's favorite tree, I spied the timid beginnings of reciprocal smiles.

Hannah Sheridan was making inroads with the resort's West Indian workers. For the life of me, I still had no idea why.

~ 16 ~

Town

To first-time visitors, Cruz Bay might come off as a sleepy Caribbean hamlet, perhaps one that's a little shabby around the edges with a few too many free-roaming chickens.

But to those of us who live on the island, it's a thriving economic hub, a bustling harbor, and basically, the center of our universe. If you can't find what you're looking for in "Town"—as it's affectionately known—you'd better find a boat.

Joe Tourist, fruitlessly punching buttons on his signal-less cell phone as he stumbles the wrong direction down the middle of a congested one-way street, probably doesn't realize just how much he's missing. Tormented by his flaming sunburn and the itch of multiple no-see-um bites, all our friend Joe wants is a nice cool drink and one of those fish sandwiches people keep telling him about.

So when Joe and his female companion collapse into their seats outside the Crunchy Carrot—at the table farthest away from the Dumpster—likely as not, they will fail to appreciate the significance of the beaten-up Jeep slowly bumping by on the main road.

The Jeep's driver's-side door is missing; the empty rusted

hinges welded to the frame are all that remains. The front bumper is visibly misshapen, the apparent loser in an altercation with a far more formidable opponent—given the concave shape of the compression, odds are, it was a tree trunk. The front windshield is cracked across its middle and in danger of falling out, and the fabric seats reek of a strange mixture of salt water and mildew that has somehow managed to compete with the Dumpster's pungent odor.

Joe Tourist looks up at the Jeep's driver—a grungy little man with wild mangy hair and several days' facial growth—and shakes his head with scornful disdain.

An island junkie, Joe thinks, hopped up on the local dope. He reaches into his back pocket to make sure his wallet is still in place. Then, he glances nervously at Richard the welcoming rooster, who is strutting amicably toward his chair.

As the Jeep slows so that the driver can lean out the doorless opening to yell at the expat crowd seated a few tables over, Joe gives up on the fish sandwich, finishes off the slushy drink in his plastic cup, and says to his wife, "Come on, Maggie, let's find a place with some air-conditioning. I'm dying in this heat."

Sadly, our uninformed tourist will never think to issue a news flash to the residents of St. John, broadcasting the spectacular event he has just witnessed.

After five years of driving around town in an anemic put-put golf cart, Charlie Baker has just purchased a brand new Jeep—well, new to him at least.

Charlie was, far and away, the most senior member of the expat group in terms of both age and longevity. He had been living in the islands for almost a decade, and, at forty-five, he had more than twenty years on Jeff and the other dive shop boys, close to seven on me.

He was a short muscular man, more miniaturized than petite, a tiny lion shrunk down in perfect proportion. Beneath the ever-present layers of sweat and grime, his facial features were delicate and refined—or they would have been with a thorough soap and scrubbing.

Charlie had thick eyelashes and a dark mane of hair that, in the few instances when it wasn't bundled up beneath his baseball cap, fell down to his shoulders. Only a couple of gray hairs at his temples and a light creasing beneath his eyes betrayed his advancing age.

He had originally moved to the Virgins with his wife and two young children, the group of them intent on enjoying the good life in the tropics.

They'd bought a small farm on St. Croix, an island about forty miles to the south. Planning to live off the land while they built their dream home, they'd sold those possessions that were too heavy to ship and headed south.

Unfortunately, Charlie's wife had never adapted to the reduced income that had come with their scenic views. After months of bitter squabbling, mostly over finances, she'd packed up the kids and returned to their hometown in Minnesota.

Charlie hadn't seen them since.

He was a private individual and rarely talked about his troubles, but when he did, he tried to make light of the situation.

"I don't have anything against *shoes*," Charlie would sum up with a rueful grimace. A slight pitch in his typically rough, scratchy voice betrayed the underlying emotion. "I like shoes. It's Mr. *Ferragamo* I've got a problem with."

Then he would clamp his sturdy hands together as if wringing an imaginary neck. "I'd like to get my hands on that guy."

From our seats at the Dumpster table, we all turned to stare as Charlie hung out the side of his newly acquired Jeep, hollering—needlessly—to draw our attention.

He wore his typical garb of cutoff camo pants and scuffed up Army-surplus combat boots, an outfit that apparently suited his daily activities as a building contractor.

Charlie had plenty of regular full-sized vehicles, including

St. John's largest tow truck (if you believed the claim of the multicolored advert painted on its side).

He was constantly transporting heavy machinery up and down the island's steep and frequently washed-out roads, but he never drove any of his work fleet into town. Simply put, there wouldn't have been any place for him to park.

The dearth of available parking spaces was a long-running beef for the island's residents. Cruz Bay's narrow streets were tightly packed with shops, bars, restaurants, vacation rentals, and the occasional residence. The few legitimate parking spots were jealously guarded, leaving the rest of the island's vehicles to compete over a handful of dubiously designated parking areas, most of which were far more vertical than horizontal in terrain. It was not unusual to see several vehicles left precariously clinging to a thirty-degree incline with half an inch of separation between them.

Some of the most violent disputes between neighbors were rooted in the impossible parking situation—hence, Charlie's use of the golf cart.

Despite the constant mockery Charlie suffered for driving it, the golf cart was the perfect solution to Cruz Bay's parking dilemma. It could squeeze into holes that stymied even the smallest model of Jeep—including the short space between the Dumpster and our table, so long as there were enough expats around to lift it over.

The golf cart, however, had a few drawbacks.

First, its miniature size made it a dangerous target on Cruz Bay's busy streets. Charlie had been nearly flattened on several occasions by disoriented tourists who had temporarily forgotten that everyone in the Virgin Islands drives on the left-hand side of the road.

Despite the best efforts of the rental car agencies, who strategically plastered shiny red stickers screaming KEEP LEFT across the front dash of their vehicles, most Americans, the bulk of the island's tourists, had a hard time adjusting to the concept of left-handed driving.

To be honest, on those rare instances when I'd rented a ride, I'd had a few dodgy moments with oncoming traffic. Instinct is a difficult trait to change.

Setting aside its susceptibility to near-fatal collisions, the golf cart's other main shortcoming was its limited power.

Charlie lived in a sprawling concrete block house perched at the top of an inland hill about a mile east from town. It was easy enough to drive the golf cart down into Cruz Bay—Charlie had amped up the cart's brakes so that you could hear its distinctive squall several blocks away.

It was quite another matter to convince the golf cart to climb back up the hill at the end of the evening. No amount of tinkering had successfully modified the engine to pull it and its driver up the incline. On more than half of Charlie's return trips, the golf cart wound up parked in the weeds at the side of the road, waiting to be towed the rest of the way home the following morning.

After several years of ranting, raving, and inflicting a significant amount of physical abuse on the cart's plastic hood, Charlie had finally tired of walking the last half mile up the hill.

As it turned out, Charlie had news to share beyond his newly purchased Jeep, although he was now, predictably, having difficulty finding a place to park.

On his second pass by the Dumpster table, he slowed the vehicle to a crawl, leaned out again, and shouted, "Who's the guy in the black limo?"

~ *17* ~

The Vultures

St. John typically saw an increase in rental vehicles around the middle of November, but the presence of a limo on the island was surprising—at any time of the year.

Each fall, as the weather cooled in the States and schoolchildren were released for their Thanksgiving breaks, vacationers began their annual migration down to the Caribbean. Extra flights from the eastern seaboard to the airport on St. Thomas facilitated the uptick in population.

The trend continued through the end of November. Then, after a short lull, the whole cycle repeated for the Christmas and New Year holidays.

All this extra traffic was generally fine with St. John's year-round residents; the high season was when those in the tourism industry made the bulk of their annual income.

I didn't know anyone, though, who didn't let out a sigh of relief in late January, when the tide finally began to ebb, and the island returned to its regular, relaxed vibe.

This November, however, a second type of visitor had begun to crowd Cruz Bay's streets. It was one of those,

I suspected, who had been riding in the limo that had caught Charlie's eye.

With the eco-resort's lease nearing its end and a likely auction of the Maho Bay real estate looming, diligence teams from various corporate entities were now arriving to inspect the property. It appeared several parties had plans to participate in the upcoming bidding process.

Even with the island's exploding tourist numbers, the real estate vultures were easy to spot, conspicuous in their business-casual clothing, leather briefcases, and flashy rental cars—the last of which they picked up on St. Thomas and shipped across on the car ferry—further exacerbating the already unmanageable parking situation.

The rental agencies did their best to prohibit transport of their nicer vehicles across the channel to St. John, where the road conditions were notoriously bad. The potholes alone could ruin the suspensions of most models. Even some of the island's "paved" roads required four-wheel drive to safely navigate.

My brow furrowed as I sipped on a frozen daiquiri from my seat at the Dumpster table. I could only imagine the conniption fit the limo owner would have if he discovered his pricey vehicle had been schlepped over to St. John. Someone was certainly going out of his way to make an impression.

We expats weren't the only ones taking note of the island's sudden influx of ostentatious wealth.

The crowds of day workers milling about the ferry building and the Freedom Memorial park across the street turned to stare with mounting hostility at each new batch of arriving power brokers—who in turn passed them by as if they were invisible. At the elementary school up the hill from the Crunchy Carrot, parents stood in the sun waiting for their children to be released from class as air-conditioned sedans drove by carrying the economic elite who would determine the island's fate.

The topic of Maho Bay also began popping up in the

Constitutional Convention debates, which the local radio stations seemed to be broadcasting nonstop.

Sensing a theme upon which to expand their base, the Native Rights advocates asked why such a pristine and valuable piece of land should be controlled by a foreign entity. Shouldn't it belong instead, they argued, to the people of the Virgin Islands?

An uneasy tension was settling in—one for which there seemed no ready means of release.

As Charlie and his Jeep made another futile pass by the Crunchy Carrot, César stuffed the last bite of his fish sandwich into his mouth, wiped a napkin across his flushed face, and waved a short good-bye. He was needed back at the kitchen.

The real estate teams were having a noticeable impact on the island's food consumption. Reservations at the higher-end restaurants had filled up as the business executives used their lucrative expense budgets to sample the best of the local cuisine.

Seats at Pesce were the hardest to come by, and César was feeling the pressure. His consumption of fish sandwiches had dramatically increased in number, even as the length of his lunch breaks at the Crunchy Carrot grew ever shorter.

Richard the rooster kept a close eye on the stressed-out Puerto Rican. As soon as César scuttled away from the table, the bird pounced on his discarded wrappings. A moment later, an excited *squawk* signaled the discovery of an overlooked French fry.

Grinning at the bird's delight, I returned my attention to the street as Charlie's limo turned the corner at the ferry building and proceeded up the road toward the Dumpster table. Squinting, I stared at the rear windows, but the tinted glass prevented any visual of the shadowed figure in the backseat.

I couldn't help but think of the large man from Miami as the car rolled slowly past.

~ 18 ~

The Invitation

A few days later, I was enjoying a morning walk through the resort when I heard the approaching hum of one of our many motorized golf carts. I stepped onto the curb of the brick path to let the cart through, but it slowed to an idle beside me.

Manto leaned out from the driver's seat and motioned for me to join him.

"Cum' on, Pin," he said jovially. *"Eye've broker'd a truce."*

A smile of relief broke across my face. Despite all my complaining, I'd missed tormenting my cranky assistant.

"She's lonely, isn't she?" I replied as I climbed into the passenger seat.

Shaking his head, Manto pressed down on the accelerator.

"How'd you get pulled into this?" I asked as we sped off toward the resort's recreation area.

"Ain't no fun wit' you two nut talk-in'." He chuckled. *"More enter-tainin' to wat'ch ya bicker."*

After a short drive, Manto parked the cart in a shady spot near the tennis courts. He turned off the ignition, reached into a shirt pocket, and pulled out a small flask of rum. Handing me the bottle, he pointed to a narrow compartment in the molding between the seats.

"Plas-teek cups een there."

Then he exited the cart and strolled off, grinning to himself. About twenty yards down the path, he turned back and pointed a finger at me.

"Play nice, Pin," he admonished with a wink. *"At least for a leet-tle while."*

I cracked open the bottle and took a sniff. If the scent was anything to go by, it was strong but drinkable. After lifting the lid to the compartment between the seats, I fished around inside for one of the plastic cups. I held the cup up to the sunlight, blew out a few cobwebs, and dumped in an inch of the dark amber liquid.

Leaning back in my seat, I let my gaze travel to the sand-filled playground near the fence surrounding the tennis courts. Several black and green torpedo-like shapes were stretched out across the shadowed ground where Fred and his fellow iguanas stalked one another beneath the jungle gym equipment.

Slowly, I brought the rim of the cup to my lips—and nearly choked as the first sip burned down my throat.

"That's not a peace offering, Manto," I muttered under my breath once I finally managed to swallow. "She'll think I'm trying to poison her."

I didn't have long to wait. A moment later, the golf cart groaned as Vivian's sturdy figure climbed into the vacant driver's seat.

"Vivian," I said with mock surprise, keeping my gaze firmly fixed on the iguanas. "How've you been?"

She assumed a similar visual stance. "Busy," she replied crisply, as she stared out over the steering wheel.

"Can I pour you one?" I asked, digging into the compartment for the second cup.

Vivian scowled. "You know I don't like that stuff."

"That's all right," I said with a shrug. "Leaves more for me."

Her thick lips pinched with disapproval. She thrust her hand into the compartment and pulled out the cup. "Fill it up, then," she grumped.

The two of us sipped in silence as the iguanas waddled on their crooked legs across the sand. They appeared to be participating in some sort of elaborate mating ritual. Every so often, they all froze in position and gave each other affectionate, lizard-eyed looks.

"I got your message," Vivian said, tersely breaking the silence. "About Miss Sheridan."

I scratched my chin thoughtfully. "Message?" I repeated with exaggerated puzzlement, already dismissing Manto's parting words of caution. It was never too soon to start pushing Vivian's buttons.

"There was nothing in her file," she said stiffly, ignoring my tease. "That's how it came in the pouch from headquarters."

She swiveled in her seat, her accusing glare turned to its highest setting. "Just like four years ago—when *you* arrived."

Fred looked up from beneath a teeter-totter as I cleared my throat uncomfortably. I'd never given Vivian credit for having that much intuition.

Vivian snorted as if she had come to the same conclusion about me.

"At least *that one* does some work around here," she added with a grumpy smirk. "More than I can say for the likes of *you*."

She lifted the top layer of papers secured to her clipboard and pulled out a legal-sized envelope. It was similar to the one that had held the Maho Bay information I'd received the previous week.

"Something came for you in the mail," she said cryptically as she handed it over.

With a sigh, I set my cup on the dashboard and sized up the envelope. Given its light weight and lack of bulging, there couldn't have been more than a single sheet of paper inside.

"More from the home office on the Maho Bay deal," I moaned.

Vivian rejected this notion with a firm headshake. "They're not in that hunt. You know they don't have that kind of money."

Perplexed, I thought back to the previous package. With a start, I realized it had come in on the same day that Hannah Sheridan had visited my office. In my mind's eye, I saw the young woman nervously crossing from the couch to my desk—and bumping into a stack of papers on its surface. Was the package a fake? Had she slid it into my inbox?

After another glance at Vivian, I pulled out a short typewritten letter from the current envelope and began reading it aloud.

Dear Ms. Hoffstra:

I look forward to making your acquaintance during my upcoming trip to St. John. Your agreeable assistant Vivian Jackson has graciously arranged our dinner reservations for a week from Friday . . .

"Agreeable assistant?" I chortled, despite my growing apprehension. I turned my head sideways toward the driver's seat. "Graciously arranged?"

Not once in Vivian's entire miserable life had she been described as agreeable or gracious, and certainly not in the same sentence.

Vivian replied with her iciest stare. "I can assure you, I did nothing of the sort."

The paper in my hands was appearing less authentic by the minute.

"Keep reading," she added with a grunt.

"Ahem," I said, briefly raising my eyebrows.

My driver will pick you up outside the front desk at five p.m.

Yours truly . . .

When I reached the signature line, there was no longer any doubt. My face paled as I read the sender's name.

The person listed at the bottom of the letter was one I'd never seen or heard of before. A final look at Vivian's skeptical face confirmed my suspicions. Despite the printed stationary and the formal-looking address label, the writer wasn't in any way affiliated with the resort's parent company.

My upcoming dinner meeting was with a man I presumed to be the "uncle" Hannah had referred to that first morning when she arrived at the resort.

I felt certain I was about to receive a visit from the wide-girthed man from Miami.

The signature line read "Hank Sheridan."

~ *19* ~

The Trunk Bay
Parking Lot

Manto hummed happily to himself as he steered a truckload
of resort guests off North Shore Road into the parking lot for
Trunk Bay, the access point for St. John's signature—and
most visited—beach.

The passengers scrambled out of the back bed's covered seating area and hurriedly stopped by his driver's-side
window to pay their fares. After making change for the last
amount, Manto tucked the residual into his bulging wallet.
Then, he climbed out of the truck's cab and watched as his
passengers eagerly approached the ticket kiosk at the edge
of the parking lot.

It had been a busy couple of days on the truck-taxi shift,
he reflected as a pleased smile creased his ruddy face. He
was enjoying the reassurance the extra dollars would bring
to his bank account.

Trunk Bay was the only beach in the national park that
charged admission, but the payment brought with it a nice
array of amenities that many considered worth the fee. In the
calm water beyond the beach, an underwater trail led snor-

kelers to a large cay patrolled during the daytime hours by a lifeguard. Shower facilities, storage lockers, a food stand, and a snorkel rental shop serviced the hundreds of vacationers who traipsed through the area during the high season.

For most of the island's visitors, it was a must-do, if crowded, experience. On a day like today, Manto mused as the line in front of the ticket booth continued to grow, the water probably held more people than fish.

He glanced down at his silent two-way radio and then checked his watch. By now, there should be plenty of trucks waiting in town to carry potential riders into the park. It was late enough in the afternoon, he decided, to wait there at Trunk Bay for the flow of tourists to reverse course from the beaches back to the resorts.

Stretching the soreness in the small of his back, he meandered over to a row of shaded picnic benches where several of the other drivers had gathered.

Throughout the daytime hours, the truck taxies maintained a visible presence throughout the national park, informally organizing into a network of impromptu drop-off and pickup points at the most popular beaches. The largest congregation of drivers were generally located at the Trunk Bay parking lot, which had a sizeable marked-off area for their vehicles. In the slow period during the early afternoon, ten or more men could often be seen sitting or standing around the picnic tables.

Manto nodded hellos as he approached. It was a cordial group, and he had known most of the men for years.

The drivers rarely competed with each other for rides; such behavior would have broken their unspoken code of conduct. Each of the men wore a quiet, detached demeanor that matched their loose-fitting slacks and button-down linen shirts. Tourists frequently misunderstood this reserved attitude for laziness, but a driver would sooner refuse a fare than take on an insulting or disruptive passenger.

The men were all wired with cell phones and walkie-talkies that squawked and chirped as they chatted with one another. The contents of several sack lunches were spread out across the tables. This was a communal time, an important social hour in their day, dedicated to a few games of chess and the exchange of local gossip. The eyes and ears of the truck-taxi drivers picked up everything that went on in this small island community. Little escaped the wide net of their surveillance.

As Manto strolled up to one of the picnic benches, he caught sight of a small transistor radio that had been plugged into the power outlet of one of the trucks' cigarette lighters.

The radio was an almost permanent fixture at the Trunk Bay truck-taxi stand. Recently, it seemed, the dial had been fixed to the station relaying the Constitutional Convention proceedings. This afternoon, Manto noted with relief, the signal had been switched over to a broadcast of an event in Charlotte Amalie commemorating the 1733 Slave Revolt.

This was a welcome change in programming—or so Manto thought until he heard an old woman's coarse, lilting voice emitting from the black box.

Despite the afternoon heat, Manto felt an involuntary shiver down his spine as the radio carried Beulah Shah's words into the Trunk Bay parking lot.

> *When thuh slave sheep arrived een Char-lut Amal-ya, thuh Amina Preen-cess wuz auctioned off to a plant-ter who had just bought a par-cel of land on St. John . . .*

The Amina Princess had suffered through several hours of pushing, prodding, and frightening confusion before finally being bundled onto a small ferryboat and transported with several other new slaves to a small mountainous plot on St. John, where the ill-favored son-in-law of a St. Thomas planter was struggling to set up a fledgling sugar plantation.

Set in the steep hills above Maho Bay, the property was

perhaps one of the worst-suited plots for sugarcane production on an island that sported several contenders for
the title. The land was covered with a thick vegetation of
jujube, mampoo, and tan-tan, the combined root structure
of which had not done much to break up the rocky volcanic
soil. The hapless son-in-law knew next to nothing about
agriculture, and his new bride was quickly losing patience
with his ineptitude.

The Princess couldn't yet understand the language of
these pale unhappy people, but she knew enough of human
nature to predict that both the union and this poorly con-
ceived enterprise were unlikely to succeed.

This island was a wicked place, the Princess soon decided.

Her native sun had been replaced by a demonic imposter, one which boiled the air's dense humidity. What little
breeze filtered inland carried a damp moisture that caused
her joints to stiffen and swell. Her fingers had never felt so
thick, so heavy. Her body was constantly covered with a
sticky, stinking layer of sweat.

At the end of each day, the Princess lay down on her designated mat, a dusty bed on the floor of the lean-to shelter
that was now her home. Tucked beneath the trees on the
slope of a hill, the meager structure provided little protection from either the elements or the pestilence of insects that
populated the island.

The Princess ran her hand up and down the surface of her
shin, her fingers counting the welts. Thankfully, the number
had begun to decrease. At last, the microscopic beasts were
starting to lose their appetite for her golden brown skin.

As she waited patiently for the rest of the small farm's
inhabitants to drift off to sleep, her hand slipped up to her
neck, instinctively searching for the iron medallion. With
the edge of a fingernail, she traced the absent circular shape
on the flat canvas at the top of her chest. The amulet's intan-
gible force was still with her. Somehow, its presence had
followed her to this miserable island.

The Princess risked a quick glance at the other women in the shack. Her fellow sufferers were a wide range of ages; their haggard faces represented an array of declining mental states. Some had been so beaten and traumatized in their travels to this remote island, they could no longer bear to remember their African roots. They refused to talk about their origins. Their spirits, she could see, had left them. Others retained scattered fragments of their essence, but it was slowly, inevitably ebbing away from them.

She clutched the phantom metal disc at the base of her neck, taking strength from the emblem's aura—that would not happen to her.

The Princess lay on the mat in the darkness of the lean-to for another half hour, until she was sure that everyone else had fallen asleep. Then she rose quietly from the floor, taking care not to wake any of the other dozing women.

As a sleeping silence fell in around the camp, the Princess crept stealthily out into the moonlight. She skirted around the edge of the clearing, her slim figure indistinguishable in the shadow of the surrounding trees.

A moment later, she crossed the fledgling plantation's scant fortifications. The owner's quarters were not much more of a lodging than her own. All construction efforts were focused on the cane mill and boiler room, which would be needed if any of the first harvest managed to ripen.

The Princess reached the far end of the wretched little settlement and paused to look back into the gray darkness. Scanning the area, she checked for movement, but not a soul was stirring.

She turned and stepped out onto the nearest trail, fully expecting that someone would call after her to stop.

All that could be heard was the buzzing of insects.

She proceeded another ten steps and listened once more.

No one had followed her. She was alone and ready to explore.

~ 20 ~

The Teepee Tent

After a long day of travel that had begun at the threshold of his Brooklyn apartment, Conrad Corsair completed his journey with a satisfying tromp up the last steps into his tent at the Maho Bay eco-resort.

With a flourish, he swung open the screen door and stepped inside. A few short steps took him across the room where he dropped his duffel bag onto the middle of a cot and slid his beat-up guitar case into the two-foot slot beneath. Sighing deeply, he straightened his short frame and stretched his arms above his freshly dyed head of ever-thinning hair.

Months of anticipation had finally come to fruition. It was the third week of November, and he had arrived at the only place on earth he felt he truly belonged.

Conrad took a slow turn around the tent's dark interior. He had reserved this exact unit for the same two-week slot, going back every year since the eco-resort first opened. He knew each scratch and divot in the wooden floorboards, every nook and cranny of the cupboards that lined the back wall.

"Ahhh," he said fondly as if greeting an old friend. "Hello, Teepee Tent."

Conrad chuckled with his squeaky, elflike laugh, recollecting how Fast Eddie at the front desk always groused about his terminology.

"You know, Conrad," Eddie would say in that dry, humorless voice of his, "technically, it's a reinforced tent. It doesn't have any structural relationship to a *teepee*."

Conrad shook his head dismissively. He wasn't one to let such minor details get in the way of his flawless reasoning.

Conrad flipped on a light, unzipped the duffel, and rummaged through its carefully packed contents. In the months of preparation leading up to the trip, the inventory list had been scrupulously reviewed, revised, and, finally, memorialized on a laminated three-by-five index card. He could recite each and every item by heart.

He checked the duffel's side pocket for his ziplock bag of guitar picks and confirmed their location, feeling pleased with his meticulous organization. The bag contained several dozen tiny plastic triangles—each painted a different color.

It was part of a new pickup line he'd developed, one he planned to debut on this trip. Once he had identified a woman worthy of his amorous attentions, he would select the guitar pick best suited for her particular color combinations.

He had options for all contingencies. He could match a pick with the woman's shirt, hair ribbon, eye color, or, if none of the above worked, bug-spray bottle—he had a special bug-spray pick he'd brought along for just that kind of emergency.

He had practiced his opening line over and over in front of the bathroom mirror in his New York apartment.

"Well, look at that, love," he would say with expertly feigned surprise as he held the pick up to the targeted accessory. "We're a perfect match."

Conrad beamed optimistically at the plastic bag. He'd passed a pretty young woman at the check-in desk earlier that evening who would be receiving the guitar pick treatment the next time he saw her.

His eyes passed over to the duffel's pile of neatly stacked clothing. Reaching out, he gave the top pair of ragged blue jeans a loving pat. These pants had made every trip to St. John with him; they were his favorite good luck charm. He'd had to lay off the jelly donuts the last couple of weeks in order to squeeze into them, but the sacrifice had been worth it, he thought, proudly rubbing the recently diminished round of his pot belly.

Conrad ticked off the duffel's remaining contents from memory: two weeks' worth of underwear and T-shirts, open-toe sandals, a well-worn shower kit, and, last but not least, a particularly offensive pair of brand new Bermuda swimming trunks that, in his modest opinion, accentuated his brawny pecs.

He flexed his arms out, imagining the scene at Maho Beach the following morning, where the Bermudas would be making their impressive debut.

Oh, and, of course, he thought, dropping his pose, there was the manila envelope, tucked into the duffel beside the pile of clothing—it and its contents were the only other items making their maiden voyage to St. John.

Conrad lifted the legal-sized envelope from the duffel and carefully placed it on a nightstand next to the cot. He stared intently at its worn, bulging surface. His aging blue eyes glittered with intensity.

This, he thought proudly, represented his life's most important achievement. He was about to make a significant contribution to this island, and, he thought with a respectful nod to the nearest screened wall, his beloved teepee tent.

Stepping away from the cot, Conrad circled around its end post to a small mirror hanging on the tent's back wall. The scattered moonlight filtering into the tent combined with the lightbulb over the bed to generate a dim reflection.

Admiring the fresh dye job he'd applied the day before, he pulled a black plastic comb out of his back pocket and carefully ran it over the top of his head. Grinning toothily, he stared at his hollowed out cheeks and skeletal smile.

Feeling confident and self-assured, Conrad returned to the cot. After moving the duffel to the floor, he flopped down onto the loose bedsprings, kicked off his sneakers, peeled off his socks, and stretched his skinny body the length of its twin-sized frame.

His hand reached into a shirt pocket for a package of cigarettes he'd purchased on his way through town—special ones to celebrate his first night back on St. John.

Opening the paper bag, he pulled out a sample. As he passed the hand-rolled cylinder under his nose, he took in a deep whiff of its unlit fragrance.

"Ah, yes," he sighed contentedly, noting the combination of grassy floral notes. "Perfect."

Conrad fished a lighter out of another pocket and lit the cigarette. The tip of the paper glowed red as he wrapped his thin lips around the opposite end and sucked heat through the interior hallucinogens. His head began to swim as a billow of smoke filled the air above the cot.

"Hey there, Mister District Attorney Man," he mumbled groggily at the tent's ceiling. "You can't reach me here—I'm *way* outside your jurisdiction . . ."

Drifting off into the hazy edges of a dream, Conrad quickly found himself in a New York City courtroom, explaining his latest astute arguments to a judge, who sat in a black robe behind an elevated desk.

But just as Conrad warmed to a critical point in his dialogue, he was interrupted by a rustling in the woods outside his tent.

"Aw, no worries, Your Honor-man," Conrad assured the tent's blank ceiling. "That's just a mongoose. Those things are half-blind. They're always rooting around down there beneath the teepee tent."

The judge leaned over his bench and cocked a suspicious eycbrow at him.

"Mr. Corsair, a witness has previously testified that the mongoose is a diurnal animal, generally active only during the day."

Conrad pulled himself upright on the cot, puzzling as the rustling sound grew nearer. It sounded as if a large creature were pacing a circle on the forest floor beneath him.

"Could be a hermit crab, Judge. Those things are crawling around at all hours."

He took another pull on the cigarette as a second noise permeated the tent—one that stopped Conrad midsmoke. He coughed spastically as the fumes stagnated in his lungs. It was a lyrical, mystical voice, singing, chanting almost, and it appeared to be coming from the nearby woods.

Conrad jumped off the cot, leapt across the floor, and swung open the tent's screen door. His eyes scanned the surrounding trees, searching for the source of the sound. There it was again. And he was certain of it now—it was coming from a woman. This was definitely something that needed to be checked out.

Cautiously, he proceeded down the wooden walkway leading away from his tent, waiting for his woman-seeking sonar to hone in on the location of the creature with the beautiful voice.

As he reached a T-intersection with one of the main staircases, he thoughtfully drummed his fingers along the rough surface of the waist-high railing. He tilted an ear toward the upper portion of the resort, where the check-in desk and the dry goods store were located.

"Nope," Conrad mumbled out loud. She wasn't up there.

He turned left on the staircase and headed down toward the beach. The wooden planks that made up the walkway creaked beneath his bare feet as he descended. His feet *thunked* faster and faster as the sound grew louder.

Little of the sky was visible through the canopy of trees that covered the stairs, but it was a clear night—he could sense it. He felt the moon's tugging pull, working in conjunction with the woman's lyrical voice, leading him down to the ocean.

He reached a flat transition point on the stairs with a bright blue recycling tub and a water spigot mounted to a wooden post. After sprinting across the ten-foot landing, he hurtled down the next flight of steps. He had almost reached the beach—he could see the bottom of the stairs up ahead.

A moment later, the overhang of limbs and leaves parted, and the stairs emptied out onto the sand. Conrad gingerly picked his way across the layer of twigs and debris that had collected near the shore. The wide looping expanse of Maho Bay stretched out before him, lit by an eerie spectral moon that shimmered in the gentle lapping waves.

At the far end of the beach, near the boulders that blocked off the curving path of the shoreline toward Mary's Point, a shadowed figure stood in the water. It was the woman who had summoned him from the teepee tent.

She wore a close-fitting beaded vest and a sarong tied around her narrow waist. From her neck hung a silver medallion—formed in the circular shape of the sun.

Conrad blinked, desperately trying to focus his drug-addled vision.

He could see her mouth moving, her lips forming the words that floated across the sand toward him.

The woman tilted her head back, so that her face caught the moon's full illumination. Her skin was a creamy cocoa color, luminous in the water's reflection. She motioned with her hand, as if asking him to join her, luring him into the ocean.

"Me?" Conrad asked incredulously, pointing at his chest.

She nodded, the springing coils of her dark shiny hair bouncing as she sang out another strange, unearthly chorus of her song. Then, with a last flirtatious wave, she dove into the shallow water and began swimming out into the bay.

Fervently wishing he had stopped long enough to change into the Bermuda swimming trunks, Conrad quickly rolled up the legs of his blue jeans. Without further hesitation, he

waded into the water and began swimming after the Amina
Slave Princess.

Northeast of the eco-resort, on a hill in the dense woods that
covered Mary's Point, Beulah Shah lurched along the faint
outline of an overgrown, long-forgotten trail.

Football-sized boulders pushed up through the dirt, their
sharp, jutting edges slicing through her thin-soled shoes.
Calabash branches scratched her face and ripped at the
sleeves of her loose-hanging navy blue shirtdress. She paid
no heed to any of these hindrances.

The tapering path's loose, rocky base became more difficult to discern as it disappeared into a tangled mass of ferns
and oversized agave plants, but Beulah needed no guide-
posts. She knew the route by memory.

Higher and higher, the old woman climbed, pushing her
way through the underbrush, swiping at the dangling cur-
tains of ropelike vines that snaked down from the treetops—
until slowly, the canopy began to fall away, revealing a
star-strewn sky and, across the water, a moonlit Maho Bay.

She reached into the holster of a ragged sport belt secured
around her tiny waist and pulled out a bottle of water.
Unscrewing the lid, she tipped the bottle to her lips. A few
gulps later, she gummed her toothless mouth and wiped the
sweat from her brow.

Taking care with her footing, she crawled onto a rocky
outcropping that gave her a better view of the bay. From this
vantage point, Beulah could see almost the entire outline
of St. John's northern coast, a ruffled skirt of tree-rimmed
beaches and the occasional odd-shaped cay dotting the water
just beyond the shoreline.

In front of her ledge, bobbing out beyond the rounded
blunt of Mary's Point, she spied a small catamaran powerboat tethered to an anchor. Red lettering painted along the
white side of the boat read WATER TAXI.

Beulah watched as a brawny, muscular man threw an

inflatable yellow dinghy over the side of the boat, and then followed it into the water. After pulling the rip cord on a tiny black motor attached to the stern, he drove the dinghy inland toward the narrow divot of an inlet cove, where it disappeared into the shadowed darkness.

To her left, Beulah's vision took in the sweep of the hillside that housed the eco-resort and its protected beach on the sand below. Her eyes squinted as she focused her gaze on a scrawny, splashing man desperately paddling out into Maho Bay.

The mysterious woman who had drawn him into the water was nowhere to be seen.

The next morning found Conrad Corsair snoring sleepily into his pillow, facedown on his cot inside the teepee tent, wearing nothing but his Bermuda swimming trunks and a fogged-up pair of goggles. His spindly arms and legs were tangled in his bedsheets, still occasionally flailing about in a paddling motion as he tried to catch up to the singing woman who had disappeared into the ocean near Maho Bay.

The manila envelope lay on the floor by the nightstand, where it had fallen the night before during a frantic search for the ziplock bag of guitar picks. The end flap had popped open, revealing a portion of the contents stuffed inside.

A ragged stack of photocopied papers took up much of the envelope's volume. The top sheet was stamped on its upper right-hand corner with the imprint of New York City's largest public library. Part of a map was visible—it appeared to be a delineation of the west coast of Africa, heavily marked with penciled annotations pinpointing the known locations of Danish slave forts from the 1700s.

A slight breeze siphoned through the tent, riffling the papers. The top sheet peeled back to reveal the surface of the one underneath.

A second map, similarly stamped and covered with penciled handwriting, portrayed a far different geographical location—the island of St. John, expanded to highlight the area around Maho Bay.

Next to the pile of papers, hanging halfway out of the package, was a leather rope necklace connected to a circular iron amulet forged in the shape of a sun.

~ 21 ~

Mary's Point

Jeff yawned as his wristwatch alarm beeped its five a.m. alert. Pushing a button to silence the beep, he rolled silently out of the queen-sized bed, taking care not to wake its other, still snoozing occupant.

With the crook of his finger, he scooped up his red T-shirt from the floor. A quick twist of his wrists turned the garment right-side out, so that the logo of the resort's dive shop was now visible. After a discreet sniff, followed by an "oh well" shrug, he stuffed his head through the neck hole.

A couple seconds later, he'd pulled on a loose pair of well-worn, knee-length shorts, slipped into his flip-flops, and ducked noiselessly out of the one-bedroom condo unit.

He stood on the doorstep and briefly scanned the surrounding area. In the predawn darkness, no one else was awake to observe his exit—save the bright green iguana staring curiously up at him from the nearest lawn. This section of the resort was slated for renovations that were scheduled to begin in a few months' time, and the outdated rooms were rarely used to house paying guests.

With another wide yawn, Jeff waved at the iguana and loped down the hill to the dive shop.

* * *

Bright lights burned through the shop's front windows, the only illumination beyond the ground lamps that lined the sidewalks leading to the resort's quiet waterfront.

Drowsily rubbing the rough stubble on his chin, Jeff pushed open the door and shuffled inside. The other crew member assigned to the morning's charter sat kicked back on a stool behind the counter, loudly slurping a cup of coffee.

Jeff groaned internally as his expressionless gaze fell upon Rick, a cheeky blond-haired kid in his late twenties who'd recently moved down to the island from Tampa. This was one of his least favorite work pairings.

Rick was easily distracted, sloppy with their safety protocols, and had an annoying tendency to disappear whenever there was work to be done. Even worse, he was apparently under the misconception that the two of them were buddies.

Jeff felt his jaw tighten as Rick greeted him with an enthusiastic, "Good morning, sunshine." He raised a knowing eyebrow and added slyly, "Sleep well?"

Issuing a noncommittal grunt, Jeff reached behind the counter for his beat-up toiletry kit. The slightest twitch creased the left corner of his mouth as he retreated out the door, but the taciturn exterior concealed a constant commentary that played inside his head.

Mind your own business, jughead, he thought with irritation.

A few long strides took Jeff around the corner of the building to a public restroom.

He dropped the toiletry kit onto the ledge near the sink, turned on the faucet, and dunked his head under the cool stream of water. Then, with a fist full of paper towels from the automatic dispenser, he scrubbed his face dry.

Jeff let out a sigh as he ran his hand through the tower of tight curls piled up over his head. The night before, he had finally given in to Pen's demands and washed his hair.

Bannanquits, he thought with a small smile, before opening the kit and fishing out his toothpaste.

Half an hour later, Jeff guided a sleepy group of hotel guests off the dock and into the dive shop's powerboat. Up in the vessel's elevated cabin, the captain reviewed his equipment checklist and confirmed the day's weather report.

Jeff scanned the boat's interior and the adjoining dock. Rick was, predictably, nowhere to be found.

Once Jeff had safely loaded the passengers, he returned to the dive shop for the rest of the day's supplies. Muttering under his breath, he picked up a crate holding a thermos of fresh coffee, a box of Danishes, a variety of juice containers, and several bottles of rum. By the time he returned with the crate, Rick had reappeared and was now aboard, happily chatting with the passengers.

Grimacing, Jeff hefted the crate over the side of the boat and began his routine inspection of the rigging. Despite the early departure—and the less-than-desirable shipmate—today's outing was a welcome break from his regular routine.

The dive shop typically ran two daytrips a week. The first route circumnavigated the straits between the U.S. and the British Virgin Islands, taking a few snorkeling stops en route to the Virgin Gorda Baths on the far east end of the BVIs.

The Baths were marked by several enormous boulders that looked as if they'd been propped up on their ends like dominoes—the huge structures could be seen from miles away. A series of trails wove in, around, and over the rocks, creating a fun, kid-friendly, but often crowded playground.

Those were busy trips, Jeff mused wearily: helping the children struggle into their pint-sized life jackets, teaching the tots how to use the snorkel gear, and constantly counting heads to make sure he didn't lose anyone. But he'd take that shift any day over the alternate route.

The dive shop's other regular excursion was a more adult-themed affair. That trip focused on Jost Van Dyke, an island positioned at the west end of the BVI chain, not far north of St. John. Due to the later departure time, the boat stopped first for lunch at Foxy's Bar and Restaurant before proceeding on to White Bay. There, the passengers swam ashore, carrying money in plastic ziplock baggies, for a taste of one of the Soggy Dollar's renowned Painkiller cocktails.

In between stops, Jeff spent the majority of his time pouring drinks, cleaning up spills, and wishing he could push his increasingly inebriated passengers overboard.

In contrast, this morning's excursion was a specially chartered voyage. Over the next couple of hours, they would slowly circle the island, stopping every so often for a scenic photo op and the occasional snorkel break. It was a refreshing deviation from the weekly schedule. And at least on this trip, Jeff reflected drowsily, there were only four guests to cater to. How much trouble could that possibly be?

A reclining Rick waved as Jeff untied the boat from the dock. "Hey, ya' need any help there, bro?"

Make that *five* passengers to take care of, Jeff grumbled internally.

The sun's first creeping edges reflected off the flat surface of the water as the powerboat finally pushed away from the pier. Jeff began passing out pastries while Rick sat sipping his second cup of coffee.

The loud hum of the engine drowned out all conversation—which was just as well. By the time they had passed the outer edge of Cruz Bay, the vigorous commentary inside Jeff's head had reached a fever pitch. His fellow passengers had given him plenty of material to work with.

The two couples who had booked the early morning charter were from Texas. Jeff had gathered as much from the snippets of conversation he'd picked up during their earlier dialogue with Rick. Their distinctive drawling accents combined with an intense debate about the current starting lineup for the Cowboys football team had given them away.

This alone would have provided Jeff with an easy hour's

worth of mocking mental dialogue—his New England–born prejudices were firmly imprinted on his persona—but the observational bonanza of these guests didn't stop with their aggressive hometown pride.

These were rich men, overtly so—in a way that had blurred their individuality as well as their common sense. Who else wore Rolex watches and expensive leather loafers on a boat, Jeff pondered cynically. Despite their request for an early morning snorkeling stop, he was willing to bet his portion of the tip jar that neither man would risk dampening their elaborate hairpieces in the ocean's salty water.

Their wives, of course, were another matter entirely. These women were the men's second, probably third iterations on the marital wheel, judging by the dramatic age differences and the females' numerous plastic improvements.

No need to worry about additional floatation devices, Jeff thought wryly. Not with the size of those implants.

The boat rumbled past Caneel Bay's pristine western shore, revealing a row of one-bedroom cabins discreetly tucked into the trees and bushes. The acres of shallow water that stretched out from the beach were populated by a wide array of colorful fish, several bobbing turtles, and a squadron of dark gray stingrays—the last of which were, in Jeff's opinion, far too snorkeler-friendly.

As they rounded the top corner of the Caneel property, the rocky outcropping of Turtle Point came into view. This protruding spit of land was the scenic location for some of the island's most lavish and extravagant weddings. The outer rim of the national park's north shore provided a stunning photographic backdrop for newly hitched couples.

Jeff's bleary eyes followed the track of the land east from Turtle Point's narrow peninsula. He knew every inch of the map by heart: the bays of Hawksnest, Trunk, Cinnamon, and Maho—then, looming in the distance, the densely wooded curve of Mary's Point.

* * *

Skimming along the well-traveled channel between St. John and Tortola, the boat didn't take long to reach Mary's outer tip. As the vessel circled the heavily forested bulge of land, the sun made its first full glowing appearance, its blinding ball playing hide-and-seek among the mounded humps of the eastern BVIs.

The captain cut the engine to a purr as they neared the first snorkeling site. The area known as Waterlemon Cay was popular for its own happy band of turtles, a colony of starfish sucking on the ocean floor, and the occasional deer swimming across the bay on a watery shortcut to the opposite side.

The women pulled their bleach-lightened hair back into ponytails and stripped down to their suits, preparing for their swim. Meanwhile, the husbands leaned over the side, puffing on cigars as they searched the water for fish.

One of the wives stood up and took a seat on the bench next to Rick.

"Oh boy," Jeff muttered to himself as the woman placed a manicured, heavily bejeweled hand on Rick's knee and smiled seductively.

Grunting an interruption, Jeff stepped across the deck and handed the woman a snorkel mask.

A few minutes later, the wives climbed down the boat's ladder and into the water. Jeff watched them float away from the vessel, internally contemplating the chances that one of the long narrow barracudas trailing beneath the boat's shadow might take an interest in the sparkling diamonds weighing down the women's fingers.

From behind his left ear, Jeff heard one of the husbands call out to the captain's tower.

"Hey, Cap—ya' got any music?"

Jeff felt his shoulders stiffen with resistance. Oh no, please don't, he pleaded inside his head.

The boat was equipped with a large collection of CDs as well as an MP3 player packed with a wide variety of tunes, but the tourists only ever wanted to hear one album.

"How 'bout that Kenny guy? Doesn't he have a house down here?"

Jeff cringed as he heard the captain push the button on the CD player. The disc that—in the eighteen months he had been working for the dive shop—had never once been ejected from its slot began spinning its music. Out of the boat's speakers came the opening strum of a guitar and the soft sound of lapping waves.

There was nothing wrong with the tune, per se. Jeff had even enjoyed it—the first one hundred and fifty times he'd heard it.

But now, the country crooner's song about his favorite blue rocking chair on a St. John beach grated in Jeff's ears like fingernails down a chalkboard. He had heard the lyrics so many times, the mere thought of a blue rocker made him physically ill.

Jeff had often dreamt of confronting the singer whose popular song had become his daily torture. The man occasionally showed up at the Crunchy Carrot and was frequently spotted walking the streets of Cruz Bay. He had a private estate, right on the water, that they had passed during their route earlier that morning.

One of these days, I'm going to jump off the side of this boat, swim up to that guy's house, and cram that blue rocking chair up his—

Jeff broke off his silent rant as he caught sight of a movement on the east side of Mary's Point.

Wait a minute, he thought with a musing grunt. *What's that?*

The rising sun illuminated the figure of a woman perched on the crest of a ridge. She was dressed in a beaded bodice and knee-length sarong. The light morning breeze lifted a thick mass of dark curly hair from her forehead as she looked down on the water.

The woman's gaze suddenly lifted, as if she sensed she'd

been spotted. She raised a conch shell to her lips and blew out a haunting, mournful call.

From the opposite side of the boat, Rick released a puff of smoke from a cigar given to him by one of the husbands and commented, "Hey, I bet that's the Slave Princess . . ."

~ 22 ~

A Heated Debate

The governor stood on the balcony outside the second floor of the Government House, looking down on the harbor as a cruise ship pulled into Charlotte Amalie.

Behind him, the door to his office stood open. Inside, a portable television set had been tuned to a local channel broadcasting the day's proceedings of the Fifth Constitutional Convention. The delegates were receiving a report from the attorneys appointed to advise the convention on their currently proposed Native Rights terminology.

An aide wearing a suit, tie, and shiny leather shoes paced nervously back and forth on the office's plush red carpet, his hands tucked into the small of his back, his face fixed with a tense expression. The governor and his staff had been apprised of the results of the report prior to today's disclosure. The legal counsel had been unable to identify language that would meet the delegates' demands without coming into conflict with the overriding U.S. Constitution.

The aide listened anxiously as the information was explained to the delegates. As predicted, those pushing the Native Rights issue were not backing down.

A woman's commanding voice squawked out of the television's speakers. "I cannot vote in favor of this constitution unless it contains a provision for Native Rights."

The remark immediately brought a mixed chorus of cheers and grumbling.

"We can't keep coming back to this," another woman replied with exasperation. "The lawyers have just told us it will violate the U.S. Constitution. If we put in a Native Rights clause, it will sink the whole thing."

She was immediately overwhelmed by dissenters. The crowd became more and more unruly; angry voices poured out of the television set. The gavel pounded, ineffectually, against the speaker's wooden platform.

"Order, order," a man's stern but ignored voice demanded. "I call this meeting to order!"

The aide scampered out onto the balcony, wringing his hands nervously.

"Sir," he said with a gulp, "things are getting out of hand down there at the convention. You're going to have to weigh in on this."

The governor inhaled a deep breath of humid ocean air. He stared out across the harbor for a long moment, his face a dark canvas of serious contemplation. Finally, he rested his hands on the edge of the balcony and metered out an even reply.

"Not yet."

~ 23 ~

Gussying Up

Friday afternoon, Vivian sat me down in front of the bathroom mirror in my condo at the resort and began tugging a comb, not at all tenderly, through my tangled wet hair. Freshly showered, I was ready to be glamorized, or at least made presentable, for that evening's dinner with the nebulous Hank Sheridan.

To avoid any awkward questions about my whereabouts that evening, we had kept with the script laid out in the invitation. Vivian had spread the word that I was meeting with an executive from the resort's home office who had been sent to St. John to conduct an appraisal of the Maho Bay property. Neither of us had any idea where he was actually staying, but according to Vivian's well-concocted story, Hank Sheridan had snubbed the rooms at our resort for more glamorous digs on St. Thomas—the man's luxurious tastes had subsequently been derided at both the Dumpster table and in the break room behind the reception desk.

Neither Vivian nor I had discussed the Sheridan meeting with Hannah. For her part, she hadn't offered any other rationale for her uncle's visit.

What would transpire next was still a mystery. Had my

time on the island run out? Was the large man from Miami coming to remove me from my post?

I would find out soon enough, I told myself. Hank Sheridan's car would be picking me up in less than an hour.

Vivian continued to torture me with her savage beautician skills, while Hamilton played on the tile floor near the bed, happily assembling a new set of Legos.

The little paper box had held just over a hundred colorful plastic brick pieces that were designed to fit together into the shape of a boat. It was one of several toy kits I had stashed away on a top shelf in my closet. There were few contingencies that I took the time and effort to prepare for—a bribe for Vivian's hairstyling expertise was one of them.

As for the rest of me, I'd picked out a mail-order dress I'd kept aside for those rare occasions where a sundress and sandals were too casual. It had left my closet only twice since my move down to the island.

Vivian twitched her mouth critically at the matching pair of open-toe pumps, which had seen a similarly limited amount of use. She pointed skeptically at the two-inch heel.

"You really think you can walk in those?" she asked dubiously.

I shrugged my response. They would have to do. They'd come with the dress—it had been four years since my feet had seen a mainland shoe store. These were the only shoes I owned that hadn't spent a deteriorating amount of time at the beach.

Muttering under her breath, Vivian gathered the back sections of my hair and began twisting them into a bun. I tried not to wince as she wound up the strands and fastened the clip. Then she spun me around and began working on my face and bangs. An army of beautifying tools lay spread out on the counter, each pencil, brush, and lipstick container diligently awaiting her next command.

"Pucker your lips," she ordered briskly.

I held my mouth as still as possible until Vivian finished with the lip liner and leaned back to check her work.

"Smile," she demanded curtly.

I posed a stiff grin while Vivian stared critically at my face. Finally, she seemed satisfied and dropped the applicator on the counter.

Ham held up his newly constructed boat. "Look what *I* made," he called out sweetly.

The faint shadow of a proud smile crossed Vivian's serious face.

Ham pushed the little boat in a circle around the upended shoe box, adding his own motorboat noises to the scraping sound of the plastic against the tile.

"My boat is sailing around the island," he explained with a loud "*vroom*."

"A sailboat is much quieter than that," Vivian replied with a sternly cocked eyebrow.

Ham revised his toy scenario. "My *motor*boat is *motoring* around the island," he proclaimed loudly with an impish look at his mother. His little lips vibrated, spitting wildly as his boat made faster and faster turns around the shoe box.

"Here, my boat is going past Chocolate Hole," he said excitedly, pausing his motoring noise long enough to give us an update on his location.

Vivian sighed and returned to her makeup kit.

"And here, my boat is making a pit stop at the ferry building," he added, twisting his toy perpendicular to the side of the box.

Eyeliner in hand, Vivian grabbed hold of my head and tilted it toward the ceiling. "Look up," she murmured, her concentration focused on my face.

Ham's squeaky voice continued in the background. "And here, my boat is zooming around Caneel Bay . . ."

Vivian botched her first attempt with the liner. After blotting out the mark with a tissue, she pulled back from my face and picked up a sharpener from the counter. As she stuck the pencil's pointed end into the device, Ham let out a squeal.

"And look, there on Turtle Point—it's the Slave Princess!"

There was a sharp crack as the eyeliner stick broke off in Vivian's hand.

~ 24 ~

Caneel Bay

The Amina Princess lay atop her mat on the dusty floor of the lean-to, her eyes tightly shut, her body curled into a ball, waiting for the rest of the meager settlement to retire for the evening. The sun had yet to fully set, but an air of exhaustion soon fell over the camp, and the area quickly grew silent and still.

The surrounding structures bore a closer resemblance to ruins than newly constructed buildings. The jungle's voracious vegetation had consumed many of the stone walls, filling the roofless rooms with a dense layer of vines.

The Princess cracked open an eyelid and carefully examined the shed's sleeping occupants. One of the humped forms sighed out a snore. From another came the involuntary grinding of teeth.

Summoning all her hunting skills of stealth, she rose from the mat and quietly crept outside, ready to begin her nightly explorations.

She allotted a few hours each evening for sleep, either immediately following sunset or just before daybreak. Despite the lack of rest, her strength and power continued to build. Any tiredness she experienced was overcome by her growing sense of independence and her increasing curiosity for the island that had become her new home.

With every step that increased her distance from the decrepit lean-to, her spirits began to lift. During this limited time span, she owned herself, and a small ray of hope began to swell in her heart.

Each trip, she grew bolder and ventured farther afield. At this point, she had covered almost the entire north shore; its hidden trails and secluded coves were all mapped in her memory.

Sometime soon, she would leave the camp's wretched confines and not come back, but she wasn't yet prepared to make that permanent break.

As the Princess skipped along through the trees, her toes gripped the rough topography of the trail beneath her feet. The island was made up of a much younger soil than that of her homeland. This brash, gritty composite had not yet learned to obey the hand of man; it was filled with sharp-edged rocks that cut and slashed the unwary.

She had hated this dirt when she'd first arrived, violently lashing out at it in those early days as she worked her designated rows of the farmer's plot. The dark volcanic loam had received every ancestral curse she could mutter.

But as the weeks passed, she had found herself gradually coming to admire its stubborn resistance, its formidable front against nature and man.

The island and its resilient earth would outlast the fledgling farmer and his domineering wife—so would she.

After a half hour's brisk walk, the dirt gave way to sand, and the Princess reached the water's edge. The top curve of the setting sun glowed through a growing bank of clouds while the ocean lapped at her feet, showering her legs with its gentle foaming spray. She set out along the beach, dancing in the day's disappearing light.

Twenty yards from the shoreline, she spied the tiny ripple of a turtle's bald head, splashing up for air before it sank back beneath the surface.

After a short invigorating swim, the Princess continued on, traveling west until she reached a narrow peninsula of rocky land that stretched out into the water to form the sweeping curve of an inlet cove. She happened upon a trail leading through the woods and instinctively began to follow it.

After leading her up over the slight roll of a hill, the trail opened out onto a clean, manicured lawn overlooking the peninsula's pointed tip.

The Princess took in the view, slowly turning in place to assess her surroundings. To her right, the sun-bleached sand of the island's north shore flickered in the sun's diminishing rays. To her front, the peninsula's top edge dropped off to an ocean channel that separated her island from its nearest cousins.

To her left, in the distance, she spied the low-lying buildings that made up the Caneel Bay resort, each pathway and entrance discretely lit by ground lamps.

A brown and white sign posted next to the clearing where she stood contained a simple label: TURTLE POINT.

The Princess spied a small herd of donkeys, grazing on the clearing's grass. The group paused in its munching and looked up at her quizzically. A cuddly foal peeked tentatively out from behind its mother's hindquarters. The largest member of the herd made a curious whinny and trotted toward her.

The Princess froze as the donkey drew close enough to touch. Her green eyes met his enormous brown ones. Slowly, she reached out her hand to pet the beast's soft sniffing nose.

As she stepped tentatively around the donkey's shoulder to stroke his mane, she noticed a far more human shadow standing on the well-groomed lawn, next to a white gazebo about twenty feet away.

Her breath caught in her chest, spooking the donkey. He jerked his head away from her hand and retreated to his herd. As the hard black hoofs thudded across the lawn, the Princess stood, transfixed, staring at the figure in the distance.

It was a man with skin as dark as the night sky. Strangely fashioned clothes draped over his body; heavy clunky shoes encased his feet. In his right hand, he wielded a long wooden spear whose end had been modified with a terrifying multipronged attachment. His face transmitted the same shock she felt coursing through her body.

For a long paralyzing moment, the Princess couldn't move. She'd broken the cardinal rule; she'd been discovered off her designated plantation. What should she do?

Finally, her legs regained their motion. She turned and ran, top speed, all the way back to the planter's crumbling encampment.

Heart pounding, she slipped into the lean-to, curled up on her dirty mat, and fitfully drifted off to sleep.

~ *25* ~

Miss Hoffstra

Once Vivian finished her beautifying efforts, I walked up to the resort's reception area to wait for Hank Sheridan's driver. A slight breeze filtered through the late afternoon sun as I took a seat on a bench by the truck-taxi stand. I had just smoothed out the wrinkles in my dress when a black town car pulled into the front drive.

Not a limousine, I noted, thinking of the vehicle spotted in Cruz Bay the previous week. Perhaps Sheridan was keeping that ride for his own personal use, I mused crassly.

A short Hispanic man dressed in a simple black suit and white cotton gloves leapt out the front of the car seconds after it came to a stop. The man's dark hair had been slicked neatly back; every strand was combed perfectly into place.

He trotted briskly around to the rear passenger-side door and, with a polite bow, swung it open.

"Miss Hoffstra," he said, with a white-gloved gesture.

"Where are we headed?" I asked, amused at his formality but nervous nonetheless about the final destination of this flamboyant ride.

"If you please, Miss Hoffstra," he replied without answering my question.

I hesitated for a moment on the curb, considering.

I had no choice, I told myself. After four years of playing the part, I had to see this through to the end—or at least to the next act.

"Miss Hoffstra, it is," I thought as I climbed into the sedan.

The door snapped neatly shut, trapping me inside, and I turned my head to glance up at the resort. The building's facade was as quiet and relaxed as ever, but I could sense the sea of eyes watching my departure.

Returning to the front seat, the driver started the engine, and we sped off down the driveway.

A group of iguanas were spread across the wide grassy lawn near the turnout for the main road, enjoying the early evening shade that had begun to seep across the island.

As the car braked, waiting for traffic to clear, one particularly bright green lizard lifted his head and gave me a reassuring wink.

Fifteen minutes later, the town car entered the outskirts of Cruz Bay. From the backseat, I looked out the tinted windows that I knew had done more to announce my arrival than mask my identity.

A number of expats lounged around the Dumpster table outside the Crunchy Carrot. Richard the rooster perched on the table's edge, near where César was stuffing down a fish sandwich. The Puerto Rican waved the last bite at the car, a jocular smirk on his face.

A couple hundred yards farther down the road, we turned the corner in front of the ferry building. The truck-taxi drivers gathered near the Freedom Memorial all turned to stare at the shiny black car, their faces stony, their postures stiff, straight, and unambiguously accusing.

Past the police station around the next bend, we came upon a bustling crowd of Thanksgiving-week tourists strolling along the sidewalk. They stopped and gawked in a starstruck manner, several pointing as if they thought the island's local country music celebrity might be hidden behind the car's dark glass.

All the while, the driver peered blithely through the front windshield, seemingly oblivious to the attention we were drawing.

We crossed through to the opposite side of Cruz Bay, which had one more row of restaurants, but the car didn't slow before entering the sweeping turn up the hill. I leaned tensely back in my seat as the driver steered us into the climbing curve. We weren't stopping in town, at least that much was now certain.

The sedan continued on over the hill's crest, passing the brown and white wooden sign that marked the entrance to the national park. Beyond this point, the road disappeared into jungle, descending into a leafy green tunnel that blocked most attempts of the fading light to breach it.

All evidence of Cruz Bay evaporated into the surge of vegetation, and a quiet stillness fell in around the car. Despite the headlights that had clicked on up front, the vehicle's flat rolling motion had the eerie feel of a creature creeping stealthily along the road, hoping to avoid detection.

I was immune, I told myself, to the restless spirits the local West Indians imagined inhabited these dark woods— to the vinelike arms that dropped down from the treetops with the coming of nightfall. But as I sat with growing discomfort in the town car's rear seat, I felt an unwanted shiver skim across my shoulders.

The driver slowed to a snail's pace as he struggled to squeeze the car's long line around the tight curves of uneven asphalt. The road was much more suited for vehicles with shorter axles, like the rental Jeeps that sped through here with terrifying frenzy, or those with elevation and extra engine power, like the truck taxis that navigated the steep hairpins with relative ease.

The chauffeur's white gloves gripped the leather-wrapped steering wheel as we traveled deeper into the road's knotted corkscrew. I wasn't sure what type of driving conditions he was accustomed to, but I suspected this was one of his first forays into St. John's national park.

As the bottom of the front bumper scraped against a steep curving upswing in the pavement, I found myself hoping he wasn't taking me on my *last*.

I sighed with more relief than I cared to admit when the trees pulled back from the road at Caneel Bay's front gates. The driver paused briefly in the stone-flanked left-hand lane before a uniformed attendant inside the turreted guard station pushed a button, activating a lever that raised a red and white striped barrier to let us through.

The place hadn't changed much since the days of its founder, Laurance Rockefeller. Its modern-day updates were carefully disguised behind the original rustic elegance.

Rockefeller had designed his resort as an escapist retreat, a back-to-nature experience intentionally isolated from the stress of everyday life. Even today, over fifty years after it first opened, the individual guest rooms didn't have telephone lines to the outside. Low one-story cabins were sprinkled across the property, their earth-toned facades fading into the landscape of flowering shrubs and low-lying trees.

Whereas my resort was set up in a typical generic Caribbean style, the kind you could find on almost any island between here and Miami, Caneel was unique, and decidedly upscale—the nightly price was almost double that for my establishment.

As part of the leasing arrangement with the park service, Caneel was required to hold open a portion of its beachfront to the public. For those willing to ignore the disapproving looks of the staff and paying guests, the snorkeling off Caneel's west-facing beach was some of the best on the island—although when I'd brought Jeff to the spot, he'd been spooked by the stingrays that patrolled the reef, and he quickly abandoned for the shore.

The gray phantomlike creatures had a habit of sneaking

up on snorkelers. They seemed to enjoy causing a fright as they crowded in on the humans' floating flippers—I know Jeff's panicked retreat had given me quite a chuckle.

The stingrays weren't the only wild creatures at Caneel that had tormented Jeff. He'd been equally leery of the rabbit-eared donkeys that roamed the grounds. The furry beasts trekked all over the island, but they appeared to use Caneel's vast manicured acreage as their home base. Their fast lips munched down leaves, grass, and whatever food guests left unguarded for more than thirty seconds. On our trip, they'd made off with three-fourths of Jeff's brown bag lunch.

My previous trips to Caneel Bay had been far more pleasant in nature, I reflected with a short grin as the town car motored past the guest parking lot and veered right toward a six-foot rock wall blooming with bougainvilleas.

But my humorous mood evaporated with the memory.

We had to be nearing the meeting point. One way or the other, I was finally about to come face to face with Hank Sheridan.

The town car motored slowly past the crumbling remains of the manor house from Caneel's 1700s-era plantation. Perched on a short rise, the dwelling was optimally positioned both for the widest view of the bay and for catching as much of the ocean breeze as possible.

A wide flight of stone steps led to the main level, which, like the rest of the ruins scattered across the island, was missing much of its upper half. The stone walls were all that remained, the roof, doors, and window coverings having long since disintegrated.

A testament to the creativity of those early builders, each wall was constructed from piles of volcanic rocks and sun-cured coral. The various shapes and sizes were pieced together like a master puzzle, and then fixed in position with a gritty sand-based mortar.

Beyond the manor house, just over the crest of the hill,

we slowed to a halt next to a much larger, bulkier, and far more intact ruin. The late afternoon sun blazed across the clearing, its near horizontal angle glowing against the gray stone walls, scattering on the rough surface of the embedded stones.

Once more, the driver jumped out of his seat to assist me.

"Please wait for Mr. Sheridan by the sugar mill ruins," he said with the same stiff and maddeningly uninformative decorum.

After stepping out of the backseat, I watched from the side of the road as the town car drove off into the resort.

"That's *Miss Hoffstra* to you, buddy," I muttered with a sigh.

~ 26 ~

Turtle Point

During my chauffeured drive from the resort to Caneel, a slight turbulence had begun to ripple through the island's upper atmosphere. A brooding cloud mass dominated the skyline to the east, a giant billboard forecasting the evening's coming rain.

Weather moved across these islands like a checkerboard, hopping from one to the next in a predictable hopscotch fashion. The storm would be on top of us within the next few hours.

I glanced down at my silk dress and high-heeled shoes.

"Should have worn a raincoat and sneakers," I sighed with a grimace.

I teetered slowly from the asphalt into the grass, the tiny pointed spikes on the bottoms of my shoes threatening to sabotage each step. With difficulty, I made it to the entrance of the sugar mill ruins. Seeing no one in the immediate vicinity, I wobbled through the stone archway of the mill's upper structure.

Inside, I found the cane-crushing arena, which was

designed so that the resulting sugar pulp would flow by gravity through stone troughs into boiler cauldrons in the attached rooms on the hillside below. The remains of a smokestack that had been used to heat the sticky juice towered seven or eight feet above the walls' top edge.

Standing in the midst of the ruins, I couldn't help but wonder what the place had been like during the colonial era. Caneel Bay had housed one of St. John's few successful sugar plantations. By all accounts, it was the site of some of the fiercest fighting at the start of the 1733 Slave Revolt.

Unlike the rest of St. John, the majority of Caneel's slave population was from non-Amina tribes. Wary of the rebels' plans of dominance, a large portion of Caneel's slaves had declined to rise up against their owners. Warnings had been discreetly whispered to nearby plantation families, giving several time to flee.

A small collection of farmers and non-Amina slaves had set up bunkers here at Caneel, while wives and children were whisked to a larger cay offshore where they could be safely ferried across the channel to St. Thomas. Cannons positioned at Caneel's front gates had provided enough firepower to hold off and repel the Amina warriors. After a lengthy standoff, the rebels had eventually retreated into the woods.

My thoughts were still drifting through the ruins' history as I left the boiler room and continued farther inside the sugar mill's sprawling compound, whose extensive network took up much of the gradual slope of the hillside. A few steps later, I wandered into a smaller two-story rectangular space positioned behind the boiler room that had, perhaps, once served as a storage area.

Caneel's diligent grounds crew kept the rest of the resort in a state of highly manicured alignment, but this spot had somehow escaped their meticulous attention. Shielded from view behind eighteen-foot-high stone walls, the jungle's ever-reaching tentacles had flourished and multiplied.

Thick vines threaded their suckers into the porous stone

substrate, inextricably embedding themselves into the grooves and crevices. Spiny clumps of tropical palms and other deciduous plants had sprung up across the floor. More sank their roots into the narrow one-inch ledges that formed between slipping portions of rock, auger-ing their unrelenting green fingers into the crumbling masonry.

I stood in the shadowed darkness, the thriving vegetation curling up around my feet, the storm brewing over my head, waiting for the enigmatic Hank Sheridan to reveal himself.

The plant-dominated silence was suddenly interrupted by the crunching of footsteps on the opposite side of the storage room's ocean-facing wall.

Sheridan, I thought as I eased across the pebbled floor, inching toward a rectangular-shaped portal near the origin of the sound.

Slowly shifting my weight, I leaned forward into the portal so that I could peer down its length to where it opened into the side of a larger cavelike tunnel built into the lower elevation on the hillside below. My cheek pressed against the cool rock surface as I listened for another movement on the opposite side.

The same shiver I'd felt inside the town car reemerged in a line of goose pimples that tingled from my shoulders down to the small of my back.

"Hey," a man whispered.

The word echoed through the rock-walled chamber, clear and distinct, as if the speaker were standing right next to me.

"What are you doing in here?" he asked.

My mouth went dry as I spun my head back toward the storage room.

"I've been looking all over for you."

He wasn't speaking to me, I realized as another voice replied. It came from an older man; his hoarse, hushed tone transmitted a deep-seated terror.

"Thees afta'noon . . ."

"Josiah, you're shaking," the first speaker said with concern. "What's got into you? What happened this afternoon?"

The older man cleared his throat in a ragged heaving sound that conveyed his emotional upheaval.

"Late thees afta'noon, Eye wuz out . . . out on thuh Point . . ."

"Ohhh." I could hear the first man's shudder. His nervous words tumbled over one another as his voice sped up. "Say no more. You know I don't go out there, not in the daylight or the dark. That place is . . ." He drew in a sharp breath. "That place is *haunted.*"

The delicate fronds of a fern brushed against the back of my leg, tickling my skin, but I dared not move for fear I'd knock a stray pebble that would give away my position. I held my breath as the older man moaned.

"Eye'd been workin' there all day . . . settin' up for the weddin' t'morrow mornin' . . ."

The troublesome fern was beginning to cause an itch. I glanced down at the persistent plant and sized up the frond's reach—just a half step forward would do the trick. Digging my hands into the sides of the rock wall, I slid my shoe farther into the slope of the portal's passage, away from the fern's clinging grasp.

The extra six inches brought me closer to the portal's perpendicular connection to the tunnel. Trying not to topple over, I tilted my head around the corner so that I could look down the tunnel's length.

The huddled shadows of two men crouched at the far end, near the opening to an interior courtyard located deeper inside the ruins. The orange glow of the looming sunset filtered through the courtyard's crumbling walls, blinding the men to my face in the tunnel's dark corner.

The younger of the pair stood with his eyes squeezed shut, his hands clamped down over his ears. The older man stood facing him, the whites of his eyes bulging out of his ruddy face, his voice steadily rising in strength and volume. Now that Josiah had started telling his story, he would not be stopped.

"Eye wuz almost dun wit the gazebo . . . twist'in thuh last bolts inta place . . . Sum leaves had blown onto the spot

where the chairs were goin' in the morning, so Eye grabbed my rake. Eye wanted to git out of there before the sun set, but Eye couldn't leave before Eye wuz finished . . ."

I looked away for a moment, feeling guilty for listening in on this private conversation. A tiny gecko hanging on the wall met my gaze, the slim razor of its body melding seamlessly into the collage of ancient stones. I was about to backtrack through the storage room to the road outside when Josiah's voice surged louder, his tone pitching with terror.

"She walked out of thuh forest. She . . . she . . . she was wit' a bunch of dun-keys. Eye think she put a hex on one of them. Then, Eye felt hur . . . Eye felt hur staring at me. Hur eyes burned a mark on my chest. Eye can feel it steel."

Blinking to refocus, I returned my gaze to the tunnel as Josiah pulled open his shirt and pointed in anguish at his torso. I could see no evidence of the scar, but the surface of his skin writhed as if it were being tormented by the searing point of a poker.

"She . . . she . . . she . . . waz standing on thuh point, on thuh edge of Turtle Point, near thuh shoreline, just above thuh rocks."

Josiah yanked his shirt back over his chest as he finished the story. *"She had thick curl-ley hair, and she wore an am-u-let around hur neck."* He held up his hands, arching his fingers to connect them into a circle. *"Een thuh shape of thuh sun."*

The other man cringed as Josiah leaned closer toward him. *"She waz an Ameena."*

Just then, a third voice—one I'd last heard four years ago at the Miami airport—whispered in my left ear. A plump hand wrapped around my upper arm and pulled me into the storage room.

"Penelope, it's not polite to eavesdrop."

~ 27 ~

Hank Sheridan

Mustering my dignity, I tried to swallow the instinctive yelp that leapt into my throat. In the storage area behind me, a man's rumbling chuckle bounced eerily off the room's stone surfaces.

The gecko skittered down the wall in a hasty departure, quickly followed by a scuffling at the end of the tunnel, signifying the exit of the grounds crew members to whom I'd been listening.

I turned to face the large man who'd sneaked up behind me and muttered a wary welcome.

"Mr. Sheridan, I presume."

I couldn't keep the sarcastic edge from my voice. We both knew that wasn't his real name—any more than Penelope Hoffstra was mine. Of course, it was to my disadvantage that he knew far more about me than I about him.

"Call me Hank," he replied with a whimsical eyebrow pump.

I stepped gingerly around him toward the middle of the storage area, feeling once more ill at ease in the room's dark confines—but this time my discomfort had nothing to do with the encroaching greenery.

"It's been a while . . . Hank," I said with an unapprecia-tive grimace.

Hank—although I had difficulty calling him that with a straight face—looked exactly the same as he had when I last saw him that rainy afternoon at the Miami airport.

He was clothed in a similar outfit of golf shirt and chi-nos, both of which were clean and recently laundered but bearing the imprints of his current perspiration. His skin had a puffy, pillowy consistency, overlaid with a layer of dampness. It was as if his body was an immense swollen sponge that, with the slightest squeeze of heat, would ooze out several ounces of sweat.

He left the tunnel's opening and joined me at the center of the room. There was an unnatural lightness to his gait that was disconcerting in a man of his heft and bulk.

"Well, Hank, to what do I owe this pleasure?" I asked suspiciously.

That he had successfully orchestrated my substitution for the original Penelope Hoffstra had been a pleasant surprise. That my presence here on St. John had gone so long without detection was an even greater wonder—but these weren't the sorts of accomplishments that garnered a great deal of trust.

The time had come, I suspected, to pay the price for my four-year island vacation.

Hank strummed his hands across his chest, a thoughtful expression on the glistening folds of his face.

"I have a favor to ask," he replied after a moment of con-templation. He fixed me with a serious stare that conveyed my compliance wasn't optional. Whatever he had in mind, his proposal was one I wouldn't be allowed to refuse.

"I was expecting as much." I sighed with muted resigna-tion. "What, exactly, do you want me to do?"

"Patience, Pen," he responded cordially. "First, let's get in out of this heat."

With a heavy hand, he cupped the crook of my elbow and led me outside the storage room and across the stretch of grass to the asphalt. I felt almost invisible beside him; his bulging frame dwarfed my smaller one.

After circling through the resort, the sedan was now parked pointed in the opposite direction, its motor idling smoothly on the tarmac.

Still chuckling at his own guile, Hank motioned for the driver to stay at the wheel. He opened the rear passenger door and ushered me through it.

"Where are we going?" I demanded. Despite his strategic advantage, I wasn't prepared to be his compliant puppet.

"I believe you were promised dinner," he provided blandly.

As our vehicle sped through the exit lane next to the Caneel Bay guardhouse, he leaned toward my shoulder and asked in a low conspiratorial tone, "Now, Penelope. What do you know about the Native Rights movement?"

The town car wound its way back out of the national park, the driver's maneuvering of the steep corners only slightly improved over the earlier inbound trip. I clamped my hand around the leather handle mounted onto the passenger-side door to keep from sliding into the middle on the curves.

The overreaching jungle was just as spooky the second time around, but I was far more focused on the whispering of my riding companion than that of the trees crowding the road outside our vehicle.

From the discussion, I gathered that Hank Sheridan—or, more accurately, the man behind that alias—was a businessman of sorts, with contacts and influence spread out across the Caribbean. He provided a wide range of services, of the sort you couldn't find advertized in the yellow pages. He was like an octopus, with multiple arms worming their way into countless commercial and private matters, all of his activities suitably masked in an inky dark shroud.

He had come to St. John at the request of one of his clients, a nameless individual (at least as far as I was concerned) who had engaged him to influence the outcome of the pending Maho Bay sale. It was for that task that he was seeking my assistance.

Pondering this latest development, I rested the back of my head against the leather seat and stared up at the ceiling.

Of course, I'd known all along that he'd had some sort of hidden agenda for placing me in position at the resort. I was an asset to be brought into play at the appropriate moment, a pawn on someone else's chessboard, my movements a minor aspect in a much larger scheme—over the four years' lack of communication, I had preferred to forget that fact. The global economic downturn that had delayed the sale of Maho Bay, I reflected, had likely given me an extra year or two on the island.

Hank cleared his throat, as if to bring me back to the matter at hand.

"Okay, let me see what you've got," I said, still grumpy for having been dragged into this ruse but, nonetheless, finding myself intrigued.

He pulled out a stack of papers from a file that had been tucked into the pocket of the seat back and handed them to me. We hit another turn as I flipped through the pages, and I momentarily lost my grip on the door handle. Sliding across the backseat, I had to scramble to avoid landing in his lap.

As my weight crashed into him, there was an artificial puff of air, like a balloon losing a fraction of its volume after having been squeezed too tightly. I had the disconcerting sensation that I had run into something other than human tissue; his pillowy girth was apparently made up of a spongy, foamlike substance that was somewhat lighter and stiffer than the real thing.

Brow furrowed, I pulled myself back over to my side of the car. I returned my attention to the file, trying not to think about the apparatus I suspected he had strapped around his waist.

The document was written to read as if it had been drafted by one of the diligence teams inspecting the Maho Bay property. Citing quotes from the recent Native Rights discussions at the Constitutional Convention, the position paper advised against acquiring the Maho Bay property, warning that public reaction against the foreign nature of the purchasing company might lead to insurmountable regulatory and permit hurdles for any future development. The writer even insinuated there was a risk the USVI government might confiscate the land for public use.

I had always dismissed the assertions of the Native Rights advocates, but, I reflected, their inflammatory rhetoric could be easily misconstrued by outsiders. The herd mentality loomed large over any auction process—no one wanted to get caught holding a lame duck. If a few bidders got cold feet, the rest would begin to second-guess their calculations.

It might be enough to shave a few hundred thousand off the purchase price, I reasoned, but it was unlikely to completely dissuade potential purchasers.

"This will certainly get their attention," I said, looking up from the papers as the town car pulled into the truck-taxi lane next to the ferry building.

The white-gloved man hopped out the front and discretely handed a wad of cash to the taxi driver who had given up his place for our vehicle. Then, he hurried off down the street toward the Crunchy Carrot, leaving me alone in the car with Sheridan.

"He's gone to pick up our dinner. I've placed an order for a couple of fish sandwiches," Sheridan explained with a wink. "I hear they're rather tasty."

For the first time in memory, the idea of one of the Carrot's fish sandwiches didn't cause my mouth to water. My stomach had taken a leave of absence—scared off, I suspected, by the shady character seated next to me in the sedan.

Hank reached into a pocket and pulled out a small disposable cell phone. "Call me once you've slipped this into circulation," he said, nodding at the file. "Let me give you the number."

I reached into my purse and dug out a piece of paper, but I found nothing to write with.

"Do you have a pen?" I asked absentmindedly.

"I have several Pens . . ." he replied with a wry smile.

My head jerked up as he pulled a stylus from the front

pocket of his golf shirt. After staring for a moment at his strange, squishy face, I wrote down the number for his cell phone.

A moment later, the driver reappeared in the distance carrying a take-out sack from the Crunchy Carrot.

I was still mulling over Hank's Maho Bay strategy. The packet of papers was unlikely to be the extent of his meddling. I had but a partial picture of his overall plan, I concluded uneasily.

I was afraid to ask the one question I most feared the answer to—whether this meant the end of my stay on St. John—so I decided to probe the issue indirectly, via the young woman whose recent arrival had nearly blown my cover.

Releasing a frustrated puff of air, I turned in my seat to face Hank.

"So," I asked tensely, "how does Hannah fit into all this?"

"Who?" he replied with a startled look.

"Hannah Sheridan," I repeated warily.

The troubled expression on his face registered a convincing display of ignorance. He cocked a perplexed eyebrow at me.

"I thought that was you."

~ 28 ~

The Uncle

Just past the wooden park sign at the top of the hill over-looking Cruz Bay, a truck taxi turned into Pesce's gravel driveway to let off a passenger in a flower-print sundress. Hannah Sheridan climbed gracefully out of the truck's back bed and paid the driver. Then, she skipped past a long black limo parked in the road's easement and continued up the stone steps leading into the restaurant's Mediterranean stone building.

The hostess nodded immediate recognition as soon as Hannah gave her name and directed her through a mahogany-walled bar to the dining area on the flat landing spanning the restaurant's oceanfront side.

The tables were, predictably, filled with several out-of-town real estate types. With so many patrons sporting casual business attire and numerous leather-bound port-folios scattered about, the occasional tourists mixed into the crowd looked almost out of place.

From the elevated perspective of Pesce's verandah, the town of Cruz Bay took on a far more pristine glow than its reality deserved. A neat and tidy collection of shops and restaurants skirted the edge of the peaceful harbor. The clutter of dust, debris, and vagrant poultry disappeared beneath the colorful canvas of low lying trees and brightly painted buildings.

To the west, St. Thomas benefited from a similarly glamorizing gloss. Distance and the span of the Pillsbury Sound hid its hordes of humanity. The twinkling lights that had begun to pop on across the island's low shadow were the only evidence of their existence.

Hannah wandered through the dining area, drawing a few curious glances as she made her way to the edge of the balcony and looked down on the harbor. Several brown pelicans swooped low across the water, diving in and out among a collection of small bobbing sailboats.

She stood, silently watching the feeding frenzy, as she listened to the murmurs of the other diners.

". . . we're putting together our bid this weekend . . ."

". . . still some questions to resolve . . ."

". . . fear the price may be too steep for us . . ."

Taking in a deep breath, she straightened her shoulders and approached the open chair next to her patiently waiting dinner companion.

". . . striking girl . . ."

". . . something familiar about her . . ."

As Hannah circled to the opposite side of the table, she glanced up at the sky where a streaming bank of clouds led the front edge of an advancing storm. The air was so thick with moisture, she could almost taste it.

The rains are coming, she thought as she leaned over the table to plant a kiss on the cheek of her beaming relative. Her face curved into a sly smile as she hooked a blue nylon satchel over the back corner of her chair.

"Hello, Uncle."

~ *29* ~

Bannanquits

I returned to the resort that night carrying half a fish sandwich still in its take-out container.

As I walked along the ground-lit path to my condo, pondering my meeting with the formidable Hank Sheridan, the wind began to bellow in from the ocean, summoning the forces of nature to this tiny speck of earth that had dared to rise up out of the sea.

A rabid confluence of seething energy swirled above my head. The sky that most days seemed so vast, so voluminous, was now crowded with rowdy boisterous characters, bumping and elbowing each other for space, edging their way closer and closer to the ground.

Inside the condo, I turned off the lights, the air conditioner, and the small rotating fan plugged into the wall. I didn't want any artificial inputs distracting my thinking. I crawled into bed, lay on my back, and listened as the long-awaited storm finally arrived on St. John.

Rain began pattering against windows and splashing into gutters. Across the island, water catchments opened wide, drinking in the downpour. The little concrete wading pool

on my back porch that had been empty all summer started
to fill with runoff.

In my mind's eye, I saw Fred and his iguana friends inching slowly across the glistening grass, moisture beading up
on their thick leathery skins, their lizard mouths munching
in peaceful robotic bliss. As my head sank into the pillow's
comforting cushion, I could almost hear their happy rumi-
nating stomachs through my bedroom walls.

A strobe of lightning flashed across the nearest window,
momentarily illuminating the condo's interior.

Even after four years of residence, there was little to
show in the way of personalization. The unit was sparsely
appointed with decommissioned resort furniture. The
pictures on the walls, along with the knickknacks on the
dresser, were all generic island chic.

Through the angle of my open bedroom door, I could
see the back of the living room couch, whose faded tropical pattern was decorated with too many stains to count.
In front of the couch stretched a glass-topped coffee table,
inlaid with seashells and pebbles from a beach—probably
not one that was anywhere near our island.

Opposite the table sat a wicker chair, whose rattan wrappings were peeling away from the frame. Many of the spines
threaded into the chair's back were missing, and the lumpy
discolored seat cushion had been soaked endless times by
wet swimsuit bottoms.

Beyond the living area, the curve of a tiled counter
marked the edge of a small kitchen. It was equipped with a
mismatched collection of rudimentary appliances: a micro-
wave, a micro-fridge, several mugs, a few shot glasses, a
toaster, and a rusted-out oven I had never attempted to turn
on much less cook with.

The lightning-lit scene returned to darkness as a wave of
thunder rocked the building, more evidence of the tempest
brewing above. A tiny popping sound followed by the hum

of the resort's reserve generators gave the subtle indication that the island's power had just gone out.

In the weeks since I'd first met Hannah Sheridan in the corridor outside my office, I'd spent a great deal of time wondering whether her appearance was a signal my time on the island was drawing to a close. I'd worried for countless hours that the man from Miami would be coming to relieve me of my post.

But now that he was here, now that I knew at least a portion of the next phase of this journey, my focus had turned to a different issue.

In the four years since I'd hopped that flight to St. Thomas, I had deliberately avoided thinking about the *real* Penelope Hoffstra, the woman whose life I had stepped into, whose identity I had assumed.

In my head, I'd convinced myself that if I didn't ask about her—if I didn't know what had become of her—I could somehow limit my culpability in her disappearance.

Now, lying in my bed beneath the storm, Hank Sheridan's cryptic words were all I could think about.

I have several Pens . . .

How many of us were out there, I wondered, living under this pseudonym?

What had happened to the original Pen? Had she ever even existed?

The front door creaked open, letting in the rain.

Wet feet squished against the living room's tile floor. After stopping in the kitchen for a glass of water, the footsteps circled behind the couch and crossed the threshold to the bedroom. Then a damp shadow crept through the darkness toward my bed.

I set aside my concerns about the fat man and his other Penelopes as the intruder leaned over my pillow and kissed my forehead. All notions of Hannah, her bouncing curls, and her silly spinning sundresses left me as I drank in the smell of his skin, a wild, wet essence of the sun and the sea.

As I reached up my hands to run my fingers through the nest of his thick tangled hair, all I could hear was the twittering of bananaquits.

~ *30* ~

A Wet Morning

Saturday morning, Manto sloshed through the puddles along the resort's front drive as he headed toward the designated parking spot for the flatbed golf cart he used when working with the grounds crew. The rain from the night before had yet to let up, and the floppy hat crammed onto his head was already damp from the drips accumulating on its brim and seeping through its worn cotton fabric.

With a groan, Manto climbed into the cart's wet front seat and plugged the key into the ignition. A moment later, he turned off the main driveway, steering the cart down a narrow brick path that curved behind a fence of bushes to a shed attached to the south side of the reception area. After unlocking the shed's door, he began loading the morning's gardening tools into the cart's back bed.

First went a plastic bucket full of hand clippers, quickly followed by a collection of larger limb-lopping hedge trimmers. The long wooden handles of several pointed hoes and rakes were stacked in next.

As the shed emptied out and the golf cart filled up, Manto leaned back and placed his hands on his hips.

He stared at the pile of tools for a moment; then he pulled

the soaked hat from his head and used it to wipe a coating of moisture from his face.

Raising a crooked finger in the air, he counted the poles laid out on the cart.

"Dahg, blast it," he muttered with consternation. *"Somemun's run off with a rake."*

Jeff had long since left the condo by the time I stumbled through the living room, intent on seeking out a fresh pot of coffee from the resort's breakfast bar. Almost as an afterthought, I grabbed Hank Sheridan's file on my way out the door.

My sleep-soaked brain had yet to devise a plan for getting the fake memo "into circulation," as Hank had put it, but, I reasoned, you never knew what kind of opportunity might present itself after a waking cup of coffee.

Five minutes later, I wandered into the breakfast pavilion by the beach. After sniffing at the coffee container on the buffet line, I sidled through the doorway to the busy kitchen area.

As I had suspected, a fresh pot was percolating in the pavilion's industrial-sized coffeemaker. I grabbed a foam cup and diverted the stream to fill it.

Sipping on the energizing liquid, I looked out into the dining room. The majority of the resort's guests had already wrapped up their morning meal, but one remaining table contained a few easily identifiable real estate types chatting over the last bites of an omelet and a Belgian waffle.

With a quick glance at the folder tucked under my arm, I flagged one of the passing waitresses, an older West Indian woman wearing a GLENNA name tag.

"Excuse me," I said conversationally. "Uh, Glenna."

She stopped and stared at me for a moment before answering.

"Ga mornin, ma'am,' " she said with a decidedly wary look.

"Hi, er, good morning," I replied uncomfortably. "I was wondering if you could help me out with something . . ."

Her right eyebrow cocked suspiciously. Her face crimped skeptically.

I decided to take a more assertive tack.

"Ahem," I said, straightening my shoulders. I summoned my best Vivian imitation, assuming a stoic, no-nonsense expression and deadening my voice to a monotone command.

"When you clean off the table out there—the one next to the two men with the briefcases—leave this file on the surface."

She gazed dubiously at the folder I handed her, and then at me. Her eyes flickered whimsically, as if she had recognized the impersonation. Instead of being intimidated, she found the whole scene amusing.

I cleared my throat and then pleaded in the manner that I always ended up using with Vivian. "Please, I need you to be discreet."

"Dees-creet?" she repeated dubiously.

"Yes, discreet." I nodded, cursing myself for acting so impulsively. It was a good thing, I reflected, that Hank wasn't here to see me bungle this.

But the second strategy apparently worked, as Glenna suddenly relented. I caught the glint of a smile on her face as she picked up a tray, positioned the folder flat on its surface, and covered it with one of the resort's laundered linen napkins.

I watched from the corner of the kitchen as Glenna shuffled into the dining room.

As luck would have it, I had picked a pro as my accomplice. Not one of the diners seated nearby appeared to notice as she cleared the dishes from the empty table, swept up the crumbs, and re-centered the salt and pepper shakers. If I hadn't been staring right at her, I would have missed the sleight of hand she used to slide the envelope from her tray onto the clean tablecloth.

She looked across the dining room and winked in my direction before continuing about her duties.

I took a sip of coffee and sat back to see if the ploy would work.

I didn't have to wait long. As one of the businessmen stood from his chair and brushed the crumbs from his shirt, he noticed the manila folder lying on the next table.

Grinning widely, I looked on as he reached over and, with a guilty glance around the breakfast pavilion, snagged the folder. The look of excitement on his face was easy to read as he pulled out the papers and realized he had scored one of his opponents' work products.

His gleeful expression soon darkened, however, when he scanned through the information detailed in the memo.

As he pulled out his cell phone and began frantically calling his colleagues, I refilled my cup and headed toward my office for a late-morning session on the balcony.

My scaly confidant clawed his way up the tree as I stretched out in the lawn chair, rinsing down my second cup of coffee with a shot of Cruzan.

"Well, Fred, it couldn't have been easier," I boasted over the balcony about my file-transfer experience.

Fred issued a silent but sarcastic blink as I pulled out the piece of paper on which I'd written Hank's phone number. I was about to start dialing it when a pair of cleaning ladies stopped to chat on the sidewalk below.

Always intrigued by the tidbits of information that floated up to the balcony, I paused to listen.

The women's conversation quickly transitioned from obligatory greetings to the coming holiday. Not Thanksgiving—that was a minor celebration marked only by expats and tourists. The November 23 commemoration of the 1733 Slave Revolt was nearly upon us, and with it, the annual revival of the tale of the Slave Princess.

It had been a busy couple of weeks for the Princess's ghost. In my four years on St. John, I couldn't remember the Princess ever being credited with a single in-person appearance. However, the man I'd overheard in the Caneel Bay sugar mill ruins was but one of many who had sworn that they'd seen her ghost in recent days.

I took another sip from my shot glass, shaking my head as one of the maids on the sidewalk below launched into her own testimonial. But as the woman continued to elaborate on the Princess's description, I dropped my cynical stance. Setting down the drink, I leaned my head toward the edge of the balcony.

The woman spoke of a slim young beauty with creamy cocoa-colored skin and dark curly hair that bounced around her shoulders. It was an eerie match to our new employee, Hannah Sheridan.

As the women's gossip continued to float up toward my chair, I reached once more for the shot glass, struck by a second observation.

I wasn't the only one to notice the similarities.

~ 31 ~

The Proposal

Later that afternoon, a catamaran powerboat rocked in White Bay's gentle waters, a few hundred yards off the coast of Jost Van Dyke. After the morning's intermittent rain, a brief window of sunshine had allowed the dive shop to run its regular Saturday afternoon trip, to the delight of the tourists who had signed up earlier that week—if not all the members of the boat's crew.

A freckled man with a mound of wild frizzy hair sat on the vessel's lower deck, pressing his face against a pair of binoculars as he watched the passengers who had just jumped overboard paddle ashore to the Soggy Dollar. Each of the swimmers gripped a plastic ziplock baggie holding damp bills that the proprietor of the Dollar would soon hang out to dry on a clothesline behind the counter where he served his famous Painkiller cocktails.

Jeff's steely blue eyes concentrated on the bobbing life jackets, counting the number over and over again as the group floated toward the beach.

It didn't take long; the tide carried the bodies inland without much effort. The return trip was a more challenging task, when the swimmers would be fighting the current with bellies full of alcohol.

As the last bar-goer stumbled onto the sand, Jeff sighed and dropped the binoculars, leaving them to hang from the strap around his neck.

He walked into the boat's kitchen area and began wiping down the counter next to the sink. After an afternoon of mixing and pouring drinks, a sticky residue of rum and punch coated almost every surface. Shaking his head at the mess, he slowly worked his way down the front of the cabinets beneath the counter. The gummy pool of liquid on the floor, he decided, would have to wait until they returned to the resort, when he'd take a pressure hose to the boat's entire guest area.

Brushing a grimy hand across his sweating forehead, Jeff returned to the boat's open back landing and leaned his body against one of the metal side railings.

The sun played soothingly on the rough brown stubble that covered the bottom half of his face as he settled into the boat's rocking, swaying motion. The waves were a pendulum that swung in time with his inner equilibrium, a comforting rhythm that had been deeply imprinted on his sailor's soul. He felt more at home on the water than off it.

He glanced across the bow at the furry green mounds of the islands that surrounded the bay. The water acted as a natural scaffold, balancing the boat at what would have been cloud level of the volcanic mountains that rose from the ocean floor, several thousand feet beneath.

He knew it was a rare and beautiful treasure to be taking in this scenic channel, enjoying the watery, rooftop view of the liquid-filled canyon below. No matter how many times he swore he couldn't take another whining tourist, he'd be a fool to ever give this up.

His mother wrote to him once a week, detailing all the latest gossip from their small New England town. It was a charming place; he didn't have anything against it. He'd spent the first twenty-four years of his life there, and the New England coast was where he'd learned to sail.

But his mother never failed to mention the weather— particularly when they'd received a foot or two of snow. He couldn't ever go back to those icy cold winters, he thought with a shiver.

It was as Jeff reflected on the dramatic climate differences between his hometown and the Caribbean that he noticed a figure seated on one of the boat's rear benches.

A large, extremely obese man lounged on the plastic cushions. His face was difficult to make out beneath the straw sunhat covering his head and the wide mirrored sunglasses protecting his eyes, but Jeff didn't recognize the man from the afternoon's list of passengers. He was oddly unfamiliar.

Jeff puzzled for a moment, his startled emotion barely registering on his otherwise blank expression. He could have sworn he had accounted for all of his human cargo as the swimmers waded onto the beach. He scratched his chin, perplexed, and then shrugged. He must have missed one.

Clearing his throat, Jeff raised a questioning eyebrow at the abandoned passenger and nodded pointedly at the water beyond the boat's railing.

The man chuckled appreciatively. "I think we both know I'm not cut out for that."

After eighteen months working for the dive shop, Jeff had seen his share of characters. People from across the U.S. and all over the world had sat on this boat as he attended to their needs, served them drinks, and kept them from unintentionally falling overboard.

He thought he'd seen it all, but there was something strange about this fellow. The guy was studying him intently, not as a deckhand on a boat, not as a paid servant, but as a person of interest.

Jeff found the sensation vaguely unsettling.

The man stroked a swollen hand across the round plump

of his chin before making his next comment—one that drew a flustered blush to Jeff's typically bland cheeks.

"I hear you've been taking nautical classes over on St. Thomas. You looking to captain your own boat one day, son?"

~ *32* ~

Cinnamon Bay Ruins

The rains resumed early Saturday evening, causing most of the island's tourists to hole up inside their hotels. Only a handful ventured out to the bars. Many of the truck-taxi drivers called it a night and returned home to their families.

Manto's half-ton pickup rolled through the unlit streets of Cruz Bay, one of the few vehicles to brave the increasingly torrential conditions. The truck's wide tires splashed through pothole puddles and streams of overflow from the road's brimming gutters as rivulets of rain ran down the pink flamingoes and brightly colored parrots painted on the vehicle's side paneling. The plastic cushions in the back passenger seating area were soaked through, the overhead canopy providing little impediment to a rain of this magnitude and persistence.

Carefully, he steered the truck around a hapless couple wading across the street, trying to reach the protection of the next building's eaves.

Both figures wore thin plastic ponchos, the kind sold by the local trinket shops. The vendors had done a brisk business in disposable raincoats over the previous twenty-four hours. This storm was predicted to last a couple of days, and few tourists brought rain gear with them to the Caribbean.

Inside the truck's front cab, Manto was safe and dry, but not making much money. Even though it had been several hours since his last fare, he had not been overly enthusiastic when this call came in.

On the north side of town, he pulled over onto a wide shoulder next to the national park's welcome center. Gulping, he ran a trembling hand over the receding hairline of closely cropped hair scattered across his scalp's dark skin. Then, he leaned across the wide bench seat to the glove compartment. With the push of his thumb, he released the latch and reached into the bin. Next to a plastic jug of candies, he found a small paper bag.

The rain blurred the windshield as Manto pulled out a bottle of rum, unscrewed the lid, and tipped the bottle to his lips. He shook his head back and forth as the liquid burned down his throat.

"S'okay, Bessie," Manto said soothingly to the truck's dashboard, *"we'll be in 'n out 'fore you know it."*

His resolve strengthened, he screwed the lid back on the bottle and returned it to the glove compartment.

He didn't want to admit it, but he knew the driver needed the convincing much more than the vehicle did.

Manto shifted the truck into gear and angled it up the hill toward the brown and white wooden sign marking the national park's entrance. The truck's windshield wipers slapped back and forth at maximum speed, its souped-up engine chugging easily over the crest.

As Manto approached the first narrow turn into the dense woods, his thick lips began to roll inward toward his gums. He kept his face pointed directly over the rim of the steering wheel, trying to keep the area beyond the curved stone gutters that lined the edges of the road out of his line of sight.

Even without looking, he could feel the presence of the spirits that lurked in the trees. He sucked nervously on the inner meat of his cheeks, certain that he was under the ghostly surveillance of countless spying eyes.

Manto thought of himself as a practical, rational man. He didn't put much stock in the island's local superstitions—most days.

But every November, when the old timers pulled out their stories of the 1733 Slave Revolt, he found himself giving the ghosts a little more credence—this year more so than usual. Not in Manto's long memory had the tales been as vivid as those that had been recounted in the last few weeks.

The details of the rebellion, of course, he knew by heart. They had been seared into his consciousness at an early age—along with that of every other school-age child on St. John.

Every so often, however, a new tidbit of information emerged from some far-off archive, illuminating another aspect of that dark, tortuous time. The Amina Slave Princess was apparently just that sort of discovery, or so he had heard from one of the drivers at the picnic tables in the Trunk Bay parking lot. While her tale was a recent addition to the rebellion folklore, it had quickly captured the local imagination.

The Princess's tragic story was haunting enough all by itself, Manto thought with a shiver. But in recent days, several drivers had begun reporting actual sightings of the Princess's ghost. This wasn't just the typical idle speculation generated by an errant cool breeze on an otherwise hot and stifling day; it was something more concrete than an odd, unsourced sound in the woods—each of the men claimed to have seen the humanized embodiment of the Princess's spirit.

Numerous supernatural beings were believed to populate the island. Even Manto's skeptical mind allowed for that. The undeveloped stretches of the north shore as well as Ram Head, along the southeastern rim, were heavily trafficked by those of the metaphysical world. But of all these beings, no ghosts were more feared, their presence more dreaded, than those of the Amina, the slaves who had rebelled against St. John's plantation owners and exacted a bloodthirsty revenge.

It was enough to get under anyone's skin, Manto told himself with a second headshake as the truck continued farther east along the North Shore Road, navigating like a boat through the pavement's waterlogged dips and gullies.

The full beam of the headlights barely made a dent in the drenching sheets of rain; the windshield was nothing but a dark blur of wooded browns and greens. Massive mounds of volcanic rock occasionally popped up along the side of the road, the chalky gray stones hazardously coming into view at the last possible moment of evasion.

Manto felt his pulse rising; he was driving more out of memory than sight. He gripped the wheel, cursing the phone call that had brought him out into this treacherous night.

He had been in the break room, chatting with the house-maids, when the resort's concierge found him. A guest had called in from a cell phone, requesting the pickup. The group had been out on the trails all day, apparently hiking through the rain, and had lost track of time. The five stranded tourists were supposed to be waiting at the Cinnamon Bay parking lot, about a fifteen minutes' drive from the national park's main entrance—more like twenty-five under these weather conditions.

Manto would have declined the job, but he knew no other driver would dare make the attempt. The truck taxis that plowed up and down the North Shore Road during the day-time hours had long since vacated the park. Few would venture into the forest after sunset.

None of them, save Manto, would be caught dead out here on a night like this.

Manto slowed the truck to a crawl as he came around the last corner before the parking lot's turn-in. The truck's heavy treaded tires squealed against the pavement. He drew in his breath; his face skewed with concentration.

"Keep it togetha, man," he muttered to himself, desper-

ately trying to prevent his panicked nerves from overcorrecting the steering wheel.

He sighed with relief as the truck taxi rolled to a stop inside the parking lot's empty U-bend. He tapped the horn lightly and waited.

The rain beat down against the truck's flat metal roof, a deafening sound that played tricks with the mind. Manto took another sip of rum from the glove compartment as he anxiously scanned the deep wet forest surrounding the lot.

Several times, he thought he heard footsteps approaching, and he braced himself for the expected knock on his window. But after fifteen long and fearful minutes, his passengers had failed to appear.

At long last, Manto had had enough. There was no one out here; the call had been a prank. He had been a fool to come.

Somewhere on the other side of the island, he thought with chagrin, someone was having a good laugh at his expense. Grumbling bitterly, he started the engine and shifted the truck into drive.

Manto reached for the radio's walkie-talkie as he steered the truck back onto the North Shore Road. He pressed a button on the side of the handheld receiver, the cranky grouse of his voice barely audible over the rain's ceaseless drumbeat.

". . . Thees here's Manto. There's no won at Cinn'mon Bay. I'm leavn' dis gud-forseken pless . . ."

His voice caught in his throat as a human figure dashed across the road in front of the truck.

"What een thuh . . ."

He blinked his eyes, furiously focusing on the flooding black tarmac. It had happened so quickly, he wasn't sure what he had seen.

"Eye gut yu now!" he exclaimed as a woman's soaking form suddenly ducked into a bank of trees near the parking lot.

He stared at the greenery where the woman had disappeared. Despite his confident shout, a shiver of apprehension was working its way down his spine.

It had to have been one of the tourists he'd been sent to collect—no one else would be out in this weather.

But why would a tourist run from his truck?

If she wasn't a tourist . . . he refused to think it.

For a few seconds, Manto's eyes remained glued to the side of the road, searching the forest for another glimpse of the fleeing figure. Then he swung his head forward, shifting his vision back to the front windshield—but he had left it a moment too late.

During his brief distraction, the truck had veered into the right hand lane. The right front wheel dipped into the trough of the road's curbed gutter, tipping the truck sideways.

Deftly, he cranked the steering wheel to the left. He could feel the back wheels skidding across the frictionless, water-slicked surface, even as the truck's front end remained lodged in the gutter. A mounded clump of wet leaves lodged beneath the gutter-trapped wheel, preventing the rubber from gaining traction.

"Oh, no yu don't," Manto reprimanded the truck. He stamped on the brakes, fervently hoping to stop its rotation. *"We're nut gettin' stuck out here. Nut wid that ghost, we're nut!"*

After a stomach-tossing swerve, the truck rocked to a screeching halt.

Manto touched his fingers to his lips and then pressed them against the roof of the cab. The vehicle was positioned at a forty-five-degree angle facing into the gutter, but three-fourths of its length was still on the road—that, he thought gratefully, was a blessing.

He would back it out, nice and easy. Simple as that. He didn't know what he had just seen, but he had no desire to investigate further.

"Cum on, Bessie," Manto pleaded. Eyes focused on the side mirror to ensure he didn't overshoot the gutter on the

road's opposite side, he straightened the steering wheel and pressed his foot down lightly on the gas pedal.

Just as the front wheel found the rocky surface beneath the leaves, the ghostly figure streaked across the reflection in the mirror. Manto cringed at the sight; instinctively, his foot stomped on the gas.

The truck lurched backward, the burst of speed taking its back wheels into and over the left-hand gutter.

Manto punched the brakes, but he had already run out of road. He braced himself as the rear taillights illuminated the stone and mortar columns that marked the boundaries of the Cinnamon Bay plantation ruins scattered across the woods behind the careening truck.

A moment later, a jarring *crunch* reverberated through the cab. The truck came once more to a jarring halt, this time its momentum absorbed by the back bumper as it collided with the nearest stone column.

Manto heard the hiss of a puncture, accompanied by a slow dip in the truck's left rear corner. He reached once more for the bottle of rum. This time, he took a long deep swallow.

Grimacing, Manto picked up the dangling radio receiver from where he had dropped it during the skid. His fingers shook as he changed the dial to a different channel.

"Char-lee . . ." his shaken voice called weakly into the receiver.

There was no response. Terrified tears streaked down his face as he repeated the name. *"Char-lee, Char-lee . . ."*

A grumbling static finally responded, "Manto, is that you?"

Manto collapsed in relief against the back of his seat.

"Charlie, mon, you gut to cum git me. Eye've gut a flat. Eye've . . . Eye've run off thuh road."

"You ran off the road?" Charlie's sputtering voice replied immediately. "What in the heck are you doing out in this weather? Manto, where are you?"

Manto's face beamed a relaxed smile as he heard the

clack of Charlie's keys in the background of the transmission. He flashed the windshield wipers for a second confirmatory look at the brown and white national park sign that marked the entrance to the parking lot where his troubles had begun.

"Eye'm jus' past the entrance to thuh Cin'mon Bay parking lot by thuh sugar mill ruins." Licking his lips, Manto glanced at the stone column in his rearview mirror. *"Vaarey close to thuh ruins,"* he added, a note of grim humor in his voice.

"Okay, stay where you are," Charlie replied grumpily. "Don't move. I'm leaving right now."

Manto sighed happily into the receiver. *"Charlie, mon, you're thuh bes . . ."* But he stopped short as the woman's image flashed once more across his side mirror.

"Noooo . . ." he moaned in dismay.

Her clothes were plastered to her skin; she was soaked through from the rain. She wore a sleeveless beaded vest and a soggy sarong. Manto couldn't quite make out her face, but she had a distinctive mop of dark curly hair with ringlets that fell to her slim shoulders. Around her neck hung a silver amulet, whose circular tooled surface glinted in the beam of the remaining taillight. She seemed a bit pale, but otherwise, the description matched that of the previously reported sightings.

It had to be—the Slave Princess.

"Manto?" Charlie broke through the sudden radio silence, his voice registering concern.

"Eye'm seeing a . . ." Manto replied. He felt lightheaded, as if he might pass out at any moment.

Then his eyes narrowed and focused in on the item the Princess held in her right hand. It was a long wooden spear with a multipronged attachment at its end.

"You're seeing a what?" Charlie yelled through the radio. "Manto, what is it?!"

"That wo-man stole my rake," Manto spat with disgust. *"Charlie, yu'd betta cum git me,"* he added hastily. Then

he dropped the receiver, leaving it dangling from the steering wheel.

Manto's forehead crinkled with a mixture of consternation and confusion as he crammed a baseball cap onto his head, grabbed a flashlight from the glove compartment, and wrenched open the driver's-side door.

He was rapidly drenched from head to foot. His sandals slid in the mud and wet leaves as he flicked on the flashlight and aimed it toward the ruins at the edge of the road. Through the sheets of rain, he could just make out a network of evenly spaced stone columns, one of which was flush with the truck's dented back bumper.

There was a movement in the darkness, and Manto swung his light to catch it.

The mischievous Princess had moved about twenty feet into the ruins. He watched as she passed in front of the main boiler room and crossed to a short flight of steps leading to the elevated embankment of the cane-crushing ring. Her sneakered feet climbed the stairs and skittered across the circular, stone-ringed structure at the top.

Manto scrambled across the clearing toward the mill, skipping around the stone columns as he chased the Princess through the driving rain. But when he reached the bottom of the stairs, she was nowhere to be seen. The rain poured down as he slowly pivoted with his flashlight, searching the wet shadows for her elusive figure—once more, she had vanished.

Still muttering under his breath about the stolen rake, Manto climbed the slippery stone steps to get a better view of the ruins. From the short height of the cane-crushing ring, he could see into the remains of the boiler room and the series of open cauldrons that had been used to cook down the mill's sugarcane juice. The building's roof had long since washed away, but the boiler room's stone walls, along with the towering smokestack on its far side, stood solid, providing an endless number of hiding places.

A sharp, swirling breeze whipped through the trees, cutting through Manto's wet clothing. The oppressive heat that had tormented the island for the last two months was now, with the arrival of this pounding storm, morphing into a chilly, bone-soaking cold.

Manto knew he should get back inside the truck, where he could warm himself with its heater and wait for Charlie to arrive. But despite the increasing chill and the lure of the warm, dry cab, he remained at his position on the ledge of the cane-crushing ring, continuing to sweep his flashlight through the ruins' crumbling stone structures.

He was determined, for once and for all, to catch this troublesome, thieving Slave Princess—and, hopefully, to retrieve his rake.

Deep down in the superstitious corners of his soul, Manto confessed that a part of him wanted to believe in the myth of the Slave Princess. Despite his childhood-instilled fear of the Amina, she represented a proud connection to his ancestors, a link to his heritage that he could boast about to his grandchildren.

But there was something definitely amiss here. In all the versions of the Slave Princess tale, and, for that matter, all the stories of the forest spirits he'd listened to growing up on the island, he'd never once heard of a ghost stealing a piece of gardening equipment.

Issuing a perplexed grunt, Manto crossed toward the opposite side of the ring, to the portion located farthest away from the road, where the land sloped gently upward to meet its top rim. He trained his light on a line of small rooms positioned behind the boiler room.

As the beam flickered across one of the many smooth-limbed, reddish-trunked bay trees dispersed throughout the mill area, a slight movement at the edge of Manto's periphery confirmed his suspicions. His spotlight found a rain-blurred face peering out from one of the stone entrances.

Manto raced to the circle's perimeter, his sandals scrambling on the slick, sodden grass. Slipping with every step, he hurtled over the stone rim, dashed around a mound of rocks, and sprinted up to the now empty doorway. Heart pounding, he stepped cautiously over the threshold and looked inside.

The roofless room was vacant, save for the spindly trunk of yet another bay tree.

His frustration mounting, Manto arched his light over the slender branches and then down to the raised roots that snaked across the volcanic-earth floor.

The sound of racing feet brought him back to the doorway. Something scuttled through the leaves to his left.

He turned, panning his flashlight toward the Princess's fleeing silhouette. His beam followed her as she scampered down a short path leading away from the mill. Then the Princess scrambled across a narrow bridge and up a stone-littered hill to the remains of the ruins' plantation house— all the while gripping the rake handle in her hand, using it like a walking stick for balance.

Flushed with chill and adrenaline, Manto wavered as his mind argued vigorously with his eyes. He knew it was unwise to follow the Princess, be she ghost or human, much farther into the ruins. But finally, he wiped the back of his hand across his rain-streaked face and continued on.

The narrow ravine beneath the bridge was quickly filling with runoff; a torrent of water rushed through its streambed. On the bridge's opposite side, the path leading up to the plantation's former living quarters was a minefield of slippery roots and loose rocks. Long vines dropped down from low-hanging branches, slapping him across the face with every step.

Between the struggle for his footing and the constant swatting of the vines, by the time Manto stepped inside the ruins of the main house, he had once more lost track of his target.

The plantation house was far more deteriorated than the sugar mill. The remaining walls were more horizontal than upright; the structure looked as if it were about to tumble down completely.

Manto aimed his shaking flashlight at the nearest room, illuminating the barely distinguishable outlines of its stove and chimney.

At least, he thought wearily, the tree cover provided some protection from the rain. Water was now coming down against his head in discrete plops.

Drop. Drop. Drop. The sound echoed in his ears, mimicking the staccato of approaching footsteps.

"You're all rig't, Manto," he told himself, trying to drum up confidence. *"She's nut a ghost."* With a clarifying gulp, he amended, *"Leas', I hope nut."*

After a quick check to his rear, Manto swept the flashlight toward the house's top corner. There, at the forest's edge, just behind the wide fan of a yucca plant, he spied the Amina Slave Princess—still grasping the handle of the missing rake.

As they faced one another over the rainy forty-foot distance, the Princess brushed her free hand through the spiraling damp curls of her jet black hair. Then her fingers dropped to the amulet hanging from her neck.

A flash of lightning blitzed across the night sky, illuminating the entire ruins in a ghostly specter of light.

Temporarily blinded, Manto blinked and refocused his gaze on the spot where the Princess had stood, but she—and the rake—were gone.

A dark-skinned man with muscular arms watched the scene in the Cinnamon Bay ruins unfold from the thick woods at the back of the property, near the entrance to a nature trail that led up into St. John's hilly center. Rain dripped down on the water taxi captain through the heavy canopy of the surrounding bay trees, but he appeared not to notice. His attention was focused on the events taking place in the ruins.

When he saw the Slave Princess make her move toward the trailhead, he slipped into a small rustic cemetery holding the remains of the plantation's early settlers and waited for her to pass. A moment later, he followed her up the trail.

As soon as the captain disappeared through the trees, an elderly woman in a soaking wet shirtdress and loose rubber sandals crept out from behind the largest of the aboveground stone coffins. Taking care to maintain a safe distance, Beulah Shah set off up the trail, falling in behind both the water taxi captain and the Amina Slave Princess.

Charlie carefully navigated his towing rig down the slick and treacherous North Shore Road, keeping his eyes peeled for Manto's disabled truck taxi. The rain was still coming down in buckets, limiting visibility, especially on the road's sharp curves.

When he finally spied the entrance to the Cinnamon Bay parking lot and, in the ruins on the opposite side of the road, Manto's disabled truck, he could hardly believe the sight.

"What—did you forget how to drive?" Charlie asked with exasperation as Manto met him at the tow truck's back hitch. He studied Manto's wet, disheveled appearance with concern. "What happened to you?"

"Eye saw a ghost." Manto gulped, his face deadly serious. *"She ran me off thuh road."*

"A what?" Charlie asked, his brow furrowed. "A ghost ran you off the road?"

"It wuz a wo-man—thuh Ameena Slave Preen-cess." Manto wiped a hand across his forehead.

"The who?" Charlie demanded, clearly confused. "The Slave who?"

Manto cleared his throat. *"She had wone of my rakes."*

Charlie put his hands on his hips. "A ghost ran you off the road with a rake?"

Manto nodded solemnly. *"Sometin' lyke that."*

Charlie covered his face with his hands. Then he pointed to the tow truck.

"Get in the cab," he said with a sigh. "We'll get Bessie out in the morning."

~ *33* ~

The Bug Mon

Jeff sent word that the dive shop had picked up a last-minute sunset charter, so I found myself without my expected Saturday-night companion.

I couldn't imagine why anyone would pay good money to sit on a wet boat on rough water out in all this rain, but there was no accounting for the wild whims of tourists. Regardless, I headed into town on my own, catching a ride on one of the few remaining truck taxis waiting in the resort's front drive.

Twenty minutes later, I dashed through the rain, up a flight of green-painted steps into the second floor of a building located to the right of the Crunchy Carrot. With the storm still emptying itself onto the island, the Dumpster table was out of the question, but the bar next door was a perfect alternative.

The Silent John had the laid-back atmosphere of an old Irish pub—that is, one that had been exposed to the open air of the Caribbean for the last forty years. The uneven wood floor and well-worn furnishings were a perfect complement to the plastic table and chairs of the Dumpster table below.

Shaking off a scattering of droplets, I crossed the room

to a counter and a row of bar stools. A couple of television screens were hooked up to a satellite feed along the back wall behind the server's station. Underneath the TVs, a rickety shelf held a line of dusty beer cans and bottles, an advertisement of the bar's beverage offerings.

The Silent John didn't serve food—which was probably a good thing, given the sanitary conditions in the place—but the waitresses from the Crunchy Carrot made frequent deliveries up the stairs.

I placed an order for a fish sandwich and took a stool at the far end the counter. As I stared up at the nearest television screen, my thoughts focused on the hot meal that would soon be headed in my direction. My stomach rumbled with hungry anticipation.

This sandwich would receive a much better reception than the one I'd received in the backseat of Hank Sheridan's sedan.

Down at the other end of the bar, a man in a Hawaiian print shirt knocked back a shot of dark amber liquid. Then he *thunked* the glass dramatically on the counter next to a dingy baseball cap. Given the molded crease in the hair across the back of the man's head, the hat had seen several days' worth of constant use.

The man licked his lips and announced in a loud drawl to the fellow seated to his left, "I'm from Murfreesboro—that's in Tennessee. I'm here on my honeymoon."

The Hawaiian shirt had been dyed an eye-popping array of vivid orange and pink, the bright-colored blobs arranged into the shapes of oversized flower petals. The top three buttons were undone, revealing the red skin of the man's neck. This was not the recent sunburn of an island vacation, but the permanent leatherizing texture accumulated over a lifetime of UV exposure.

Beneath the shirt, the man wore a pair of ill-fitting, roughed-up blue jeans. A circular impression had been worn into the left rear pocket, the residual imprint from countless tins of chewing tobacco. A pair of pale hairy feet poked out from the jeans' rolled-up cuffs. Chipped, yellowed toenails wiggled freely in cheap discount-store sandals.

"Have you ever heard of Murfreesboro?" he yelled loudly into his neighbor's ear. *"Merf-fees-buro?"* he repeated, his voice slurring even as he overenunciated each syllable.

The recipient of all this attention was a dark-skinned man with wooly dreadlocks and a tired, blistered face. The West Indian's body was covered with a permanent layer of long-unwashed grit and grime. The rags of his clothes hung with the same limp, dirt-laden droop. A vacant, drug-numbed expression clouded the man's eyes. The stench of human decay wafted all the way down the bar to where I was sitting, but the Tennessean appeared not to notice.

"Actually, this vacation is part honeymoon and part fishin' trip." He shrugged his shoulders affably. "A bit more fishin' than honeymoon-in'," he confessed with a gap-toothed grin that was as ragged as his toenails.

The man's grisly neighbor had yet to register any indication that he had heard or understood this unsolicited information, but his stoic demeanor did nothing to dampen his new friend's enthusiasm.

"I packed a whole extra suitcase full of miniature Jack Daniel's bottles," the Tennessean said, shaking his head remorsefully. "And then, in all the excitement with the weddin', I forgot to bring 'em to the airport."

I glanced wryly at the waitress behind the bar. Still awash in cheap rum over three hundred years after its first sugarcane distillery, the Caribbean seemed an odd place to bring a case full of Jack.

Tourists, I thought, always overpack.

"I've been having a great time anyway," the man said cheerfully as the waitress refilled his shot glass from a bottle of whiskey that looked as if it might have been part of the Silent John's original inventory. The label was peeling off, and a thick layer of dust caked the bottle's exterior.

He nodded at his noncommunicative neighbor. "How 'bout one for my buddy here too."

The waitress hesitated only a moment before bringing another shot glass from beneath the counter and filling it. The volume of liquid in the second glass, I noticed, wasn't quite as full as the Tennessean's, but neither man appeared to notice.

The honeymooner raised his shot into the air and suggestively waved it at his drinking partner.

Without a word, the second man suddenly reached for his glass. His bleary, bloodshot eyes honed in on the liquid with a raw intensity that was almost a terror to behold. A deep resonant voice poured smoothly from his chapped lips.

"Salute."

The pair began the shot together, but the West Indian downed his in half the time as his sponsor.

The Tennessean finally finished the shot, smacking his lips to emphasize his accomplishment. "Ahhhh," he sighed, leaning back on his stool.

His eyes scanned the dusty scene on the server's side of the counter. Then his reddened face lit up as if he'd just received a liquor-inspired insight.

"You know what this island needs? Do ya?" he asked the other man, who had resumed his laconic, nonverbal state.

"An exterminator. Yep. A specialist in insect eradication."

The Tennessean spun his baseball cap on the counter's sticky surface and pointed to the cap's front logo. It depicted a cartooned mosquito in sneakers that appeared to be running for its life.

"That's me! I run an exterminator business back home in Murfreesboro. I've been talking to the missus about it. We could move down here, set up shop."

The waitress looked down the bar toward me with a grin. She'd heard variations on this discourse hundreds of times before.

For most visitors, it doesn't take more than a day or two before they begin asking themselves the inevitable what-if question: what if I just packed it all up and moved here?

Many dream about it, but few actually take the leap.

When faced with the true spreadsheet of plusses and minuses, only a handful of people are willing to commit to an island lifestyle—it was one that I was still desperately trying to hold on to.

There is nothing wrong, however, in enjoying the fantasy.

"I've got a name all picked out," the exterminator said enthusiastically as he tapped the West Indian on the shoulder. "What do you think of this? I'll call myself 'The Bug Mon.'"

~ *34* ~

The Signal

I left the bar and strolled out onto the balcony overlooking the street. For the last several weeks of still, dripping heat, the Silent John's second-floor bar area had been an almost unbearable location—which was a shame, because the balcony that ran along its front windows was the best place in town to watch the action on Cruz Bay's new roundabout.

Construction of the project had wrapped up a couple of months ago, but local fascination with the traffic structure had yet to wane. Located near the center of town, across the street from the main grocery store and not far up the hill from the Silent John and the Crunchy Carrot, the roundabout's purported rationale was to alleviate traffic—but none of St. John's residents actually believed that. Everyone knew the roundabout's primary function was to provide entertainment.

According to my calculations—based on anecdotal evidence and a random sampling from several late-afternoon sessions on the Silent John's balcony—at least sixty-five percent of the rental Jeeps approaching the roundabout entered it from the wrong direction. Luckily, the Jeeps were equipped with plenty of traction and maneuverability, so the panicked, befuddled drivers generally wound up off-roading over the roundabout's center or backing out the steep side slope against the flow of traffic. I've never seen such a snarl of misguided vehicles, terrified honking, and obscene gestures.

To clarify—the situation is lucky for those of us onlookers.

I can't remember what we did for amusement prior to the roundabout's installation; whatever it was paled by comparison to the action at the new traffic structure.

With the onset of the tourist season, huge throngs of locals had begun gathering around the spectacle, observing in bemused amazement. The front stoop of the grocery store was almost always filled with gawkers, while others crowded the surrounding sidewalk. But in my opinion, the Silent John's front balcony was the best viewing position, one that came with both comfortable wooden stools and cool refreshments.

Of course, not even fascination with the roundabout could draw people out during weather like this. With most of the tourists hibernating at their hotels, there wasn't enough traffic in the roundabout to warrant interest anyway.

Only one other person had ventured out onto the balcony that evening. A wiry little man hunched over a wobbly table tucked in under the eaves, near the corner of the building where it turned inward to accommodate a dart-throwing lane.

He was facing the opposite direction, so that I had a perfect view of his scraggly reddish brown ponytail. A hand-rolled cigarette dangled from his left hand; the plume of smoke hanging over the table reeked of marijuana. The New York hippie seemed abnormally serious as he studied a pile of tattered, dog-eared papers heaped up on the table next to a blue nylon satchel.

"Conrad Corsair," I called out as I strolled across the balcony toward him.

I'd grown fond of Conrad in the years since our first

meeting. He was like a crazy neighbor whose eccentricities slowly grew on you over time. This tempered affection notwithstanding, I refused to go anywhere near the Maho Bay campground when Conrad was in town for fear I might be unwittingly lured into his infamous teepee tent. Here on the Silent John's balcony, however, I felt I could easily evade his overamorous attentions.

Conrad's bony head jerked up as I called out his name. The startled expression on his skeletal face quickly stretched into his toothy attempt at a seductive smile. If Conrad had one thing going for him, it was his eternal optimism.

"Pa-hen," he replied as he scrambled to scoop up the pile of papers. He tapped the bottom edge of the stack against the sticky surface of the table. Nervously, he shoved the pile into the blue nylon bag, pulled the top flap over the opening, and secured its latch.

"Well, if it isn't my favorite St. John resort director," he said brightly as he jumped up from the table and swung his arms around my shoulders. I grinned through a grimace as he made a show out of dramatically kissing me on each cheek.

"So . . . good . . . to see . . . you," I replied haltingly as I stepped back against the wall, suddenly remembering that a little bit of Conrad went a long way.

Conrad's googly eyeballs bulged with excitement as he reached back to the table for the nylon satchel. "I've got something I want to show you . . ."

Before he could finish, the lights in Cruz Bay clicked off. It was the second power outage in as many days—always a bad sign. Likely as not, the temporary fix from the night before had just come loose.

The streetlamps that hovered over the road below stood lifeless, their powerless metal stems drooping like useless antennae. The windows to the Silent John and the Crunchy Carrot were nothing but black, empty sinkholes.

A bank of clouds moved across the moon, swallowing its meager light and leaving us in a moment of wet blindness.

Inside the Carrot's kitchen, I heard the hiccupping hum

of a generator as its engine struggled to kick in, a hopeful sign for the prospects of my fish sandwich. But before the motor worked up enough speed to reignite the lightbulbs, a hand reached out for my left arm.

"Conrad, let go," I said sternly, not the least bit amused.

A deep voice whispered in my left ear. *"Peen-ello-pee . . ."*

I tried to release my arm, but the man's grip was too tight.

"That's enough, Conrad," I replied tensely, wondering how such a tiny man could wield so much strength.

And then I caught a whiff of the body attached to the clenched hand. My nose filled with the sweaty, smoky stench of stale whiskey.

"Lees-en for thuh seeg-nul," the voice admonished firmly. *"Wens-day at noon."*

Before I could process the message, the hand released my arm, and the stench disappeared, as if its source had evaporated into the rain.

With a few strobing flashes, the lights inside the Silent John flickered on, and I found myself alone on the balcony.

I stepped back inside the bar as the television sets crackled with static while they attempted to reestablish their satellite connection. A white plastic sack holding a foam box with my fish sandwich waited at the end of the counter.

The Tennessee exterminator sat on his stool with a blank, expressionless look on his face. I wondered if he'd even noticed the blackout in his whiskey-induced stupor.

My gaze honed in on the empty seat to the exterminator's right that had been occupied by the grisly haired West Indian. I rubbed my arm where the man's fingers had wrapped around it, puzzling as I scanned the room.

Neither Conrad nor the smelly man who'd issued the warning were anywhere to be seen.

~ 35 ~

The Haircut

That same dark rainy night, a shirtless man with frizzy brown hair sat on a wooden stool in the center of one of the many elevated tents at the Maho Bay eco-resort.

Jeff's flat, freckled face bore a clear expression of discomfort. The bare skin on his hairy chest twitched as a young woman danced circles around his stool. The woman's fluid movements caused her spinning sundress to cast rippling shadows against the tent's canvas walls.

Hannah reached out to Jeff's head and teasingly pulled her fingers through the thick tangles of his hair.

Grunting with concern, he shifted his weight, tilting his head away from her hand. "Nobody said anything about a haircut," he muttered grimly.

Giggling shyly, Hannah raised a pair of cordless battery-powered shears and flicked the handle's on switch.

Jeff flinched at the subsequent buzzing hum. His hands clenched the rim of the stool as Hannah carefully brought the shears in toward his wild mass of hair. The approaching vibration tickled his ear, and he jerked his head away once more.

"I can't . . ." he said, shaking his head. The typically

immobile contours of his face twisted into a pleading hound-dog expression.

Hannah turned off the shears and bent down in front of him. Her voice was calm and soothing as she lightly touched his knee.

"You want to captain your own boat, don't you?"

Jeff blew out a frustrated sigh; his shoulders sagged in defeat. He nodded and closed his eyes submissively.

The shears returned to life as Hannah brought the tip to the nape of Jeff's neck. With quick, upward, sweeping motions, she began running the razor's head along his scalp.

Large frizzy clumps soon floated through the air, falling like New England snowflakes as they drifted down to the tent's wooden floor.

Crouched in the forest outside, an elderly woman watched the pair through a back window screen. Beulah Shah's wizened face pinched with thought as the pile of hair beneath the stool continued to grow.

~ *36* ~

Lost

I staggered outside the condo Monday morning, grumpy, hungover, and decidedly out of sorts. The bright sun beat a hammering blow through my aching head, a painful reminder of the bottle of Cruzan I had finished off the night before.

It had been two nights now with no sign of Jeff. I had done enough snooping around the dive shop to confirm that Saturday's sunset charter had been a fiction. No one had seen him since he returned from the weekly trip to Jost Van Dyke. He had simply disappeared.

I'd spoken to one of Jeff's dive shop buddies, a soppy blond-haired guy named Rick, who had taken his last sailing shift for him. It had been a particularly disturbing conversation—during which Rick had luridly insinuated that he would be happy to fill in for more than just Jeff's dive shop duties. I had resisted the urge to slap him.

Around the resort, no one thought Jeff's departure particularly unusual. The lower-level dive shop employees were transitory types, and he had been here longer than most. With his nautical classifications, he could take his credentials anywhere in the Caribbean. Dive shops were always looking for capable hands.

Likely as not, most reckoned, he would pop up in some other beach town in a few days' time. Not that anyone would likely ever know one way or the other—among islands, even thirty miles of ocean translated into a significant geographic barrier.

So far, I was unconvinced of this reasoning. Jeff wasn't the typical wandering deckhand, I thought with frustration as I sulked my way toward the coffee cart in the reception area.

At least, I didn't want to believe that he was.

A part of me, of course, realized that perhaps this was just Jeff's way of ending our relationship. Ours had been one of wordless commitment, a dating arrangement whose meaning was subject to evolving interpretation. I had never pressed the point, and he had never vocalized his feelings.

I had always known that I wouldn't have him forever—the difference in our ages guaranteed that. But, like my stolen time here on the island, I had been desperate to extend that franchise for as long as possible.

I wasn't quite yet ready to concede defeat—on either count.

Still mulling over the puzzle of my missing boat boy, I plucked a foam cup from the reception area's dispenser and began filling it. As I lifted the steaming cup toward my nose and took in a deep whiff of the pungent liquid, a man's voice trickled into my periphery.

"Excuse me, miss," he said affably. "I was hoping you could settle a dispute we've been having."

"I'll do my best," Hannah's pleasant, cheerful tone replied.

The coffee kiosk was pushed up against a column, and the concierge desk—where Hannah was apparently stationed—was positioned on the opposite side.

Mere proximity to Hannah rankled my already sour disposition. The finest coffee in the world couldn't coax me to stand there any longer than necessary. But I figured I'd get at least one refill before Hannah—the still maddeningly unexplained, Slave Princess–impersonating Hannah—drove me from the coffee kiosk.

"This Slave Princess everyone's been talking about. They say she hangs out at Maho Bay."

Slurping down the burning hot coffee, I tilted my head around the side of the column to get a peek at the concierge counter. The man posing this offbeat question was one of the many real estate lawyers staying at the resort.

"I've been all over the island this last week," he continued. "I have to say—it seems to me, if I were going to do myself in by jumping off a cliff, I'd pick Ram Head. That place has the best cliff overhang I've ever seen."

"I hope you're not planning to test this theory," Hannah said with a gracious smile.

The lawyer persisted. "I'm starting to think maybe this Maho Bay business is just a ruse." He pointed his finger at his companions. "To scare off us real estate types."

Smart fellow, I thought, nearly spilling coffee down the front of my shirt in my eagerness to eavesdrop on the conversation.

"The Princess does have a connection to Ram Head," Hannah replied diplomatically. "But it was at the beginning of the revolt, not the end. They say she and the other Amina met on the cliffs—the evening of the revolt, after the initial slaughter was completed. The rebels reportedly had a hideout up there. From that angle, you can see the entire southern half of the island."

She glanced back toward the coffee stand, and I had the sudden impression that she was just as much aware of my presence as I was of hers.

Her voice lowered conspiratorially as she leaned toward the lawyer. "But I can assure you, the locals swear her ghost haunts the grounds of the eco-resort up at Maho Bay."

The lawyer chortled loudly. "Well, then I hope she likes company. We're going to build a huge resort on that property."

The Computer Programmer

Late Tuesday afternoon, the clouds were still hanging low over St. John.

The constant gray drip had begun to dampen the spirits of the island's vacationers. While the rain was good for the island's fragile ecosystem and cistern supplies, it was a bust with visiting tourists. The intermittent electrical outages of the last few days hadn't improved the overall temperament.

Vivian stood on the resort's dock, a tented poncho hanging from her sturdy shoulders. She stared stolidly out into the bay, one hand gripping the handle of a bright-colored umbrella, the other wrapped around her ever-present clipboard.

Beside her, the staff of designated greeters awaited the afternoon arrival of the resort's double-decker powerboat from St. Thomas. The shuttle service transported guests directly from the airport to the resort's pier, bypassing the public ferry taken by other travelers.

A dozen tiny plastic cups filled with a cheap rum cocktail waited on a tray, ready to hand out to passengers as they stepped off the boat. The ship was running a little later than usual, given the delays of the incoming flights and the rough water in the Pillsbury Sound. The ice cubes had begun to melt, raising the liquid's volume dangerously close to the rims.

Vivian didn't mind the cooler temperatures, she reflected as the drip intensified against the outer surface of her umbrella, but even she had to admit that their guest-greeting routine was much better received on a sunny afternoon. The palm-tree-lined beach and half-acre swimming pool lost much of their tropical aura when shrouded in cold cloudy rain. This kind of weather, she knew from experience, brought out the worst in new arrivals.

Vivian checked her watch and, with a sigh, pointed toward the pavilion at the end of the dock. Her relieved staff immediately moved under its cover. If they were about to receive a boatload of cranky guests, they might as well be dry.

When at long last the boat pulled into the bay, the rain had accelerated to a full-on downpour. As soon as the rigging was secured to the pier, the first guests began hurrying down the metal gangplank, sprinting for the pavilion's overhead cover.

The computer programmer was the last to disembark. Carrying a canvas toolbox and a roll-around suitcase, the large man stepped carefully onto the temporary walkway, as if unsure of his footing. Despite the heavy rain, he took his time walrus-ing his hefty mass down the dock. He was thoroughly soaked by the time he reached the pavilion's protection.

Dourly, Vivian offered him a plastic cup filled with a now watery concoction of rum and punch. "Welcome to St. John," she said stiffly.

Cracking a weary smile, the computer programmer waived off the cocktail. He remembered the assistant manager from his last visit to the resort—four and a half years ago—but, just to be sure, he tilted his round head to read the printing on the tag pinned to her shirt.

"Nice to see you again, Vivian."

With a grunt, she checked the last guest off on her clipboard: Howard Stoutman. The man had used a different name the last time they'd met, but she'd recognized his large bulky form immediately.

"I see you're here to set up our wireless Internet," she confirmed tensely. "You'll need access to the main circuit boards. They're mounted to the wall in the storm cellar beneath the administrative building. I'll take you down first thing in the morning."

Her sharp eyes summed up his sizeable girth. "It's rather close quarters in there," she added pointedly, "in case you don't remember."

The programmer sighed tiredly and glanced at his watch. "Any chance you could let me in this afternoon?" he asked, clearing his throat to emphasize the request. "I'd like to get a head start if I could."

Vivian huffed impatiently. "We'll have to hurry," she replied testily. She shifted the clipboard to her hip so that she could reach into her pocket for a large key ring. "My son will be getting in from school in about fifteen minutes."

She motioned to a staff member sitting behind the wheel of a motorized golf cart. With a nodding jerk of her head, Vivian dismissed the driver and slid into his seat. She grabbed a towel from the center console compartment and wiped off the raindrops that had splattered across the dashboard.

The programmer hefted his roll-around suitcase into the rear cargo space and squeezed himself into the passenger seat.

Vivian muttered something under her breath as the cart groaned beneath his weight, then she pushed the accelerator to the floor.

After a jerking start, the golf cart chugged off down the red brick path leading into the resort.

A few minutes later, the computer programmer stood in the administrative building's dimly lit basement. Fingering the bent and rusted key Vivian had entrusted to him, he turned to glance anxiously back at the dusty concrete steps leading up to the ground floor.

Outside, the rain had provided a cooling respite to the island's heat, but here in the basement's claustrophobic confines, conditions were stuffy and hot.

Best to get in and out of this place as quickly as possible, he thought as he wiped a layer of sweat from his flushed face. He had one more task to complete—delivering the contents of the canvas toolbox—then he would lay low until it was time to hop on the late-night water taxi back to St. Thomas. The resort was long overdue for Wi-Fi Internet access, but he wouldn't be the one installing it.

The programmer jiggled the ill-fitting key in the lock until the teeth finally found the right groove. Once the interior bolt slid free of the latch, the heavy metal door swung open with a loud *creak*.

Spying a triangular chunk of wood in the corner of the stairwell, he pushed the door against the concrete wall and crammed the nose of the piece of wood into the half-inch space beneath its bottom width.

Dusting his hands off on the back of his pants, the programmer slipped the key into his right pocket and picked up his bags. He stepped into the storm cellar and parked his roll-around near the door. Turning, he flipped a plastic switch on the wall nearest the entrance, but the low-hanging fluorescent bulb dangling in the center of the concrete-walled room failed to illuminate. Unhooking a penlight from his shirt collar, he panned the narrow beam across the cellar's interior space.

A rudimentary toilet and makeshift shower were sequestered in the back corner. A rotting plastic chair had been upended on the sand-coated floor. Moldy, decaying cardboard boxes lined one of the walls. The boxes were presumably filled with a stash of provisions, should anyone be unlucky enough to find himself stranded inside.

The programmer shuddered. The cellar's isolation was the reason he'd selected it as the drop-off point, but he'd rather drown in a hurricane than be trapped indefinitely within this room.

The programmer righted the chair and set his toolbox on its seat. As he unzipped the top opening, a scuttling sound scratched against the concrete floor in the corridor outside the cellar entrance.

Had he been followed? The programmer closed his eyes for a long panic-surging moment. Summoning his inner reserves, he calmly reopened them to the sight of a crusty hermit crab carrying its shell across the threshold.

"Hello, my friend," he said with a laugh. He walked over to the small crustacean and bent down to get a better look. "Welcome to my humble abode."

The crab eyeballed the wide heft of the man hovering above him, scurried to the nearest corner, and retracted into its shell.

With a sigh of relief, the programmer crossed to the far side of the room, where a large metal cupboard containing the electrical boards had been mounted onto the wall. He could hear the crab slowly creeping along behind him, the hard surface of its claws clacking against the gritty concrete floor.

"Glad for the company, little buddy," the programmer said as he thumbed through his pockets for a second key.

Tack. Tack. Tack.

Friendly little guy, he thought, dismissing the sound. He inserted the second key into the cupboard's lock and wrenched open the metal casing. Waving the penlight up and down the electrical box, he searched for his package.

"Ah, there you are," he said with chuckle, reaching for a paper bag crammed into a crevice in the back wall.

He tipped the bag sideways, sliding out a wad of bills. His thick fingers quickly thumbed through the stack, sizing it up for a quick estimation. Four years' worth of embezzlement through the resort's water taxi and overtime expenditure account had racked up a nice pile of cash, his payment for relocating Vivian and her son here from the Bahamas.

Tack. Tack. Tack.

"Hey, pal," the programmer said nervously, turning his light toward the floor to look for the crab, "don't think I'm going to cut you in on this . . ."

The words died in his throat. The crab was still curled up in the corner near the door, in the same tucked-up formation it had assumed a few minutes earlier. The seat of the plastic chair where he'd set his canvas toolbox was now empty.

The color drained from the programmer's face as the heavy metal door began to swing shut.

"Who goes there?" he called out tentatively.

The door thumped against the threshold, and the lock clicked in its fittings. With clammy, fumbling fingers, the programmer reached into his pocket, desperately searching for the main key.

"Hey!" he yelled angrily as he discovered the empty pocket. "Hey!"

No one answered. The programmer and the hermit crab were locked together in the darkness of the storm cellar.

~ *38* ~

Beneath the Sea

The public power grid for St. John relied on a network of submarine cables that connected it to the Red Hook power station on the east end of St. Thomas. The lines lay at the bottom of the Pillsbury Sound, where the brilliant crystal blue water of the shoreline darkened to a deep murky gray.

Lobsters skulked along the sand's swirling surface, probing the cylindrical tube with their claws as they searched for prey hiding in the loose crevices beneath. Stingrays skated through the deep water, their dark menacing cloaks silently stalking the power line's endless snake. Occasionally, the white-tipped jaws of a shark playfully mouthed the cable, leaving behind a telltale imprint of pointed indentations.

Every so often, a storm rolled across the Virgins that generated enough surface turbulence to disrupt the creepy quiet of this underwater scene, roiling the aging cables until a weak spot was exposed.

The lights of St. John flickered so regularly that no one questioned the cause of this latest power outage. The larger resorts, several of the bars and restaurants, as well as most permanent residents relied on backup generators to mitigate the constant power inconvenience.

Few people knew that these most recent blackouts were no act of nature.

Beulah Shah, who slipped the cellar key into a pocket of her frayed shirtdress as she limped up the stairs to the administrative building's first floor, was one of those few.

It would be at least twenty-four hours, if not more, she thought as the canvas toolbox swung from her bony hand, before anyone came to check on the resort's main electrical box in the cellar where the computer programmer was now trapped.

~ *39* ~

The Jeep

Early Wednesday morning, November 23, I sat on a bench under the eaves outside the resort's reception area, waiting in the darkness for my ride. Although the rain was still smattering down, a coming break in the storm pattern promised a brilliant, clear sunrise—but that wasn't the reason I had risen so early.

The battered, doorless Jeep that rattled up the entrance leg of the horseshoe-shaped drive was unlikely to be confused with any of its rental counterparts. I yawned sleepily as the vehicle slowed to an idle in front of the reception's entrance. After a brisk skip through the raindrops, I opened the passenger-side door and climbed inside.

The freshly showered man behind the wheel was almost unrecognizable. Charlie Baker's hair was damp, neatly combed back, and uncovered by its habitual dirty baseball cap.

I couldn't imagine where he'd found the white cotton shirt and pressed khaki shorts he was wearing. They couldn't possibly have come from his regular closet.

"Look at you," I greeted him sleepily as my gaze swept from his clean scalp to the sharp tan line on his lower shins.

His pale feet sported a new pair of leather sandals. "All cleaned up and ready for your big trip."

Charlie glanced sheepishly down at his wardrobe and shrugged his shoulders.

After many months of wrangling, his ex-wife had agreed to bring their kids, now teenagers, down to the islands for Thanksgiving. The group of them would spend the rest of the week together in one of Charlie's rental villas on St. Croix.

Located only thirty miles to the south, St. Croix was a world away from St. John.

Despite the short distance, it would take Charlie the better part of the day to get there. After the ferry ride to Red Hook, he'd catch a taxi across St. Thomas to Charlotte Amalie. There, he would board a seaplane to Christiansted, St. Croix's main port.

The largest of the Virgin Islands, St. Croix fell within the confines of the U.S. Territory more by happenstance than geography.

Seeking additional arable land for sugarcane production, the Danish purchased the island from the French in 1733. It was because of this land deal that the French sent soldiers to help the Danes put down the slave revolt on St. John later that same year. Many of the farmers displaced by the St. John attacks eventually settled on St. Croix, whose flat southwestern quadrant far surpassed St. Thomas in its agricultural potential.

The resulting development led to a much more diversified economy than that of the northern Virgin Islands. Over the years, agriculture had been replaced by an immense oil refinery business and several rum-distilling operations. Even in modern times, tourism was but a minor component of the island's overall revenue.

While connected governmentally to St. Thomas—and the oft-forgotten St. John—St. Croix looked and felt like a whole other country.

* * *

Charlie spun the wheel to turn the Jeep down the resort's front drive as I snapped what remained of the passenger-side seat belt into its latch. He'd agreed to let me borrow his Jeep while he was away—if I dropped him off at the six a.m. ferry.

I tried to will myself awake with a second wide yawn. The early morning errand was a small price to pay for access to a set of wheels.

"Whatever you do, don't let Manto near the Jeep," Charlie admonished as I bounced along in the passenger seat, longing for a cup of coffee. "It took my guys three whole days to fix his rig."

Charlie shook his head in consternation. "He tried to tell me that a *ghost* ran him off the road the other night. Some woman the locals call the Amina Slave Princess."

I gripped the door handle as Charlie swerved around a pothole. Hannah, I reflected, had certainly been busy.

Charlie gave me a sideways glance and chuckled. "I don't know why I think you'll be a better driver," he said sarcastically.

He lifted a hand from the wheel and pointed emphatically at the doorless opening beside him. "Just remember, Pen. Keep *left*."

By the time we reached the outskirts of town, the sun was beginning to crack the horizon. As the clouds parted and light flickered across Charlie's tense face, I could see the joking had been a cover for his growing apprehension.

He'd pulled out all the stops for this half-week experiment; he had numerous activities planned for the kids and had made reservations at the island's best restaurants.

For his sake, I just hoped his family actually showed up.

"What are you going to do if . . . ?" I asked as the Jeep pulled to a stop in front of the ferry building. There was no need to fill in the rest of the sentence.

Charlie hopped out and trotted around to the rear storage compartment to retrieve his luggage. I met him on the curb as he set his bag on the wet pavement.

He let out a volume of pent-up air, as if he'd spent the entire morning steeling himself for the possibility that this might end up being a solo excursion.

"Well, then I'll have a big house party down on St. Croix," he replied with forced optimism. "Don't suppose you . . . ?"

He cut short his offer with a flat smile that conveyed he was as yet unaware of Jeff's sudden leave of absence.

"No, I guess you wouldn't."

Before I had time to correct him, he tossed his hands in the air and headed toward the ticket booth, his new shoes squeaking on the pavement as he walked.

~ 40 ~

Keep to the Left

I climbed through the Jeep's open doorway and adjusted the seat to my slightly longer legs. Punching the release button on the gear handle, I shifted into drive and carefully began threading my way through the milling crowd of truck-taxi drivers, arriving day workers, and scurrying chickens.

It was a jumpy ride, and the steering wheel had a lot of extra play in it, but I wasn't complaining. To have a vehicle on the island was an expensive luxury, one that I'd rarely indulged in.

By the time a car traversed all the water between Miami and St. John, it racked up several thousand dollars' worth of transportation costs. On top of that, gas here was significantly more expensive than up in the States.

Like most of the other expats, most days, I got around just fine on foot, by truck taxi, or bumming rides from friends. But after four years of depending on others, I found it liberating to finally be piloting my own ship.

I'd only driven a few times during my years on the island, but the tales of my inability to stay on the left side of the road had been widely circulated by the Dumpster table gang. I had, of course, protested that these stories were greatly exaggerated—but in the first hundred yards of manning Charlie's Jeep that morning, I did little to put those rumors to rest.

Several well-intentioned honks, followed by energetic finger pointing greeted me as I merged onto the main thoroughfare. After a dicey turn through the island's new roundabout—during which time I vowed I would never again make fun of another confused tourist—it was with great relief that I found myself back on the road to the resort.

The entrance to the resort's U-shaped front drive was the only hurdle that remained. I slowed the Jeep as I neared the dual prongs of the turnoff, concentrating to ensure I wouldn't end up on the wrong side of the loop.

Halfway up the drive, I realized I'd picked the wrong leg of the horseshoe. By that point, it was too late to back up. Best, I reasoned, to power through to the top of the circle and hopefully turn around before anyone caught sight of me.

I knew I wouldn't be that lucky.

Vivian and Hamilton stood waiting for me out front of the reception area as I pulled up from the wrong direction.

Mother and child were dressed in clothes typically reserved as their Sunday best. Vivian had donned a linen dress that hugged her many curves, while Ham wore a starched white shirt, tan slacks, and dark green tie.

I had agreed to give the pair a ride to the Moravian church at the edge of Coral Bay on the far east end of the island. They would be joining the group marching to the old Danish fort, or Fortsberg, as it was officially called, later that morning for the annual commemoration of the 1733 Slave Revolt.

With all of its Native Rights undertones, this wasn't the kind of event Vivian normally would have been caught dead at, but Ham had talked her into it. Several of the children from his school would be there, and he was eager to participate.

To Vivian's chagrin, her son couldn't stop talking about the Amina Slave Princess, who, it was rumored, would be making an appearance somewhere along the route.

I sat in the Jeep, waiting for the inevitable critique of my driving skills.

Vivian stared for a long moment at the vehicle, her eyes skeptically scanning its dented front bumper and missing driver's-side door.

Then, she narrowed her focus on me. She crossed her arms in front of her body and shook her head dismissively, before striding purposefully to the doorless driver's-side opening.

"Move over," she said in a no-nonsense manner, hands firmly planted on her hips.

I strummed my fingers across the steering wheel's sun-hardened plastic. "What's wrong, Vivian?" I asked teasingly. "You don't trust my driving?"

"No," came her immediate response.

Vivian was nothing if not direct.

"Fine," I said, winking at Ham as I unbuckled my seat belt. "Fine, fine, fine," I grumbled loudly while walking around the dented front bumper to the opposite side.

Vivian helped Ham climb into the tiny back passenger area, then she settled into the driver's seat and cranked the engine.

"As if I would let the likes of *you* drive *my* son," she muttered under her breath.

I glanced over my left shoulder and shared a grin with Ham. The rant continued as we rumbled off.

"Smells like something died in here . . ."

~ *41* ~

The Brown Bay Ruins

The Amina Slave Princess woke to a light rain tapping against the canvas roof of her tent at the Maho Bay eco-resort. She rolled out from under the bedsheets, placed her bare feet on the tent's wooden floor, and stretched her arms toward the ceiling. Her eyelashes fluttered in the predawn darkness, shaking loose the last remnants of a restful night's sleep.

She dressed in a T-shirt, blue jeans, and sneakers, then she loaded her beaded vest, knee-length sarong, and wig of bouncing black curls into a small satchel. The residents of the eco-resort tended to be early risers, and she had almost been spotted leaving her tent several times over the past week. After a few close calls, she had taken to bringing her costume along with her, so that she could change in and out of it a safe distance from the eco-resort.

Pulling the plastic sheath of a disposable raincoat over her head, she slipped the satchel beneath it and looped the strap over her shoulder. Cautiously, she sneaked out the tent's front door.

The dripping rain drowned out the light tread of her foot-steps as the Princess disappeared into the darkness. She made a quick stop to dig her spear out of the pile of leaves where she had hidden it the previous evening, then she trotted down the wooden walkway, ready to begin her daily explorations.

So far, all was quiet in the eco-resort, with snores still droning from several of the elevated units. The Princess climbed the short flight of stairs to the dry goods store, taking care not to wake any of the camp's peaceful sleepers. Once there, she crossed the last of the elevated walkways and proceeded down a washed-out gravel road that served as the resort's driveway.

By the time she reached the far edge of the grounds, her tennis shoes were soggy and her jeans were wet up to her knees. Her head, however, felt fresh and clear, invigorated by the cooling rain. She twirled the pole of her spear in her hands, eager to set off on her journey.

The Princess couldn't say what compelled the direction she chose that particular morning. But, as she reached the pavement at the bottom of the dirt road, her feet turned, seemingly of their own volition, toward the east, down a paved artery that fed into the island's main north shore thoroughfare.

Fifteen minutes later, the Princess had circled around the back side of Mary's Point and picked up the shoreline on the opposite side of its bulge. A mile-long trek along the water led her to the curving beach that lined Waterlemon Bay. There, she veered inland on a dirt path leading up a steep, rocky incline.

The rising sun broke through the clouds to illuminate the muddy trail's sharp twists and turns. Damp jungle moved in around the Princess as she climbed toward the summit, steadying her footing by wedging her spear into the thick roots that crisscrossed the ground.

What had started off as a cool, wet morning quickly transitioned into a daytime's steam. Halfway to the trail's summit, she had to remove the raincoat to keep from overheating.

It took some effort, but she finally cleared the crest. As a playful breeze brushed against her face, she had the sense that this morning's excursion would be different from her previous outings.

Having caught her breath, the Princess resumed her hike, continuing across the hilltop until she reached a fork in the trail. Brow furrowed, the Princess stared at a brown metal post with white markings planted next to the path. The post's block letters were similar to the ones she had encountered a couple days earlier on the sign near the donkeys at Turtle Point.

Her eyes honed in on a white-painted arrow pointed east.

Temptation tugged at her for only a moment before she made her decision. She licked her upper lip resolutely and began her descent on the Brown Bay Trail.

The Princess skipped lightly down the hill, instantly disappearing into the swampy forest. The sun did its best to infiltrate the netting of leaves and vegetation above her head, but she soon found herself immersed in the jungle's dark shadows.

As the path sank to sea level, its route curved along a bog of mangroves grown up in a brackish salt pond. The Princess left the trail, veering off into a thick patch of grasses. She pushed her way deep into the marsh and stood there in silence, her body moving in perfect time with the swaying reeds, as she absorbed every detail of her surroundings.

Once she was satisfied that she had not been followed, she waded closer to the shore, her progress as indiscernible as that of the island's tiny biting insects.

The roaring punch of the ocean greeted her at Brown Bay's pebbly beach. The sky glowed with a full morning's heat, flushing her cheeks as it warmed her skin.

The Princess walked along the rocky shoreline, using her spear to navigate over several slick boulders, until she happened upon the rough remains of a low rock wall tumbling out of the woods. Curiously, she peered into the dense brush, searching for a larger structure that might explain the wall's existence.

The tree limbs spread low, hugging the ground, impeding her progress. Her body bent into a crawling position, trying to find an opening through the network of roping vines that barricaded every ingress.

After fighting about twenty yards inland through the overgrowth, she came across the ruins of a small settlement, hidden in the trees.

Holding her multipronged spear at the ready, the Princess carefully circled the ruins. The buildings were ancient, abandoned, and looked as if they had been built by a people who had inhabited the island long ago. In the middle of the settlement, a small courtyard formed a pen that likely had been used to hold livestock. Off to one side, the stone ring of a drinking well encircled a dark gaping hole.

A rickety two-story structure in the center of the area appeared to have been the main living quarters. The building had long since been taken over by the forest's jungling arms; moss covered most of the stone surfaces. One of the structure's disintegrating side walls provided a precarious staircase to its upper level, with pseudo-steps formed out of loose stones that had not yet fallen away from the wall.

The Princess's tennis shoes wobbled on the shaky steps as she climbed to the top floor. Brushing aside the spiderwebs that crisscrossed the doorless entry, she peered inside.

There on the leaf-strewn floor, nestled in a corner, lay a small wooden box.

With her spear, the Princess cleared a path through the leaves, testing the floor with its pronged end before trusting it with her weight. Her heart beat heavily within her chest as she drew close enough to the box to unhook the rusting metal clasp that held the lid shut.

Carefully, she lifted the cover, generating a loud *creak* that echoed through the stone-filled room.

Inching nearer, she peeked over the rim to look inside. In the bottom of the box lay a blue nylon satchel.

The Princess stretched her hand out to touch the fabric. The material was slick and shiny, yet seemingly durable. She unsnapped the satchel and looked inside.

A large sheaf of papers filled up much of the space, but there at the bottom of the pouch was an item that immediately caught her attention.

The Princess blinked in disbelief.

She couldn't imagine how it had followed her all these many miles across the ocean, but she knew *this* was the reason she had set out on the easterly path that morning.

There, inside the blue nylon satchel, lay her precious medallion.

~ 42 ~

The Blue Nylon Satchel

Slowly, the Princess extended her hand into the satchel. Her trembling fingers hovered over the amulet, afraid it might disappear if she tried to touch it. Every ridge and contour of the medallion was just as she remembered—a blazing circle of the sun, a halo of rays streaming out from its burning center.

Sucking in her breath, she willed herself to capture the last inch of space separating her from the trinket. As the familiar cool metal surface pressed against her skin, she felt the transfer of its power course into her fingers and up through her arm.

Just then, the Princess heard a commotion at the beach. Pulling the medallion toward her chest, she scurried back to the top of the rickety steps. Crouching behind the corner of the second-story wall, she spied two figures stumbling through the underbrush toward the ruins.

The first to emerge from the thicket was a small bony man with thinning brown hair tied in a limp ponytail at the back of his neck.

"It's in here, Eddie," he called back to his companion, a tall skinny fellow with a bald head and a full beard who was still struggling through the overgrowth of shrubs and low-hanging branches.

"Conrad, you crazy hippie," Alden Edwards muttered under his breath as a curtain of ropelike vines smacked him across the face.

His eyes widened as he noticed a bustling wasp nest attached to a dangling vine about a foot to his right. Nervously, he ran a hand over his bald—and exposed—crown as he counted close to a hundred stingers in the pulsating mass of insects.

"What have you dragged me into?"

Gripping the handle of her spear, the Princess watched as the two men approached her hiding spot. The shorter of the pair paused at the bottom of the steps leading to the second floor of her building, and she backed farther into the stone recess to avoid being seen.

"Come on, Fast Eddie," Conrad encouraged. "Hurry up, or I'll have to find you another nickname."

Eyes rolling, Alden staggered forward, his back bent almost horizontal to duck beneath the hanging vines. His feet slipped on the wet ground, narrowly missing the edge of the well. He paused to poke his head into the deep hole, trying to determine its depth, but he could see nothing but a dark seeping pit.

"I'll be lucky if I make it out of here alive," he groaned as Conrad began climbing up the side of a crumbling brick wall, using the exposed rocks as footholds.

The nimble New Yorker quickly reached a landing on the second floor of the ruin. He turned and waived enthusiastically down at the eco-resort manager.

"Tell me again," Alden groused, "why we couldn't have

done this back at the campground?" With a wide yawn, he added, "And a couple of hours later?"

Conrad propped his hands on his slim hips. He stood mere inches away from the Princess, who had crouched behind the nearest wall to stay out of Alden's line of sight.

"I have to keep it hidden—to protect it. You'll see." Conrad jerked his head toward his left shoulder. "Get on up here, and I'll show you."

The Princess wrapped both hands tightly around her spear's wooden handle. Her eyes focused in on the skinny ponytail tied at the back of the man's neck as she prepared to strike.

Grumbling uneasily, Alden placed a first foot on the bottom rock.

Conrad smoothed a hand over the top of his head and straightened his ponytail. "When I read about the Maho Bay sale in the papers, I knew I had to do something. I couldn't let anything happen to my teepee tent," he said as Alden took a second tentative step onto the shaky stones.

"I began searching through the Rockefeller archives at one of the New York libraries. They had stuff going all the way back to before the island's transfer—from the Danes to the Americans. It took some digging, but I finally got to what I was looking for. This little sheet of paper is going to make a big difference around here."

He poked his narrow chest out boastfully. "You can start unpacking your boxes, Eddie, and book my reservation for next year, and the year after that, and the year after . . ."

Conrad's elflike body suddenly jerked sideways as he disappeared behind the wall into the second floor of the ruins.

Alden heard a strange rustling sound.

"Conrad, are you okay?" he called out with concern.

He took another wobbly step up the rock wall of stairs. "Conrad?"

Alden bent to his knees, trying to gain enough balance to climb the rest of the way up the wall. But before he could scramble the remaining five feet in height, a wild figure exploded from the second floor landing.

Brandishing the spear above her head, a blood-curdling scream trilling from her throat, the Amina Princess leapt from the top of the steps to the forest below.

As Alden dove for cover, he caught only a glimpse of a curly-haired woman in a beaded vest and sarong flying through the air.

A silver medallion hung from her neck on a leather cord. The handle of a blue nylon satchel was wrapped around one wrist; in the opposite hand she held a rake that looked as if it been stolen from one of the resorts.

~ *43* ~

Coral Bay

Throughout the entire drive over Centerline Road to Coral Bay, Vivian continued to mutter about both the decrepit state of the Jeep and my abysmal driving skills—each instance of which Hamilton found enormously amusing. By the time we turned into the parking lot outside the Moravian church, he had nearly worn himself out from giggling.

Despite being at the epicenter of St. John's original colonization, nowadays Coral Bay was associated with the less-populated side of the island. To modern eyes, this was an "up and coming" area, ripe for future development.

Coral Bay's loosely defined boundaries included a small handful of restaurants, a gas station (which had changed hands countless times and was only sporadically open for service), several less-expensive villa rentals, and numerous lots touting their suitability as building sites. It was home to a roaming herd of stubborn goats, many of whom had no intention of yielding to vehicular traffic. A flock of Richard's feathered cousins also frequented the area, monitoring the leftovers at the tables outside one of the harbor-front restaurants.

If—or when, depending on your point of view—a large resort was built out on this sleepier quadrant, the island's dynamics would change dramatically. Many speculated that Coral Bay might one day overshadow its sister city to the west as the focal point of the island's population and tourist activities. Until then, what little there was of the tiny town lined an inlet offshoot of Hurricane Hole, a harbor named for its long-serving role as a boat sanctuary during major storms.

The remains of the original Danish fort, Fortsberg, sat on a low hill overlooking this quiet rural scene. The ruins were located on private land and generally off-limits to visitors. But on the yearly anniversary of the 1733 Slave Revolt, the property owner relented and allowed the commemorative march to make its pilgrimage to the site.

The parking lot in front of the Moravian church was already filling with marchers when Vivian stopped the Jeep and secured its hand brake.

Still sitting in the driver's seat, she opened her purse and removed a pad of red arrow-shaped sticky notes. She peeled off one after the other and began pressing them onto the dashboard, the sunshade—any flat surface that would accept their adhesive.

With the placement of each sticky note, she turned her head toward me and barked sternly, "*Left*. Keep to the *left*."

Finally, she climbed out and flipped her seat forward to help her son exit.

Hamilton grinned cheekily. "Left," he mimicked with a cute grin, pointing his finger across his chest.

"All right, already," I deflected. "I've got it under control."

Vivian shot me a dubious look.

When I pulled out of the parking lot a few minutes later, I could hear Ham's squeaky voice hollering, "*Left!* Penelope, keep *left*!"

* * *

This second attempt at driving Charlie's Jeep, I did manage to stay on the left side of the road—at least most of the time.

I backtracked about a quarter of the way across Centerline before turning right on a connector to the north shore. In the backseat, next to where Ham had been sitting, rode my flippers, snorkel gear, and a beach towel. I'd been wearing my swimsuit beneath my T-shirt and shorts since Charlie's predawn pickup. It was finally time to hit the beach.

The Jeep bounced along the asphalt, its spongy tires dipping in and out of the potholes that pitted the surface. A pleasant breeze floated through the driver's-side opening, whispering against my bare legs.

I leaned my head back, soaking in the sense of freedom and escape—until a blaring horn drew my attention back to the road, and I swerved left to return to my lane.

The Trunk Bay parking lot was almost empty when I pulled in. Despite the island's crush of Thanksgiving-week tourists, the beach would be deserted for at least another hour.

I parked near the truck-taxi stand and slid the keys under the seat. With the door missing, there was no point in locking it. And besides, I shrugged, who would steal a Jeep on an island?

I hopped over the loose chain draped across the entrance, bypassing the four-dollar entrance fee since there was no one at the kiosk to collect it. My flip-flops crunched down a sandy trail, past the locked showering and changing facilities. About a hundred yards later, I stepped out onto a white beach and a wide swath of perfect blue water.

There's nothing quite like the feeling of being the first to set foot on a clean stretch of sand, taking claim to a virgin plot of unmarked beach. The morning sun spread across the sky as I sat at the water's edge and let the gentle waves lap at my legs.

Tiny swells ebbed in and out, taunting and teasing my toes. Every so often, a rush of water would rise up in a triumphant *oomph* to splash across my shins—only to collapse into an apologetic retreat of sweeping curls on the sand's wet pancake.

After pulling on my snorkel mask and fins, I began swimming out toward the underwater trail of placards identifying fish and coral formations along the ocean floor, gradually making my way to a clump of boulders that formed a cay at the center right of the bay.

Head turned toward the ocean floor's wondrous landscape, I slowly drifted from the clear aqua blue of the shallow water near the beach into the murkier indigo of the deeper depths. The water pressed against my ears, a blanketing vacuum that obliterated all sound but the occasional gurgle of a bubble escaping from my mask.

Floating passively with the current, I drifted into a school of sardines, whose millions of members swam right up to my treading fingertips, expertly maneuvering away at the last second to avoid touching my skin. A rolling tide caused a ripple in the crowds of needle-shaped fish, and the school parted to reveal the elephant hump of a tarpon tracking below.

When I could no longer stand the suctioning pressure of the mask against my forehead, I paddled back to shore. After the inevitable awkwardness of the de-snorkeling procedure, I collapsed into exhaustion on the beach.

Flipping over onto my back, I turned my gaze skyward. White cotton-ball clouds streamed across the blue canvas, their rounded shapes slanted from their hurried pace, leaving a trail of discarded tufts in their wake.

A gray-headed pelican swooped into view, hunting for its breakfast. White-tipped wings spanned by dark brown feathers swooped over the water, the bird's sharp eyes searching for the cylindrical shadow of a fish.

Once the target was cited, the pelican's wings angled toward the sun, feinting an arching, roller-coaster maneuver. Up, up, up it went—before its body suddenly rotated to dive, straight down, into the shallows.

The tip of the bird's beak hit the smooth, mirrored surface with a loud *smack*, as its pointed head jackhammered against the ocean.

The feathered body popped up immediately, a fish-shaped bulge poking out of the spongy skin of its long stringy neck.

I lay there on the beach, thinking about the fish's perspective, as it found itself transferred, in a flashing instant, from one liquid medium to another—and wondering how long it took before the fish realized it had been trapped.

~ 44 ~

Centerline Road

Gripping the spear near its rakelike attachment, the Amina Princess sloshed through the marshy salt pond and sped up the narrow dirt path, each step increasing her distance from the Brown Bay ruins. The amulet swung from her neck as she ran, the shiny metal disc pumping its strength through her veins.

Her feet skimmed effortlessly past the sharp ledges of rock that cut across the trail. She leapt over a fallen tree, her body lifting into the air like a gazelle. Her lungs filled with the island's moist air; she could go on like this for days— now that she had been reunited with her beloved medallion.

She reached the clearing at the crest of the hill, and the sun's bending rays blessed her curly wigged head. The wilderness of this once fearsome place was now her ally. Her bleary world had suddenly become clear and distinct.

She knew what she must do next. Nothing could stop her from completing her next task.

The Princess paused to change out of her costume, exchanging the wig, beaded bodice, and sarong for her blue jeans and

T-shirt. She tucked the garments into the blue nylon satchel and set off along the shoreline, reversing her previous route.

Despite the early hour, she occasionally heard voices floating through the trees. Every so often, she came across a pair of snorkelers paddling in the shallow water. She gave them a casual wave, confident she wouldn't be recognized in her modern-day attire.

Eventually, the Princess picked up the North Shore Road. As she walked along its shoulder, a truck taxi motored by, carrying the day's first load of tourists to the national park beaches. A second vehicle turned into the parking lot for Trunk Bay, and she fell back into the trees to follow it.

The rusted red Jeep stopped at the far end of the lot, closest to the beach entrance. Since the driver's-side door was missing, the Princess had a clear view of the woman behind the wheel.

After parking the Jeep, the woman yanked the key from the ignition and slid it under the front seat. Then she grabbed her snorkeling gear and headed off toward the beach.

The Princess kept a safe distance as she tracked the woman through the gates of the empty ticket booth, around the edge of an outside shower center, and past a locked food and beverage hut. The woman's path soon opened up to a wide sweeping bay, with shimmering blue water dotted by a large cay about a hundred yards out from the shore.

The woman stripped to her swimsuit and sat for a short while on the sand before wading into the ocean—all the while oblivious to the figure creeping stealthily along the forest floor, monitoring her every move. A few steps from the beach, the woman sank into the waves, letting the water sweep her under. Then, her head broke the surface about twenty feet from the shoreline.

Once it became clear the woman was intent on a lengthy swim, the Princess raced back to the parking lot. A quick surveillance confirmed no one else had arrived during her detour to the beach.

Scanning the trees for potential onlookers, the Princess fed the pole of her spear through the Jeep's passenger window. Running around the dented front bumper, she climbed into the driver's seat—and immediately clamped her hand over her nose.

The Jeep's interior smelled like moldy fish.

Holding her breath, the Princess puzzled for a moment over the assortment of red sticky notes plastered across the dashboard and sun visor. With a shrug, she reached beneath the seat and found the key.

Seconds later, she was speeding along the North Shore Road, the breeze whipping through the open door a welcome respite from the stench of the seat cushions.

The Princess steered the Jeep down the road's winding asphalt trail, passing the entrance to another beach and, later, the stone gates leading into the Caneel Bay plantation.

After a short drive, the roadway climbed a steep hill, peaking at an overlook that provided a sweeping view of island's main town.

The Princess slowed the Jeep as she looked out over the busy harbor. Brightly colored buildings spanned the cusp of the bay, and several sailboats bobbed in the water as the eight a.m. ferryboat from St. Thomas chugged into the dock.

Having taken in the view, the Princess guided the Jeep down the opposite side of the hill into Cruz Bay. A few of the day workers milling about the ferry building pointed quizzically at the rake sticking out of the Jeep's passenger-side window. Most, however, were focused on the gathering in the park across the street.

An elderly woman stood on a green bench beside the Freedom Memorial, spinning yet another version of the tale of the Amina Princess who had arrived on a slave ship in 1733 and gone on to lead her people into a revolt that had—for a time—controlled the island. With a demure nod at the rickety woman on the bench, the Princess carefully maneuvered the Jeep through the crowds and turned onto the main thoroughfare.

A dingy little bar came into view on her left. Several white plastic tables were arranged out front, one of which appeared to be awfully close to a blue Dumpster.

The Princess turned her head to sniff the delectable smell of a hot fish sandwich floating out the bar's kitchen window. She hadn't had time to stop for breakfast . . . Then she slammed on the brakes to avoid a plump rooster brazenly strutting in front of the Jeep, a greasy French fry hanging from its beak.

About a hundred yards beyond the bar, the roadway merged into a confusing circular traffic structure. The Princess spun the wheel, gunning the engine to avoid an oncoming vehicle. After a short detour that nearly landed her on the front porch of an adjacent grocery store, she veered onto Centerline Road, the main east-west thoroughfare across the island's center.

A green and white sign posted beside the roadway depicted an arrow, pointed east. Writing beneath it read CORAL BAY.

Back in the Brown Bay ruins, Alden Edwards sat on the main structure's second-floor landing, his long legs hanging off the crumbling wall of makeshift steps.

Stroking his wild unkempt beard, he studied a sheaf of papers the Princess had thrust into his hands before making her dramatic departure.

After a few minutes of reflection, Alden looked up from the documents, and a broad smile broke across the previously glum lines of his face.

~ 45 ~

The Convention

Shaking sand and ocean from my hair, I wrapped my towel around my body, gathered up the rest of my gear, and headed back through the Trunk Bay facilities to the exit. The ticket booth attendant was just arriving as I stepped over the chain by the kiosk. She gave me a simple wave as I crossed through to the parking lot.

Pausing to resecure my towel, I noticed the truck-taxi drivers had begun to congregate near the picnic tables. A thermos of coffee was passed around as someone plugged a radio into a truck battery. After a short squawk of feedback and a couple seconds of static, the audio cleared to a broadcast of the latest Constitutional Convention proceedings from a hotel on St. Thomas.

Thinking of the large man from Miami and his misleading memo, I wandered to the edge of the crowd and leaned against the side of the nearest truck, listening to the escalating ruckus emanating from the radio. Frustratingly, Hank Sheridan's cell phone had gone straight to voice mail every time I'd dialed the number to try to reach him. Perhaps, I mused, he'd gone over to St. Thomas to observe the proceedings in person.

* * *

Angry voices spit out of the radio's cracked and dusty speakers, incongruous against the serenity of the Trunk Bay parking lot. The drafting process had already taken far longer than originally anticipated. The budgeted funds to support the convention were about to run out—and the group was no closer to reaching a consensus on the controversial Native Rights language.

Every so often, a speaker came close enough to the microphone to break through the background noise.

"Only Native Virgin Islanders should be writing this constitution," a man's indignant voice shouted. "Only *they* should be eligible to vote for our government. We have been inundated enough with outsiders. This is the only way we will be able to protect our rights to our land, to our beaches—to keep them from being bought up by external interests and walled off from us.

"Native Rights *must* be in the constitution," he concluded. "That is not negotiable."

Several agreeing murmurs supported this sentiment, before a younger man's thin voice objected.

"And how, pray tell, do you purport to define who is a Native Virgin Islander?" he asked plaintively. "We have heard from the lawyers. The language you have given them is not suitable."

A woman's voice cut in with a sharp response. "Who is writing this constitution?" she demanded, and then filled in her own reply. "It is the responsibility of the *elected delegates*—not the lawyers."

A round of cheers almost drowned her out, but she persisted. "We have discussed the definition for many days now. A Native is someone who can trace his or her roots back to the time of acquisition. A Native has direct ancestry to someone living on the island on or before the transfer date—1917."

The tone of her voice made it easy to imagine her indignant expression. "These are the people whose rights have been trampled, who have never been compensated. They were simply bought and sold from one colonial power to the next."

The thin voice returned again, sputtering in frustration. "We all understand. We all have the same concerns about the Continentals and the resorts that have come down here with their money and driven up the cost of real estate. There are many of us who are struggling to stay in our homes, struggling with the rising cost of living."

He took in a huge breath of air, trying to keep his emotions in check. "But, your definition is so narrow. What about the people who have come here from other islands? People who have lived here for forty, fifty years? Some of them have been born here. They are a part of this community. How can you exclude them?"

There was a tense silence before the woman replied, her voice rigidly calm. "To my mind, they are not Native Virgin Islanders. If they do not like it here, they can go back to where they came from."

The room erupted into a discordant mixture of applause underlaid with grumbling disagreement.

Another man sang out, "This is a question of our identity, pride in who we are, where we belong. These are the generational rights for the descendants of the people who worked as slaves on this island. We must honor our heritage, our history of enslavement. No compensation will ever right that wrong, but we can make a start . . ."

He paused to clear his throat. There was a jostling sound as someone apparently handed him a glass of water. After a quick sip, he continued.

"We can start by giving Native Virgin Islanders a property tax exemption on their primary residences. This is a small measure to protect our ancestral homes. Otherwise, we will be forced off our land by these extortionate property taxes."

Other voices began to chime in. "What about homesteading rights—some land should be set aside where Native Virgin Islanders can set up homesteads."

"That's right, that's right. Our land is being sold right out from under us. We need protection. America could sell us tomorrow if it wanted to. We are just bartered citizens to them."

"It should be the best land on the island. This Maho Bay property on St. John the foreigners want to purchase for their next big hotel—that is where the Native Virgin Islanders should be living."

The young man returned to the microphone, exasperation in his voice.

"Can't you bend a little on this? Native Virgin Islanders make up less than half of the population. This language will never pass in a general election. You are proposing to give a minority of citizens special rights. We need to find some way to compromise."

An angry voice howled from across the room. "The only compromise I have for you is a stick of dynamite!"

There was nothing new in the level of vitriol, the ardent opinions expressed on the matter, or even the suggested remedies. I had heard them all before—and had always assumed that the moneyed interests that controlled local politics would prevent the Native Rights proponents from taking any serious action.

But as I studied the stolid, somber faces of the truck-taxi drivers listening to this dialogue, I began to second-guess that assumption. To a man, I noted uncomfortably, they seemed to side with the sentiments of the dynamite-wielding commentator.

It was then that I realized the contents of Hank Sheridan's memo might have been far closer to the truth than even he intended.

~ 46 ~

The Windmill

The Amina Princess drove the rusted red Jeep along Center-line Road, gazing at the stunning scenery from the elevated ridge that cut through the island's middle. Peek-a-boo views of the neighboring Virgins flashed through the trees, while a steep drop-off showcased sweeping green valleys.

The red sticky notes fluttered in the wind, but the Princess had yet to appreciate the significance of their left-pointing arrows. Blaring honks from oncoming traffic caused her to veer from side to side. After a few close calls, she assured herself, she was starting to get the hang of things.

From the right side of the road, she waved happily at the frustrated motorists who dodged around her, receiving numerous emphatic pointed gestures in return.

As the Princess approached the island's centermost peak, a familiar brown and white national park sign appeared on the roadside. Next to the sign, a family of donkeys nibbled the tender shoots of grass that had sprung up along the road's shoulder.

The donkeys looked up from their grazing as the Princess turned in front of the sign and headed off on a rutted dirt road that quickly disappeared into the forest. The donkeys' bleached gray muzzles twitched silently while they contemplated the large round dent in the Jeep's front bumper; then they resumed their eating.

About a half mile down the rugged lane, the Princess reached the remains of an enormous stone windmill. The wind-catching vanes that had topped the mill had long been destroyed, but the conical tower that had supported the spinning blades was still largely intact, giving some sense of the structure's once massive size.

The Princess jerked the Jeep to a stop in a clearing beside the abandoned mill, and, jumping out, ran toward the entrance.

A stone ramp took her to an arched opening at the bottom of the tower. She stepped inside and positioned herself in the center of the circular-shaped floor. Curved stone walls soared thirty or forty feet above her, their top edges turreted like that of a castle.

Pivoting in a slow circle, she scanned the tower's interior for the package that had been left by her accomplice—but the area was empty.

Undeterred, the Princess reversed course down the ramp and slipped into one of the tunnels that ran beneath the mill. An extensive network of cavelike passages had been built into the structure's rock base, linking storage cavities for the products that had once been ground by the mill's turbines.

Windows cut into the outer walls allowed in some exterior light, but the deeper the Princess ventured into the honeycombed base, the dimmer the rooms became. She was about to return to the Jeep for a flashlight when she finally stumbled across the item she'd been looking for.

Hidden behind a round column directly beneath the windmill's tower, lay a small canvas toolbox holding the materials she would need for the next stop in her journey.

~ *47* ~

The Cannon

A festive atmosphere filled the Moravian church parking lot near the north end of Coral Bay's sparse settlement. Volunteers busily distributed water bottles, granola bars, and pieces of fruit as Manto's truck taxi pulled in with a last load of participants.

The gathering point for the Fortsberg march had drawn a few community leaders, a handful of confused tourists, and a couple of visiting Danish anthropologists, but the majority of the crowd was made up of parents and their school-age children, the latter of which had been given the day off from classes so they could join in.

Although the organizers had brought signs and banners for the marchers to carry, the children were encouraged to create their own. Hamilton and several of his friends gathered together on a sidewalk with paper pads and crayons, chattering excitedly about the Amina Slave Princess as they worked on their individual placards.

With a flourish, Hamilton picked up his drawing and held it over his chest, proudly displaying it for the others to see.

Vivian stood nearby, frowning as she watched her son's enthusiasm.

"You'd think she was Santa Claus," she grumbled under her breath.

The Princess drove the Jeep past the crowd gathered outside the church, slowing behind a flamingo-decorated truck taxi as it pulled into the lot. Half a block later, she reached Coral Bay's main intersection—a T-juncture that marked the end of Centerline Road.

She turned south and parked the Jeep in the lot of the boarded up gas station. Before stepping out of the driver's-side opening, she reached into the rear seat for the canvas toolbox and the blue nylon satchel containing her costume. Gripping her packages, she returned to the intersection and veered right.

Around the next curve, she slipped into the driveway for an emergency fire and rescue center, and then ducked into a dense stand of trees.

Blocked from the view of the road, she quickly switched back into the Princess outfit. She buttoned the beaded vest across her chest, tied the sarong around her waist, and crammed the dark curly wig onto her head. After stuffing her street clothes into the satchel, she hid it in the trees. Still carrying the canvas toolbox, she headed up the path to the fort.

The medallion, of course, had never once left her neck.

As the Princess reached a small bluff, she paused to look back toward the church.

The marchers had left the parking lot and were now progressing slowly along the path behind her. The children ran circles around the group, chasing one another through the trees. Their peaceful, meandering pace would give her enough time to complete her task, but not much extra.

The Princess continued on through the cactus-strewn forest, following in the 1733 footsteps of the original Amina. She imagined their shadows walking beside her on the trail as they advanced on the Danish soldiers. The phantom forms bent beneath the bundles of firewood stacked on their shoulders, but the weight of the wood was eased by the knowledge of the machetes hidden inside. She felt buoyed by the presence of the ancient spirits; they accompanied her all the way to the fort's crumbling boundary.

There, the Princess waged her own hand-to-hand combat with the brambling bushes as she searched through the overgrown ruins for the sole remaining cannon. After a frantic hunt, she finally found its iron barrel, mounted onto a rock wall so that it pointed out over Hurricane Hole.

The fort's four hundred feet of elevation gave it a commanding 360-degree view of Coral Bay, the harbor, and the protecting arms of land that curved around it. The Princess's eyes swept across the scene. It was from this location that the Amina's signal of success had been sent far and wide across the Virgins.

The cannon was old and long past the point of use, even if she had been able to locate a ball of ammunition to fit into its tube—but she had a far more expeditious means of communicating her message.

The Princess unzipped the toolbox, reached inside, and pulled out a long cylinder, followed by a plastic-wrapped lump of putty.

She unwrapped the putty, kneaded it with her fingers, and smashed it around the cylinder's explosive device. Using a pair of the computer programmer's pliers, she readied the device for action, then she attached the whole contraption to the cannon's long outside wall.

With a last glance back at the approaching marchers, she pulled a matchbook from her pocket and lit the fuse.

The marchers were about a hundred yards away from the fort when those at the front of the crowd spied a figure sprinting headlong through the trees.

Hamilton was the first to point and cry out, "There she is!"

The boy next to him squealed, "It's the Slave Princess! The Amina Slave Princess!"

Vivian squinted skeptically at the fleeing woman. She wore a knee-length sarong tied around her waist and a tight-fitting beaded vest over her narrow chest. She was too far from the group for Vivian to get a clear identification, but the mass of dark curly hair springing around her shoulders was unmistakable.

"Whut is that wo-man doin'?" Vivian muttered under her breath.

A moment later, a series of three loud booms echoed through the forest, shaking the ground beneath her feet.

~ 48 ~

The Signal Is Heard

A bright green iguana dug his claws into the tree behind the resort's administrative building, steadily making his way toward the limbs that reached out over the second-floor balcony. Fred's long lizard shape blended seamlessly into the leaves, the multiple shades of green camouflaging his stiff jerking movements.

When at last he reached his favorite branch, he settled in on a flat portion of the bark that his leathery body had smoothed down over repeated sitting sessions. One of his front legs dropped over the edge and dangled in the morning's breeze. Turning his head toward the office, his beady eyes scanned the interior, searching for the woman who habitually sought his guidance, but he saw no sign of her there that morning.

Fred stretched his neck toward a nearby stem and plucked off a plump red berry. With his tongue, he rolled the fruit in his mouth, expertly positioning it under the sharp point of his teeth.

Just as he bit down on the juicy morsel, the first explosion echoed through the air.

*   *   *

Outside the Crunchy Carrot at the white plastic table farthest from the Dumpster, Joe Tourist and his wife sat soaking in the sun while they sipped on frozen fruit drinks in flimsy plastic cups.

Music from inside the bar filtered out onto the street. A country music crooner strummed his guitar as he began his signature St. John song. A background track of waves lapping soothingly on a beach was soon replaced by the crooner's smooth, slightly twangy voice describing his favorite blue rocking chair.

Between the music, the truck taxi rumbling past, and the numbing effect of their drinks, the pair failed to notice the cannon-fire-mimicking explosion that ricocheted across the island.

After a long slurp from her strawberry concoction, the woman turned to her husband and said, "Honey, maybe we should think about moving down here."

Fifteen feet away, beneath the Dumpster table, a black rooster with a plump belly and a colorfully plumed tail gobbled hungrily on a small pile of discarded French fries. Richard's head bobbed up and down as he worked the long pieces of fried potato down through his stringy neck.

More alert than the tourists, the bird immediately picked up on the irregular nature of the explosions.

Upon the third booming blast, he scooped up the last of his treasure trove and took flight to the protection of the alley behind the Crunchy Carrot.

In Pesce's hot, steaming kitchen, a Puerto Rican sous chef wiped his forearm across his greasy, sweating forehead and leaned back from a counter filled with the day's fresh seafood delivery. Several dozen fish had been apportioned into a myriad of piles, each grouping designated for a specific component in the night's appetizer and entrée menu.

Stepping away from the counter, César used his elbow to turn the lever for a nearby faucet, then he thrust his hands beneath the resulting stream of water and let the cool liquid wash the slimy coating from his fingers. After wiping his hands on the nearest clean dish towel, he turned back to the fish and picked up his knife.

"Now," he said, surveying the piles with a weary cackle, "who wants to go first?"

Swinging a pointed finger over the counter, he chanted, "Eeny, meeny, miny . . ."

On "moe," the first explosion rocked through the kitchen.

Startled, César grabbed the edge of the table, in the process catching the tip of a finger with the knife blade.

Sucking on the wounded appendage, he left the fish counter and wandered into the dining area. From the verandah, looking east toward Coral Bay, he could just make out a tiny plume of smoke.

On the oceanfront side of the resort's reception area, an elderly cleaning woman stood in the middle of a crowd of service workers. Several maids, waitstaff, mainte-nance workers, and members of the grounds crew encir-cled her as she cupped a hand around her ear, waiting for the signal.

When the first thudding *boom* echoed through the air, Beulah raised a pearl-colored conch shell to her lips and blew out a long mournful wail. Many others within the crowd followed suit. Someone began to beat a portable drum. One of the grounds crew slid a coconut-chopping machete from its sheath and raised it in the air.

Chants, conch wails, and drumbeats filled the air as Beu-lah led the group through the reception area, past several dumbstruck real estate attorneys, and out to the truck taxis waiting on the front drive.

* * *

Inside the storm cellar beneath the administrative building, a sweaty, seemingly deflated man sat on a plastic chair, eating a cold can of baked beans with a plastic spoon. A tepid bottle of water sat open on the rickety plastic table beside him. As he reached the bottom of the can, the man spooned up a small bean and bent down to the sand-covered concrete floor.

"Here you go, Stanley," the programmer offered to the hermit crab ogling up at the chair. "It's not in my regular diet either, but we have to keep our strength up. No telling how long we'll be stuck down he—"

He broke off his sentence as the first *boom* shook the concrete floor.

As the third explosion rumbled across the island, the computer programmer heard the grating metal sound of a key scraping in the cellar door's lock. Before he could leap up from his chair, the door swung open, and a young woman's tentative face peeked inside.

Her green eyes shone, even in the room's dim light. Dark curly hair hung down to her shoulders. She wore a flowered sundress made up of a light, floating fabric.

The programmer stared at her for a long moment before clearing his throat. He stood from the plastic chair and extended his hand.

"Hannah Sheridan, I presume."

Across the Pillsbury Sound, on the second floor of the Government House, the governor sat at his desk perusing the local newspaper. He had read halfway through an article reporting on the latest proceedings of the Constitutional Convention when his phone rang.

Calmly, he set the paper on his desk, reached for the receiver, and lifted it to his ear. He listened for a long moment to the voice of the water taxi captain on the other end of the line; then a serene smile stretched across his face.

"Thank you for the update."

Back on St. John, a middle-aged woman walked through the Trunk Bay parking lot, intent on climbing into her vehicle and driving back to the resort for a quick shower and a change of clothes.

The triad of booms failed to break through her deepening concern as she stared at the empty parking space where she'd left her ride.

"Hey," she cried out in disbelief.

"What happened to the Jeep?"

~ *49* ~

The Missing Jeep

After walking back and forth across the black tarmac, desperately searching the ever-growing collection of rental cars for the rusty bumper of Charlie's Jeep, I returned to the empty slot where I'd parked it.

Standing on the hot asphalt, clutching the beach towel around my waist, I finally reached the inevitable conclusion: the Jeep was gone.

One thought coursed through my head: I would never hear the end of this from Charlie and the rest of the Dumpster table gang.

This was rapidly followed by a desperate attempt at mitigation. The only way the Jeep could leave this little twenty-square-mile island was via the car ferry. I had to get down to the dock as quickly as possible.

A short distance away, I spied Manto striding toward his truck. He climbed inside and immediately cranked the engine.

Gripping the towel with one hand, waving in the air with the other, and all the while hollering at the top of my lungs, I ran toward the parking lot exit. After initially speeding up, the truck braked, allowing me to catch up to it.

"Manto," I panted into his open window. "Someone took Charlie's Jeep. I've got to get back to town. When does the next car ferry leave?"

His ashen face turned toward me. The lines across his forehead seemed to have suddenly deepened. *"Pin, no ferry's goin' ta leave tu-day."*

"Oh, good," I said with relief. Puzzled, I stared at his worried face. "What's wrong, Manto?"

"Didn't yu hear thuh booms?" he asked.

I nodded, vaguely recalling the sounds. I had dismissed them in my search for the missing Jeep.

"That wuz thuh seeg-nal."

"The signal?" I replied, recalling the whispered message from the Silent John balcony a few nights before.

"Thuh seeg-nal from thuh Slave Preen-cess—she's takin' over thuh eye-land."

~ *50* ~

A Leet-tle Chaos

The ground shook beneath the marchers' feet as the fuse ignited the first explosion at the Fortsberg ruins. Screams rang out, and smoke filled the air. All along the trail, bodies dove for cover.

By the time the third reverberation echoed from the cannon, Vivian had pulled Hamilton into the brush, ready to buffer his short body with her stout one. The two of them lay in the leaves, Ham with his hands cupped over his ears, Vivian with her arms wrapped tightly around his shoulders.

After a few minutes of silence, the marchers slowly began to raise their heads. Coughing and choking sounds mixed with those of bewilderment.

As they straightened and looked up the hill toward the ruins, the smoky haze began to clear, concentrating down to a dark gray plume.

Near the main road, the Princess crashed through the trees to the spot where she'd hidden the blue nylon satchel with her change of clothes. The marchers' muffled cries of confusion drifted down the trail as she hurriedly slipped out of the costume and exchanged it for her blue jeans and T-shirt.

Slinging the satchel over her shoulder, she walked down the road and around the corner to the gas station parking lot. After dislodging a rooster who had taken up residence behind the wheel, she hopped into the Jeep and motored off.

Manto barreled down the North Shore Road, heading east toward Coral Bay, intent on getting to Vivian and Hamilton as quickly as possible. I struggled to slip my shorts and T-shirt on over my still damp swimsuit as the truck swung dangerously around the sharp corners. Meanwhile, a chaotic chatter crackled from the two-way radio.

"I'm here at the ferry building. People are converging on the park. Blowing conch shells. Ai-yep. That man's got a machete." A scuffling sound broke off the transmission.

A second report followed. "Everyone's leaving the resort. I'm taking a truckful into town. I've got people hanging off the side."

A woman's voice cut in. "Have you all gone mad? What is this nonsense?"

Manto's truck creaked as it sped up the bumpy connector to Centerline Road. We reached the intersection to find a stream of cars traveling in both directions, panicked looks on the faces of both drivers and passengers.

I closed my eyes as Manto gunned the engine to slip into a tiny hole in the traffic.

"Cum on, Bessie," he bellowed over the screech of horns.

A few minutes later, we descended into the melee outside the Moravian church.

Coral Bay was a mass of disheveled people, many of them standing on the side of the road looking up toward Fortsberg and the column of smoke rising from its ruins. Sirens wailed in the distance as a team of fire trucks and ambulances sped through the wilderness to the site.

Vivian rushed up to the truck as Manto pulled into the church parking lot. Her arm was tightly wrapped around Hamilton, whose rumpled hair and clothing gave him the appearance of having been partially smothered.

"What happened?" I exclaimed as I opened the door and stepped out of the cab so that the two of them could climb inside.

I had never seen Vivian in such a state of rage—and I had plenty of examples stored in my memory banks for comparison.

She lifted Hamilton into the cab and then turned back to face me.

Her livid voice was thickly accented as she spit out, *"Eye know who haz been play-ing thuh role of thuh Slave Preen-cess."*

~ *51* ~

The Condo

At the far edge of the resort, in an area slated for upcoming renovations, a former dive shop employee sneaked across the deserted lawn toward the entrance of a one-bedroom condo unit.

A midsized duffel was slung over the man's shoulder. The bag was about half full, the contents representing almost the entirety of his earthly belongings. There's not much room on a boat for extraneous possessions.

Jeff ran the palm of his hand over his newly shorn head as he paused and glanced around the lawn, checking for any onlookers. His eyes found only a bright green iguana, studiously chewing on a piece of grass.

"Haircut," he explained to Fred's questioning gaze. Then he fed a well-worn key card into the lock.

Inside the condo, he quickly retrieved the item for which he'd returned. In the top drawer of the dresser, the one Pen had set aside for him, he found a single clean shirt. Like always, she'd put it through the resort's laundry service with the rest of her clothing.

Slinging the shirt over his shoulder, he shuffled briskly out the bedroom and headed for the front door. He didn't want to be caught inside the condo when Pen returned from her trip to the beach.

Midway around the couch, however, his hurried pace slowed. He turned toward the tile counter that separated the tiny kitchenette from the living room. On its surface, he spied a ballpoint pen and a pad of paper, both stamped with the resort's name and logo.

Jeff held his hand out over the pen, his fingers wavering for a long moment before they scooped it up. Using his thumb, he clicked the end button, engaging the metal ink tip. With his free hand, he gripped the pad of paper as the pen wavered above it.

He thought about all the things he might say . . . all the things he should say. But after a long moment, he carefully placed the pen on counter, leaving the paper blank.

With one last look around, he walked outside and pulled the door shut behind him.

~ *52* ~

Clean Towels

Manto's truck was one of the first to return to the church parking lot, so it was soon loaded with marchers, who—after the morning's unexpected excitement—were eager to return to Cruz Bay. We packed as many as would safely fit into the truck's back seating area; then I squeezed into the cab with Hamilton and Vivian. Slowly, we creaked out of the lot and turned onto Centerline Road.

Vivian's furious mutterings were difficult to interpret, but thanks to Ham's frequent interjections, I was able to determine the general gist of what had happened.

The explosions, I gathered, had gone off just as the marchers neared the fort's ruins. A figure in a knee-length sarong, beaded vest, and dark curly hair had been seen fleeing through the woods. The identity of the perpetrator, however, was the subject of some debate.

"It was the Amina Slave Princess," Ham's little voice peeped with impish delight, clearly still enamored despite the cannon fire and chaos. "I saw her with my own eyes."

"It was that Hannah Sheridan *wo-man*," Vivian corrected him bitterly. "We're lucky no one was killed."

Ham peeked around his mother's chest. *"Slave Princess,"* he mouthed at me with an assuring nod.

After her flash appearance running through the woods near the old Danish fort, the Slave Princess had temporarily dropped out of sight. No one knew where she would show up next, but many were placing odds on the Freedom Memorial across from the ferry building.

Following that lead, the majority of Manto's passengers disembarked at the outskirts of Cruz Bay, which was as close as he could get due to the gathering crowds.

The truck was nearly empty by the time we finally reached the resort. It had been several hours since Charlie had first picked me up there that morning. I was famished and long past ready to change out of my swimsuit.

I hopped from the cab and headed into the reception area, my thoughts firmly focused on picking up lunch and taking it back to my condo—unfortunately, food preparation was one of the many services temporarily on hold.

I ran smack dab into a confused and complaining mass of forty or fifty guests, none of whom I was eager to comingle with. By way of escape, I slipped behind the unmanned front desk. The following snippets of conversation reached me as I crawled along the floor:

"I called for clean towels an hour ago," a woman snapped. "I don't understand. It's like there's no one here."

"I saw them all leaving," a man replied. "The cleaning staff hopped onto the truck taxis and bolted out of here. I think it's a strike."

After keeping well below the counter to avoid being identified as someone who might be sought out to address these concerns, I made my way down the hallway toward the break room, where the few staff who hadn't left for Cruz Bay had collected.

Vivian had beaten me there, wisely circling around through the service entrance to avoid the reception area.

She strode back and forth in front of the metal lockers, her face fuming in anger.

"How long is this supposed to last?" she demanded of one of the maids.

The woman shrugged her reply.

Vivian muttered something inaudible under her breath. She sucked in a huge volume of air and then slowly breathed it out.

"Where's Hannah?" she asked firmly. "Hannah Sheridan. She's got some explaining to do."

Slowly, I backed out of the break room, trying not to draw attention to myself. Using the side service door, I returned to the front drive.

Recalling Hannah's conversation with the real estate attorney at the concierge desk, I could guess her current whereabouts—and the location of the Slave Princess's next appearance.

I just hoped she was the one who had run off with Charlie's Jeep.

~ *53* ~

A Darkening Drive

Manto's truck was still outside the reception area, parked in one of the taxi slots near the front door. Manto had taken Hamilton over to the playground by the tennis courts to keep him occupied while Vivian sorted out the mess inside the resort.

I rushed over to the cab and peered in the window. As was customary among the truck-taxi drivers, Manto had left the truck's keys on the dashboard in case someone needed to move it while he was gone.

Clearly, he hadn't learned from my experience with Charlie's Jeep.

With a brief flash of guilt, I climbed inside and grabbed the keys. A few moments later, I was bumping down the road that tracked the southwest shoreline. With all of the island's traffic now concentrated in town, I reasoned, it would be far more expedient to detour around Cruz Bay to get to Centerline Road.

If I was a hazard driving Charlie's Jeep, I was a menace in Manto's truck. The side mirrors had been angled to suit

Manto's much larger frame, and they were hopelessly out of whack for my shorter height. The wheelbase was so wide, it took up nearly three-fourths of the road—or, at least, that's how it appeared from behind the steering wheel.

I felt as if I were piloting a tank. The big engine rumbled like a freight train as I powered up the hill toward Centerline; at its juncture, I turned east toward Coral Bay.

Just past the island's crest, the afternoon sun illuminated the mounded tops of the surrounding islands, their dark green cones floating in a murky blue ocean. Storm clouds stretched across the horizon, raining out the sun above the boulders of Virgin Gorda. The next soaking would reach St. John within the hour.

As I thought grimly about the chance of lightning striking my intended destination, a static-laden voice crackled from the radio.

"Pin," Manto said with exasperation. *"Where have yu gone wit' my truck?"*

I reached for the handset and clicked on the receiver.

"Sorry, Manto," I replied. "I'll bring it back when I'm done. I promise."

"Mek sure yu re-fill thuh tank," he said with a sigh.

By the time I reached the T-intersection at Coral Bay, much of the earlier chaos had dissipated. The majority of marchers had either returned home or convened on the Freedom Memorial in Cruz Bay. I waved off the few stragglers who tried to flag down the truck taxi for a ride.

Rain began to spit against the windshield as I swung the truck south onto the road that tracked Hurricane Hole's outer rim. The dark blanket of the advancing squall line billowed over the harbor, smothering the afternoon's bright sunshine.

I'd have to hurry if I was going to catch up to Hannah before the storm hit.

* * *

Past the shuttered grocery store that demarcated the end of Coral Bay's sparse settlement, I pressed on the gas, pushing the truck as fast as I dared along the twisting, winding road.

A short stretch of humping hills rose up to meet the truck's charging tires. Power lines looped from pole to pole, crisscrossing the road in a low swinging lattice. It was as if the truck were riding a roller coaster's rails; I was merely a passenger, strapped in for the ride.

The island's arid southeastern climate took over the landscape. The trees shrunk in size, giving way to multitudes of succulents—all manner of cacti and yucca plants that thrived in the hot, dry exposure. The harsh moonscape mirrored the blunt force of the wind whipping through the driver's-side window as the untamed emptiness of my uninhabited surroundings joined me inside the cab.

The road crested near the entrance to a rough parking lot that served this lesser-known portion of the island's national park. The trail to the Salt Pond and, beyond, Ram Head, was marked by the park's signature brown and white signage, but little else.

The looming storm had chased off the few swimmers who had ventured out that morning. A couple of rental cars drove out of the lot as I pulled in, leaving behind just one other vehicle—a beat-up Jeep missing its front driver's-side door.

~ 54 ~

The Salt Pond

I parked Manto's truck in the widest portion of the lot in the hopes that I wouldn't have to reverse it in order to steer back onto the road. I didn't imagine I'd receive a lot of sympathy if, after having borrowed it without permission, I managed to get it stuck in the mud.

Meanwhile, the cloud bank swept in; its howling wind buffeted the cab as raindrops began to shoot across the windshield. The automatic daytime headlights switched off when I killed the engine, increasing the dim, dreary mood of the location.

I rolled up the driver's-side window and stared out at the abandoned Jeep. There was something strangely amiss about this already odd situation.

Stretching my arm across to the glove compartment, I pushed the button that released its latch and reached inside, searching for a flashlight. In so doing, my fingers brushed against a worn paper bag containing a small glasslike object. Grinning, I retrieved both the flashlight and the bottle of rum.

"Manto, my friend," I said appreciatively, "you prepare for everything."

Unscrewing the lid, I gulped down a burning dose of the sugary brown liquid.

If I hadn't just closed the window, I would have spit it out.

"Good grief, Manto," I said, smacking my lips—at least that portion of them that hadn't been numbed by the drink. "That's horrid."

Armed now with the flashlight and rum-weakened inhibitions, I stepped out of the cab and crossed the parking lot to Charlie's Jeep.

It appeared to be empty, but I approached cautiously all the same. The dampening dirt caked the soles of my flip-flops as I aimed the flashlight's narrow beam at the Jeep's front seating compartment. Once I confirmed that it was empty, I turned the light's focus to the tiny rear seat.

On the cushion lay a canvas toolbox—empty except for a pair of pliers and a scrap of cellophane wrapping. Leaning in, I picked up the wrapper, flattened it out, and held its surface beneath the flashlight.

Enough of the wrapper remained intact for me to read the labeling for the contents it had once held: a special kind of putty used to affix explosive devices.

I found the key beneath the front seat. Tucking it into my shorts pocket, I stepped back from the Jeep and scanned the scrub brush forest that surrounded the edge of the parking lot. I'd found the Jeep; that was the main purpose of my mission—but I still had questions for the mysterious Hannah Sheridan.

My eyes stopped on the trailhead sign.

SALT POND TRAIL
SALT POND BEACH 0.3 MI
RAM HEAD 1.2 MI

* * *

It was a short five-minute walk to the beach, down a wide but steep and increasingly slippery trail of loose rocks and gravel. The path was built up on either side with a dense vegetation of spiny cactus, agave plants, and scrubby trees that, despite their short height, managed to further darken the muddy path.

Wiping the rain from my face, I gripped the flashlight's metal barrel as the path sank deeper and deeper into the brush.

A few minutes later, the brush gave way to an enormous scallop-shaped cove. Low-rising hills on either side protected this picturesque stretch of sand, which was fronted by a shallow coral-filled bay.

Everyone on the island called this beach the Salt Pond, but that was a bit of a misnomer—the brackish, uninviting swamp of saltwater that leant the area its name was about half a mile off in the brush.

Less visited by tourists due to its inaccessibility—the truck taxis charged an arm and a leg to ferry passengers out this far—the Salt Pond offered some of the island's best snorkeling. Shyer underwater creatures like octopi, lobsters, and turtles could still be seen here even when those near the north shore beaches had been scared off by hordes of curious swimmers.

On a normal sunny day during the island's high season, this beach would likely see a small scattering of swimmers. But with the rain now pelting down, it was deserted of human activity. The energy in the sky above roiled the usually placid cove; footprints that had been left near the water's edge were quickly disappearing.

I set off along the beach, the storm quickly drenching me as the waves kicked sun-bleached pieces of coral up onto the sand. The T-shirt and shorts that I had pulled on over my swimsuit were soon soaked.

Wet and increasingly chilled from the wind, I was about to give up on Hannah and return to the parking lot.

Just then, I caught sight of a movement on the opposite

side of the cove, in the rolling hillside leading toward the cliffs above the famous Ram Head bluff.

Through the blinding rain, I could make out only a few details of the human figure climbing the trail. It looked to be a woman with dark curly hair wearing a knee-length sarong and a close-fitting beaded vest. In her right hand, she held the pole of a rake that she was using as a walking stick.

I slapped the rod of the flashlight against the palm of my hand, my confidence surging with the proof that my guess had been correct.

I had found the infamous Amina Slave Princess.

~ 55 ~

Ram Head

The Princess had been waiting for the better part of an hour in the brush at the far end of the Salt Pond's beach. She knew it was only a matter of time before Pen would show up.

When the Princess caught sight of the resort manager's soggy form staggering across the sand, she stepped out into the open and waved the rake in the air to ensure she'd caught the woman's attention. Once the Princess had confirmed Pen's continued pursuit, she began hiking up the trail leading to the Ram Head cliffs.

With the help of her trusty spear, the Princess easily navigated the narrow rocky path as it wound through a cactus-strewn thicket of shrubby, twisted trees, heading south toward the mouth of the cove.

A half mile later, the route dropped back to the shoreline and a shorter, less protected beach that was covered about a foot deep in piles of dried coral. The smooth stones clattered beneath the Princess's feet as she slid across them, the slightest weight sufficient to move their light, hole-filled masses.

At the end of the coral beach, the Princess picked up

the next leg of the trail, a barely discernable opening in the overgrowth of ferns and shrubs.

As the path left the shoreline, it scaled steeply upward. The earlier arid vegetation gave way to a barren hillside dotted with the prickly barrels of red-hatted cacti.

With every step of elevation, the Princess was now more and more exposed to the elements. The wind tore at her wig, nearly ripping it from her head; the fabric of the sarong flapped about her bony knees. Gray streaks of armor streaked over the cliffs, rumbling as if in anticipation of the coming showdown.

The Princess laughed off the approaching thunder; she paid no heed to the menacing weather bearing down on the trail.

This was the day she'd been waiting for—ever since that discovery, several months earlier, in the New York library. Nothing could stop her plan from coming to fruition.

I sprinted across the Salt Pond beach to the marker for the Ram Head trail, trying to keep Hannah in my sights. The brown and white sign gave the remaining distance to the cliffs as one mile. Surely, I thought as the wind and rain began to mix with thunder, she wouldn't make me chase her all the way to the top.

After a stretch of deep sand, the path gave way to the island's sharp volcanic rocks. Cursing the persistence of the woman on the hill up ahead of me, I clambered over the twisting trail, grabbing on to branches and boulders in my haste to propel myself forward.

Drenching sheets of rain fell out of the sky as I reached a second stretch of beach, this one filled with sun-hardened coral. I glanced up at the cliffs, nearly twisting my ankle on the slick, rolling surface as I searched for the Princess's fleeing figure.

"You'll have to stop sooner or later," I muttered as I caught a glimpse of her flapping sarong in the middle of the cactus field about a hundred yards above. Hannah was almost to the cliffs. Pretty soon, she would run out of island.

Clattering over the coral beach, I staggered into the brush, thrashing around in the ferns until I found a pig trail that led me to the main path. Panting, I raced up the last incline to the cliffs' bald hump.

Taking care not to slip, I eased toward the precipice and looked over the edge. The waves pounded below, the tentacles of a hungry beast eager for the chance to grind up the tiny morsel of my being. The sea frothed like a mammoth monster, one that stretched hundreds of thousands of miles across, chewing and gnawing at this tiny spit of land—slowly, inevitably consuming it.

Suddenly, a strange singing cut through the wind. It was an odd caterwauling wail, almost painful to the ears. A shuffling of rocks drew my gaze to a frail figure scrambling up the last twenty feet to the uppermost overhang.

A bolt of lightning crashed across the sky, illuminating the person perched on the boulders' highest ledge . . . jauntily holding a rake in one hand, waving to me with the other.

I puzzled for a moment at the worn face beneath the dark curly hair. Wiping my hands over my eyes, I blinked to adjust my focus.

Beneath the flapping sarong were knobby knees—and hairy shins.

The scrawny man flashed me a toothy smile as I stumbled up the path to him.

"*How-dee*, Pen," he called out cheerily.

I stood there, stunned, before spitting out his name.

"Conrad?"

~ 56 ~

The Impersonator

The wind howled as I stared at Conrad, his ridiculous getup, and his joyful, half-crazed expression. A gust swirled around us, pushing a wet whiff of cannabis into my nose.

"Pen, Pen, Pen," he babbled as he threw his bony arms around my neck.

I grabbed on to his bare shoulders and shook him forcefully.

"Conrad, what's going on?"

"Teepee tent," he trilled out merrily as he released his hold. "The Slave Princess is here to save my teepee tent."

Hands now on my hips, I continued to stare at him, unable to understand both what he was saying and why it had led him to masquerade as the Slave Princess.

"What?" I hollered with exasperation.

Conrad leaned toward me, his squeaky voice barely audible over the rain.

"I read about the Maho Bay sale in the newspapers, so I started doing some research. I'm pretty good at finding things out, you know."

He tapped a knobby finger against his temple. "I've got

sources in law enforcement. I have to stay one step ahead of that district attorney man . . ."

He noted my pained expression and returned to the topic of Maho Bay.

"Anyway, I stopped by one of the libraries there in New York to see what I could dig up. I got into the Rockefeller archives—they had stuff going *way* back, some of it to before the transfer. I was reading through a pile of papers that detailed the accounts of the early Danish settlers . . ."

He paused to catch his breath. "That's when I found her."

"Found her? Who did you find?" I asked suspiciously.

"A beautiful woman." He gestured with his hands to form the shape of an hourglass. "With golden brown skin, luminous green eyes, and"—he pointed to the wig—"curly dark hair. She was the Amina Slave Princess—the *real* Amina Slave Princess."

Conrad's last batch of doobies must have contained an extra hallucinogenic ingredient, I thought with a sigh. I was about to dismiss all this as the rantings of a lunatic, when he issued one last statement that caused me to reconsider.

"The Princess told me to wait for you at the Salt Pond," he said with a toothy grin. "She knew you would follow me up here to Ram Head."

With a suggestive pump of his eyebrows, he offered me the crook of his arm and gestured toward the trail.

Never in my wildest dreams did I imagine I would find myself nodding with agreement in response to Conrad's timeworn solicitation.

"Pen, would you care to accompany me to the eco-resort? I've got something to show you in my teepee tent."

~ *57* ~

The Leap

Wednesday afternoon, the storm continued to move across the island, sending its drizzle into Cruz Bay. Few of the day laborers gathered around the Freedom Memorial, however, appeared bothered by the damp weather. Most of the faces in the crowd were turned toward the machete-wielding statue and the green bench beside it where Beulah Shah stood addressing her audience.

The old woman's hoarse, lilting voice rose above the rain. *"When thuh French troops sailed een-to 'Urricane 'Ole and bee-gan their assault on thuh eye-land, the Ameena soon realized they were out numbered . . ."*

From her lookout on the Ram Head cliffs, the Princess tracked the French ships as they sailed around the island's southeastern tip and headed north toward Hurricane Hole.

The sight of the massive wooden structures instantly brought back memories of her voyage from West Africa. She shuddered with remembrance. She could still feel the rocking, heaving motion of the boat, the dry thirst in her mouth—and the heavy weight of the chains hanging from her wrists and ankles.

But as she continued her surveillance, the trauma of her past was quickly overshadowed by apprehension over her future. As she counted the soldiers patrolling the decks and squinted at the powerful weaponry glinting in the sunlight, a tension began to knit across her chest.

The Princess leaned back from the ledge, her head pounding with the realization of this latest development. She and her tribesmen had controlled much of the island for the past six months, but their reign would soon be coming to an end. The French reinforcements had just tipped the balance—seemingly irreversibly—against them.

The soldiers began a systematic sweep of St. John, marching in formation through both parched scrubland and thicketed forests. The troops quickly secured the plantations and the main roads, torturing and killing anyone they suspected of colluding with the Amina. A new reign of terror gripped the island—one that appeared headed toward a gruesome, bloody end.

As the noose began to tighten, the rebels faced their unthinkable reality.

They had little choice of what to do next. There was nowhere to run, no place to hide—and only one way to escape the prolonged agony of their fate.

The only question was how to achieve it.

One by one, the suicides began.

The Princess watched with increasing horror as her tribesmen slashed at their throats and aimed pistols to their heads, leaving their bloated bodies to rot in the sun. The empty, frozen faces littered the landscape, abandoned by the spirits that had inhabited their once soft contours.

She knew that she would soon be departing this island, her new home that she had come to love, but she was determined to do so on her own terms—and in a manner that would give her flesh a more suitable resting place.

When the last of her warriors lay prostrate on the ground, the Princess set off into the woods, following a trail that tracked deep into the dense jungle that covered Mary's Point.

The greenery leaned in over the path, providing cover for the Princess's fleeing figure; the vines that dropped down from the treetops wrapped around her shoulders as she passed, buoying her with their caressing touch. The rocks and boulders of the volcanic earth pushed up against the soles of her feet, carrying her momentum forward.

After an hour's brisk hike, she reached a bluff overlooking the island's north shore.

With a last look at the channel's stunning vista of brilliant blues and greens, she stepped toward the overhang. Her pace increased as she neared the edge, gradually building to a full-on sprint.

Her feet left the ground, sending her body tumbling through space, momentarily weightless as the sea reached up to catch her.

Murmurs circulated through the gathering of day laborers surrounding the Freedom Memorial. A seam began to form on the outskirts of the crowd as a young woman with curly, dark hair wearing a flowered sundress slowly made her way toward the front.

Whispers murmured through the mist as she climbed onto the green bench next to Beulah Shah.

The voices grew louder.

"That's her. That's the girl from the resort."

Someone pointed and pronounced the crowd's conclusion.

"She's the one. She's the Slave Princess."

~ 58 ~

The Eco-resort

Conrad and I bumped along the muddy road leading up to the eco-resort in the front cab of Manto's truck taxi. The earlier storm had passed, leaving behind a clear backdrop for the day's sunset, and a slick, treacherous surface on the steep, unpaved route. Given the challenging road conditions, I'd decided the truck taxi had a better shot of making it to the camp. The Jeep would be safe enough at the Salt Pond parking lot, I reasoned, patting my hand against the pocket where I'd stored the key.

Twenty minutes later, I steered the truck taxi into the eco-resort's gravel parking lot, which was filled with several rental cars and a mud-spattered limo. I stared at the limo, wondering how it had made the trek up the hill, as Conrad— still in his Slave Princess getup—jumped out of the truck.

A handful of lawyer types milled about the cabin that housed the check-in desk where the resort's bald-headed, full-bearded director, Alden Edwards, handed out stapled packets of photocopied paper.

I trailed Conrad through the mumbling crowd, every

member of which appeared to be intensely reading the document. From the comments I picked up as we walked past, I gathered the lawyers had just come from Cruz Bay, where they'd been nervously observing the gathering of day laborers at the Freedom Memorial.

Their reporting memos had been revised several times over the last few days; the events of the past six hours would require yet another rewrite. Despite the morning's disruptive walkout, however, several groups still intended to advise their clients to make a bid.

Alden Edwards had one more dampening piece of information for their reports.

"Here you go, fellows," he said, beaming broadly as he handed packets to the latest lawyerly pair to arrive. "Freshly unearthed documentation for you."

I peeked over the nearest shoulder to read the top page. Bold block print proclaimed: "Remains of the 1733 Amina Slave Princess believed buried on Maho Bay Property."

"This is going out to the local media as I speak," Alden added with a confident smirk.

Conrad waved at Alden from the edge of the crowd, giving the eco-resort director a cheeky smile before setting off down one of the walkways.

As I scampered through the lawyers to catch up to the skinny little man in Slave Princess garb, I couldn't shake the nagging question in my gut. The Princess's connection to the property seemed a little too convenient.

Joining Conrad on the walkway, I leaned toward his head and whispered under my breath, "Conrad . . . did you?"

He winked slyly at me.

I glanced back at the crowd, silently pondering. I counted at least three or four of the assembled attorneys who looked unconvinced. We were a ways off yet, I feared, from the resolution Conrad so desperately sought.

I didn't have long to worry about Conrad's forged burial document, for I soon found myself standing in front of the infamous teepee tent. It looked, incidentally, exactly the same as the rest of the eco-resort's canvas-walled structures. It didn't bear any resemblance to a teepee, at least not to my way of thinking. After all these years of hearing Conrad rave about it, I confess, the reality was a bit of a letdown.

Thumping up the wooden steps to the entrance, I was immediately hit by a thick smoky fragrance that intensified as Conrad swung open the screen door and beckoned me inside.

"What have I gotten myself into?" I muttered as I followed his swishing sarong through the doorway.

Perhaps this had all been an elaborate ruse to lure me to the teepee tent, I thought ruefully, as I tried to remember exactly why I had accepted Conrad's invitation in the first place.

The erstwhile Slave Princess skipped over to a cot on the opposite side of the room and began digging through a duffel bag laid open on its surface.

"So, Conrad," I began warily, positioning myself next to the door in the hopes of catching a breath of fresh air. "How did you come up with the costume?"

A chuckle gurgled up from the bed as Conrad continued searching the duffel bag. "My niece seems to think she might have been the inspiration."

"Your niece?" I repeated, as the first inkling of realization began to hit me.

"Yep," he said, reaching into his back pocket. "She's been helping me save the teepee tent."

He turned and stepped toward me. "My sister married a fellow from this area, not long after I first started coming down here." He cleared his throat and frowned sadly. "She passed away during childbirth. Then, her husband—well, he pretty much lost his mind with grief. He still lives here on the island. Used to be, you'd find him hanging around the bars most days, but a couple of months ago we managed to get him a job at one of the rental car places over on St. Thomas."

Conrad's face scrunched up into a grimace. "I don't think

that's going to work out." He jerked his head toward the parking lot. "I reckon they're going to want their limo back here pretty soon."

I stood there, my jaw slowly dropping, as Conrad flipped open his worn leather wallet and thumbed through the contents.

"Anyway, my niece grew up with my folks in New York. It was only recently that she started asking questions, wanting to know more about her father's side of the family. She's working at your resort this summer. I'm sure you've seen her around. I've got a photo of her in my wallet."

He held up a picture of a young woman with green eyes, cocoa-colored skin, and dark, curly hair.

"Her name is—"

The full implication of his revelation finally hit me, and I cut in before he could finish.

"Wait—*you're* Hannah's uncle?"

I was still processing that last piece of information when a commotion outside the teepee tent interrupted our conversation. I climbed down the steps to the wooden walkway, straining my head to catch a glimpse of the ruckus going on in front of the check-in cabin.

During the few minutes we'd been inside the tent, crowds of day laborers had descended upon the eco-resort, swamping the lawyers who were still studying Alden's pamphlets.

The new arrivals, wielding conch shells, horns, and the occasional machete, had quickly snatched up copies of the Slave Princess burial documentation. None of these readers, I noted, appeared the least bit skeptical of its claims, and they, I suddenly appreciated, were a far more important audience than the whole cadre of lawyers.

As I surveyed the scene outside the check-in cabin, Conrad skipped up next to me on the walkway and tapped me on the shoulder.

"This is for you," he said with great formality. In his hands, he held out a blue nylon satchel. He issued an informative nod and added, "One friend to the other."

"Thanks," I replied. The satchel rustled as if it held a stack of papers inside. More Slave Princess propaganda, I assumed.

I glanced up at the sky, which was quickly dimming toward darkness. The next front of clouds had already filled in the eastern horizon. The sooner I managed to get Manto's truck taxi down the hill, the better. Besides, I had no intention of returning to Conrad's teepee tent.

"I'll take a look at this later," I said with a wave. Then I slung the satchel's strap over my shoulder and headed toward the parking lot.

"Later, Princess," I called out, still shaking my head with bemusement as I trotted off down the walkway.

~ *59* ~

The Pen

It was with great relief that I finally pushed open the door to the condo late Wednesday afternoon. It felt like an eternity had passed since I'd left it that morning to meet Charlie and his Jeep.

I walked wearily across the living room, intent on getting out of my swimsuit and into a hot shower as quickly as possible. Midway around the backside of the couch, however, I stopped. Something felt amiss—something other than my salty swimsuit and the disturbing image of Conrad in his Slave Princess costume now imprinted on my brain.

I scanned the area, searching for the out-of-place item. My eyes passed over the glass-top coffee table and the expiring wicker chair, finally landing on the kitchen counter and the pen lying on its surface next to the blank pad of paper.

Crossing the room, I reached out for the pen. Slowly, I turned it over in my hands. The interior rod was cocked to its on position, as if someone had held it, intending to write a message.

Lightly tapping the tip of the pen against my lips, I walked into the bedroom. After a moment of hesitation,

I pulled open the top drawer. It was empty—Jeff's spare shirt was gone.

My wordless boyfriend, I mused with chagrin, had left his good-bye.

With a sigh, I trudged to the shower, desperately trying to ignore the doleful tweets of the bananaquits sadly swooping about my head.

~ 60 ~

The Client

Vivian leaned tiredly against the reception desk's front counter. After several hours of filling in for room cleaning, laundry service, and otherwise dealing with frustrated guests, she was exhausted.

She hadn't seen Hannah Sheridan—or Penelope Hoffstra, for that matter—since returning from Coral Bay that morning. Vivian was ready to wash her hands of both women, although at this moment, Hannah was at the top of her list of people she would like to throttle.

According to the reports she'd picked up from her two-way radio, her missing crew members were still running around the island, chasing down rumored sightings of the Slave Princess.

"Slave Preen-cess," Vivian muttered bitterly under her breath. *"If Eye ever git mye hands on yewe . . ."*

She looked up as the computer programmer leaned over the reception desk and placed a chubby hand on its counter. All of her venom and pent-up frustration immediately transferred to his portly figure.

In the midst of the day's chaos, she had temporarily forgotten about the man who had arranged for Hamilton's and her transfer to St. John—and the payment he had required in return.

"You found everything you needed?" she asked stolidly, trying without success to keep the loathing tone from her voice.

"Yes, I did," he replied with a nervous glance around the reception area. "I'd like to be on tonight's water taxi." He cleared his throat uncomfortably. "If you can arrange it."

Vivian grunted tensely. "Of course."

She flipped through the sheets attached to her clipboard and then looked up at him suspiciously. "I already have your reservation."

"You do?" he asked uneasily.

Shuffling feet crept toward the counter as a bent, broken figure hobbled down the hallway from the break room. Beulah's bony face peeked around the edge of the front desk.

Her hoarse voice whispered loudly, *"What-ter taxi . . . what-ter taxi . . . ohhh, no . . ."*

A startled expression crossed the programmer's face as Beulah sidled up next to Vivian.

"Eye doon nut lyke thuh what-ter taxi . . ."

The programmer stared in disbelief at the name tag pinned to the front of the old woman's frayed shirtdress. He shook his head, blinked, and then read it again.

Beulah . . . surely not. This decrepit creature couldn't be *his* Beulah—not Beulah Shah, the woman who had paid for his Maho Bay services.

But as he stood there next to the reception counter, the woman's ragged face fixed on his thick neck. A constricting pressure clamped down on his chest, squeezing the air from his lungs. As her gaze lifted, and their eyes met, his doubts left him. This was, indeed, Beulah Shah.

The programmer stepped back from the counter, gulping in a deep breath.

He'd had some bizarre clients in his day—that was the nature of his employment—but *never* one quite as unexpected as this. And never, he thought grumpily, had one locked him in a cellar overnight. He wiped his wrist across his sweating brow as he turned away from the reception desk.

This would be the last time he took on a project for Ms. Beulah Shah.

"What-ter taxi . . . what-ter taxi . . . ohhh, no . . ."

Vivian gave Beulah a sideways glance and pursed her lips, but the old woman continued her lament, her dark eyes intensely focused on the back of the retreating computer programmer.

"Beeg sheep go down slowe . . . Small sheep go down fest . . ."

Vivian rolled her eyes. "We haven't lost anyone yet," she said sarcastically.

"Ack, Eye doon nut lyke the what-ter taxi . . ."

With a sigh, Vivian scribbled Beulah's name on her clipboard, adding her to the list of the night's water taxi passengers.

"I'm sure you'll be fine."

~ *61* ~

The Paper Bag

A shower made the post-Jeff world look a little better, even if I'd had to scrounge around for a clean towel and the water's temperature had been lukewarm—the resort's generators were having a hard time keeping up with the demand for hot water.

My bathrobe wrapped around me, I wandered through the living room to the kitchen. The blue nylon satchel lay on the counter where I'd tossed it on my way to the shower. I still hadn't looked at the papers inside.

Oh boy, I thought as the image of Conrad in his Slave Princess costume flashed across my brain.

First things first, I thought with a shudder. I removed the bottle of Cruzan from its shelf and lifted it toward the light, sizing up the number of remaining shots. I was about to fill my glass when I heard a knock at the door.

I stood there, holding the bottle in the air. After the day I'd had, there was no one I wished to see. But a second rap indicated a level of persistence in the knocker, so, with a sigh, I set the bottle on the counter and crossed to the entryway. Squinting through the peephole, I spied an old crippled woman in a housemaid's uniform.

Hoping she was there to drop off a clean set of towels, I opened the door.

The maid pushed past me, limping forcefully into the living room. In one hand, she carried a rumpled paper bag. Her feet clunked across the tile floor in oversized rubber sandals as she glanced at the shot glass and the half-empty bottle on the kitchen counter. Then she turned and whispered hoarsely to me.

"Ya look lyke yewe lost somethin'."

Her thin body was clothed in one of the resort's standard-issue shirtdresses, but the garment was decidedly more tattered and frayed than those worn by the rest of the women. She had a toothless mouth and frizzled gray wisps of hair. My eyes focused on the name tag pinned to her chest, which read BEULAH.

I leaned sideways as she bent toward me, her brown eyes studying me intently.

I tried to form a reply to her strange introduction, but my throat suddenly dried up. The air died inside my lungs, leaving me with no source of oxygen. I couldn't breathe, couldn't move.

"Fat man took 'eem," Beulah wheezed. She stepped back and licked her cracked lips, releasing me from her hypnotic hold.

"The fat man?" I asked in bewilderment after gulping in a deep breath. The image that immediately came to my mind couldn't possibly be the man to which she was referring.

Beulah stretched her hands out into the air and waddled back and forth in front of the kitchen counter. Then she crossed her arms over her chest, tilted her head to one side, and said softly, *"Thuh wone who brought ya here."*

"The fat man took—*who*?" I managed to gasp out through my surprise.

"Your boy," she replied.

She raised a bony hand to her head and wiggled her fingers above her thinning scalp. It took me a moment to interpret her gesture; she was mimicking Jeff's wild, frizzy hair.

"Ya kin steel cat'ch up to heem—if that's what yewe want."

I shook my head in confusion, struggling to understand her meaning.

Beulah pointed a knobby finger toward the blue nylon satchel. She sighed, as if disappointed in me.

"You didn't look een thuh bag."

Tightly gripping my robe, I turned to the counter and opened the satchel. It contained a file folder with a small sheaf of papers. With a curious glance at Beulah, I pulled out the folder and perused the contents. My eyes passed over sheet after sheet of routine overtime and water taxi expenditures—each one with the same looping signature of Penelope Hoffstra—each one bearing a stamp from a police evidence file.

"Where did Conrad get this?" I asked in amazement.

As I reached the page at the end of the package, my brow furrowed with concern.

It was a log from the water taxi company the resort used, detailing its transfers and pickups. Handwritten in the margin was the number of reimbursements I'd signed for—a number that far exceeded the actual water taxi shuttles. Each trip, individually, cost less than a hundred dollars, but over the course of the last four years, the accumulated bogus runs had tallied to a significant sum.

I thought back to the endless reams of expense reports flagged with red sticky notes, and my hands began to tremble.

Sheridan hadn't brought me here to help him with the real estate deal. He hadn't sought me out for my legal expertise. I hadn't been stashed away all this time in inactive exile; I'd started working for him the minute I stepped foot on the resort.

I dropped the papers back into the nylon satchel, my face paling.

I was nothing but the fall guy for his embezzlement scam.

I remembered his voice from the backseat of the sedan: *I have several Pens.*

And now, it seemed, he was about to expand his collection to one frizzy-haired dive shop employee.

Beulah bent toward me once more, her stale breath oozing out of her toothless mouth.

"You've gut wone chance, 'fore he disappears for good," she said, handing me the paper bag.

Then, she let loose an eerie cackle.

"Thuh Slave Preen-cess . . . she's nut dun yet."

~ 62 ~

A Boat of His Own

A tall New Englander with a recently shaved head sat in the captain's chair of a white catamaran powerboat. Red lettered paint across the boat's side read WATER TAXI. The current captain stood beside him, running through the ship's controls, explaining the nuances of the boat's navigational equipment.

"You think you're ready to man a rig like this?" the dark-skinned man with bulging biceps asked with a smarmy grin.

Jeff smoothed his hands over the steering wheel's worn plastic rim, his chest swelling with anticipation.

The captain let out a loud guffaw as he slapped Jeff's pale scalp.

"You'd better get some sunscreen on that noggin or it's going to blister."

~ *63* ~

The Water Taxi

Beulah Shah limped down the path leading to the dock, her rubber-soled shoes thumping across the wooden boards as the lights of the water taxi appeared in the distance. Slowly, she approached the spot at the end of the pier where the computer programmer stood waiting.

Patches of moisture had begun to spread across the heavy man's golf shirt, and his wire-rim glasses were fogged with steam. But Beulah's arrival appeared to generate far more physical discomfort than the night's dense humidity.

After a tense, awkward moment, he issued a stiff greeting.

"Ms. Shah."

She nodded with a silent leer; her eyes twinkled with devilish enjoyment.

He sucked in his breath and managed a calm statement.

"I trust you were satisfied with the services I provided."

Beulah's thin lips stretched into a smile—a superior, knowing expression, as if she were holding on to an enormous secret.

The programmer turned, dismissing the old woman. The water taxi pulled next to the pier, and he lumbered aboard. Taking a seat on the boat's back bench, he folded his hands together across the paunch of his chest and closed his eyes. He was ready to put this trip to St. John behind him.

Beulah watched from the pier. Then her voice creaked out a low whisper, *"Your services are nut yet complete, Mr. Stout-man."*

"Wone more pass-enger," Beulah said hoarsely to the boat's captain as he helped her onto the boat. *"She'll be here een jest a meen-nut. Forgut somethin' back at hur room."*

The captain stared down at the feeble maid, somewhat perplexed. He thought back to his meeting at the Government House on St. Thomas. The smelly West Indian limo driver he had met in the governor's office had mentioned there would be one additional passenger on this trip. What had he said her name was? His eyes honed in on the name tag pinned to the woman's worn shirtdress. Beulah. That was it. Beulah.

The old woman shuddered, as if upset by her pending ride on the water taxi.

"What-ter taxi . . . what-ter taxi . . . ohhh, no . . . Eye doon nut lyke thuh what-ter taxi . . ."

The captain rolled his eyes. The old bag was really milking the drama tonight. She could bloody well swim across to Red Hook, then, he thought with a smirk.

As the captain turned his attention to the empty pier and the path leading up to the darkened resort, he missed the sharp gleam in Beulah's eyes.

Hannah Sheridan ran past the resort's long sloping lawns, a slight breeze rippling through her spinning chiffon sundress and wig of dark, curly hair. A blue nylon satchel swung from her shoulder as the soles of her shoes slapped against the red brick walkway.

Despite the surrounding stillness, she was well aware of the eyes of the resort watching her sprinting figure. These

were the countless observers that would later report seeing her last-minute departure on the late-night water taxi.

Rounding a corner, she nearly squashed an iguana out
on his evening stroll. The lizard skittered beneath a bush,
puffing out the ruffles of skin around his neck to show his
offense at her rudeness—but the woman was already pounding down the path heading toward the dock.

The next wave of rain clouds had begun to move across
the island. The first cooling drops pattered onto the woman's
bare shoulders as a golf cart zoomed up behind her.

She glanced at the driver. Beulah must have sent him to
fetch me, she thought with relief.

"Don't worry, Hannah," Manto said with a wink at the
real Hannah Sheridan, who was dressed up like the fake
one. "He will wait."

~ *64* ~

The Sinking

Beulah grinned with satisfaction as the golf cart screeched to a stop at the dark end of the pier. I kept my head tilted downward and my eyes averted as the captain grabbed hold of my arm and yanked me onto the boat.

Wearing the wig, sandals, and sundress that I'd pulled out of Beulah's paper bag, I must have made a close approximation of the resort's now infamous employee. That, or the captain was in such a hurry to depart, he didn't notice that I was a much older Hannah than the one he had been hired to pick up.

I sat nervously on the boat's back bench, trying not to think about where the wig had been—given the smoky, herbal scent emanating from its fibers.

The rain picked up in intensity as the catamaran powered up its engine to high speed and sped out of the cove. I kept my gaze fixed straight ahead, not daring to look at Beulah, who perched on the bench to my left, or the large man from Miami, who spilled over the seat to my right.

The boat pitched and jumped in the rough water, as if it were struggling to break free from the ocean's tugging grasp. Beulah's lilting, singsong voice somehow managed to rise over the drowning sounds of wind, rain, and motor.

"*What-ter taxi . . . what-ter taxi . . . ohhh, no . . . Eye doon nut lyke thuh what-ter taxi . . .*"

I clenched my fists around the edge of the bench.

It's now or never, I thought, as I staggered to my feet and wobbled toward the entrance to the below-deck quarters.

My hands gripped the metal railings of the ladder leading into the hold as the boat heaved and rolled. I struggled to find the footholds, but finally reached the bottom. Turning, I brushed back the wig from my face to find a surprisingly bald Jeff staring quizzically up at me.

His face registered surprise long before he recognized me as the woman beneath the disguise. The corners of his mouth twitched in confusion.

After six months of dating, I was highly skilled in interpreting the minuscule changes in Jeff's facial expressions.

He hadn't been expecting Hannah, I realized. I turned my head toward the ceiling, mentally picturing the crafty old woman sitting on the bench above. After the day's events, it would have been too risky for Conrad's niece to return to the resort. I had been the Hannah meant for this water taxi all along.

Pushing out a frustrated puff of air, I returned my attention to the befuddled Jeff. I started a futile attempt at explanation, but before I could speak, the motor slowed to a halt. Seconds later, the captain stuck his head into the hatch. After a puzzled glance in my direction, followed by a quick shrug, he called out to Jeff.

"You ready?"

Above deck, a bright yellow self-inflating raft lay pumped up and ready for deployment in front of the rear deck's passenger seating. The captain brought out a small portable motor from a storage locker, laid it next to the raft, and carefully began checking its settings.

Satisfied with the safety review, the captain grabbed the yellow boat, wrapped an attached rope around his wrist, and tossed it into the water. Then, handing the tether to Jeff, he disappeared over the railing. Jeff leaned over the side and lowered the motor.

Hank Sheridan—which I suppose was as good a name as any for him—was now very much awake. He had begun protesting as soon as Jeff emerged from the below-deck hold. He directed his complaints not at the boat's captain, but at the old woman. From what I heard of their conversation, it seemed Mr. Sheridan had not intended to be on *this* water taxi.

After a terse back and forth, Beulah apparently won the argument. A victorious grin on her face, she handed him a life jacket and pointed at the water.

I watched, dumbstruck, as he fitted the jacket over his enormous form. Then he waddled to the side of the boat and, with a last loathing look at the old maid, jumped overboard.

Beulah was the last to depart. Her bony face studied me for a long spooky moment before suddenly cracking into a maniacal smile.

~ 65 ~

The Beach

Jeff and I left the yellow life raft and its three discordant passengers near a buoy, where they would be easily spotted by the Coast Guard.

The water taxi motored away into the darkness, disappearing forever from the waters of the Pillsbury Sound. Even as we sped along St. John's southern shore, the "sinking" catamaran was already becoming a permanent fixture in the local lore of superstitions.

I stood in the captain's cabin next to Jeff, the blue nylon satchel still looped around my neck. Several times, I reached my hand inside to pull out the papers. He should at least have an idea of the strings that were attached to his new position, I told myself.

But each time I summoned the courage to show them to him, I caught sight of his face, reflected in the boat's front exterior lights.

I'd never seen him so happy. It was too late now to change his decision. I'd lost him for good—not to a curly haired younger woman, not to a blubberous criminal mastermind— but to a boat.

Jeff steered the catamaran into the Salt Pond's wide protective cove, killing the motor about fifty yards from the outer shoreline. That was as close as he could get without risking running up against the coral.

The rain pelted down as he strapped me into a life vest and helped me to the side railing. I looked out across the dark beach and, above it, the rocky terrain devoid of any human habitation. It was a manageable swim, I told myself—although it would have been a lot less daunting in a daytime's bright sunshine.

He touched my shoulder and I turned to face him. Like so many times before, no words passed between us.

With a grimace, I pulled the wig from my head, pushed it down over his bald crown, and jumped out into the water.

I found Hannah waiting for me on the coral beach portion of the Ram Head trail, exactly where Beulah had said I would. The rain drenched down on her curly head; the drops streamed across the smooth, cocoa-colored contours of her skin.

She smiled, demure to the end. That night, standing on the beach, I had no more insight into her inner motivations than I'd had the morning she'd turned up at my office.

"Which way are you headed?" I asked, more out of curiosity than anything else as I unbuckled the life vest and handed it over to her.

"South," she replied, in a tense tone that warned me not to follow. She hesitated, her face transmitting an inner conflict between the prudence of secrecy and her innately polite nature.

"There's a place in Christiansted that will paint the boat," she finally added. "It won't be recognizable as the water taxi once they finish with it."

I watched her fasten the last buckle on the life vest, my own mind at odds of how to assess this moment. Hannah had played a crucial role in revealing the mess I was in at the resort, but I couldn't decided whether I felt gratitude or hate for that intervention.

Either way, there was no more time for delay.

"Take care of him," I said with a last glance at the boat bobbing in the bay. "Good-bye, Hannah."

That was, I suspected, the last time anyone would ever call her by that name.

"Good-bye, Pen," she replied with a wave.

I heard the light splash of her body wading into the water as I set off across the dried coral, headed inland toward the Salt Pond beach.

Manto sat in the cab of his truck taxi, waiting in the parking lot where he'd dropped off Hannah a few minutes earlier.

He beamed a jocular smile at my soaked dress and soggy sandals.

"Jus' wanted to mek shure you steel had thuh key," he said, jerking his head toward the only other vehicle in the lot, a rusted red Jeep missing its driver's-side door.

With a smile, I reached into a side zipper of the blue nylon satchel and pulled it out to show him. The photocopied papers containing the incriminating evidence of the water taxi reimbursements had been soaked during my swim ashore, but I no longer needed them. I was happy to add this packet to the list of that night's disappearing items.

Holding up the key, I waved at the truck taxi.

"You're the best, Manto."

I watched him drive off; then I climbed into Charlie's Jeep and drove it slowly, thoughtfully back to the resort.

Epilogue

I sat at the Dumpster table the following morning, looking out at Cruz Bay's quiet downtown scene. The town had quickly returned to normal; little physical evidence remained of the crowds that had gathered there the day before. While hushed whispers filled every corner of the island, St. John's inhabitants had returned to their regular work routines.

I flagged the waitress on her next trip to the trash bin. She looked up at me with a smile.

"Throw me on a fish sandwich, if you don't mind," I called out.

She waved an acknowledgement and returned inside to relay the order to the cook.

This would be my last session at the Dumpster table, my last disposable plastic cup filled with a semifrozen drink, my last fish sandwich—of the Crunchy Carrot variety anyway. A dusty roll-around suitcase packed with the few belongings I had chosen to keep lay on the ground beneath the table. My stay on the island was about to come to an end.

* * *

At last check, Beulah Shah was resting comfortably in the St. Thomas hospital where she'd been delivered by the Coast Guard rescue team. According to the morning's reports, she had adapted well to hospice care and was thoroughly enjoying being waited on by the nursing staff. They would have a difficult time discharging the old woman, I thought ruefully.

Meanwhile, the water taxi captain was holed up in his one-room Red Hook apartment, avidly surfing the Internet for his new craft while he waited for the proceeds from his insurance settlement to arrive. A cursory investigation by the local authorities blamed the sinking on inclement weather. Dive teams had attempted to locate the wreckage, but, it was believed, underwater currents had carried the remains of the water taxi from the site of the sinking.

The computer programmer had disappeared in the melee of gawking spectators and emergency vehicles that had greeted the Coast Guard ship when it pulled into Red Hook with the shipwreck survivors. Likely as not, Mr. Sheridan had already caught a flight off of St. Thomas, I mused. He would be difficult to recognize, I suspected, minus his inflatable body suit.

Maho Bay appeared destined to remain in the hands of the eco-resort—at least for the near future. In the aftermath of last night's sinking, none of the local West Indian workers were willing to set foot anywhere near the place for fear of disturbing the ghost of the Amina Slave Princess. Any new resort that attempted to build there would have to contend with the superstitions of the local workforce.

That left only Hannah Sheridan, whose last vaporous remnants were quickly melting away like the ice cubes in my plastic cup.

She'd begun to disappear four years ago at the Miami airport, when I abandoned my nylon pantyhose and tired business suit. She'd started to evaporate the moment I boarded that plane to St. Thomas. Now, as I prepared to set out on a similarly unpredictable journey into the unknown, Penelope

Hoffstra—at least *my* Penelope Hoffstra—was about to join Hannah in that oblivion.

Richard the rooster nosed his beak through the crumpled wrapper from my now devoured fish sandwich. He gave me a recriminating look for not having left any crumbs as I leaned back in the white plastic lawn chair, slurped down the last bit of slurry from the bottom of the cup, and pushed it away.

I stood from the table and extended the handle of the roll-around suitcase. As I began walking toward the ferry building, my hand slipped into a ragged shorts pocket, and my fingers wrapped around the tiny quill of a faded yellow feather.

Beneath the ferry building's colorful covered pavilion, I waited patiently for the boat's arriving passengers to disembark. Then I handed my ticket to the crewmember manning the gangplank and steeled myself to take the next step.

My feet carried me up the wooden walkway, steadily building pace as I approached the edge of the passenger entrance. Holding my breath, I took the final step onto the boat—and off the island.

From one of the benches near the boat's stern, I looked out across Cruz Bay's busy little harbor. The morning's regular commotion filled the air, bustling, squawking to and fro.

Chickens scurried through intersections. Truck taxis warmed their engines. Tourists chatted on cell phones.

But I heard none of this.

As the boat began chugging toward St. Thomas, another sound drowned out all the others. A faint smile creased my lips as I listened to the twittering in the trees along the shore and the frenetic nonstop harmony of the bananaquits.

**"[A] wild, refreshing
over-the-top-of-Nob-Hill thriller."**
—*The Best Reviews*

THE *NEW YORK TIMES* BESTSELLING SERIES FROM
· Rebecca M. Hale ·

HOW TO MOON A CAT

A Cats and Curios Mystery

When Rupert the cat sniffs out a dusty green vase
with a toy bear inside, his owner has no doubt this is
another of her Uncle Oscar's infamous clues to one of
his valuable hidden treasures. Eager to put together
the pieces of the puzzle, she's soon heading to Ne-
vada City with her two cats, having no idea that this
road trip will put her life in danger.

facebook.com/TheCrimeSceneBooks
penguin.com
howtowashacat.com

M14G0610